# a novel prototype

## Book One

## The Possession Series

# GRETCHEN de la O

Edited by
Nichole Strauss, Perfectly Publishable

Original Art and cover designed by
Sommer Stein, Perfect Pear Creative Covers

Interior Design and Formatting by
Christine Borgford, Perfectly Publishable

**early praise**

"*Sexy and suspenseful, Prototype is one surprising romance you do not want to miss. I was captivated by the unique storyline and incredible characters told in a way that only Gretchen de la O can ... with potent, powerful words that will leave you falling in love with these characters and a little terrified by the believability created in this edge of your seat, futuristic romantic thriller.*"

— **A.L. Jackson, New York Times Bestselling Author**

"*A genre-warping and deeply original suspense.*"

— **Renée Carlino, USA Today Bestselling Author**

**acknowledgments**

There are no words that exist which could possibly embody the gratitude I have for the people who have supported me and gave of themselves so unconditionally in the birth of **Prototype**. From the moment I pushed my pen to paper way back in 2009 to the moment I typed out these acknowledgements in 2014 there has been many hands which have contributed to **The Possession Series**. First I want to thank my family, **Ed, Jared, Kyle, Nathan**, and my mom, **Gramma K**. They have lived with my crazies for quite a long time. Their patience and understanding has been beyond priceless. Thank you for believing in me! I want to thank my editor, **Nichole Strauss** and formatter, **Christine Borgford** from **Perfectly Publishable**. I can only hope someday you both will truly know the deep authentic love I feel for both of you. Thank you to **Sommer Stein** from **Perfect Pear Creative Covers** for the best cover ever! She is the swirl in my gut, the creator of my brilliant BIG O brand and truly etched into my heart. Thank you to my original beta readers **Debbie Shess, Karley Bohner**, and **April Sembrat**. These women have been with me since I first scraped of the pen across the paper. I have such gratitude and deep love for them. Thank you to **Nicole Westmoreland Radlow** for your help back in 2009 and telling me the story had good bones! Thank you to my loves **A.L. Jackson, Renée Carlino, Gail McHugh, Julie Prestsater,** and **Mia Sheridan,** my sisters in the creative process, and the women who had my back when I needed them. Your time and input was so valuable, (I have such a girly crush on them). I want to thank my girls over at **Authors Off the Shelf: Amy, Julie, Renée, Hadley, Toni, Emmy,** and **Becca** your support has been amazing. A BIG O shout out and thanks to my street team, **The Big O Babes (BOBs)** for pimping my work, your support and love! Lastly, **Becky Codere,** there are no words sis, you survived another creative birthing process! Thank you, for keeping me breathing, being there as I pushed, and cutting the cord before we gave **Prototype** to the world. I love you more than my luggage!

**foreword**

Falling in love is as dangerous as murder. That is the true dichotomy of life. Murder will always be seen as wicked and immoral, while love, the thieving of someone's heart, will always be seen as heroic and gallant. The emotions read with the same vehemence; love and hate, life and death, good and bad.

To most people I am Lauren Matthews, nothing more than an average woman who lives in the small town of McLean, Virginia. To others, I am a sales pitch that went unsold, a test that went astray, a lesson learned; and to the errant few who know what I am capable of ... I am a weapon designed to control populations, build governments, and make profits into the hundreds of billions of dollars. But, to one man, I am the woman he must possess, an existence he will consume, and the only conquest he is equipped to endure.

Pick your poison; that's what people say when faced with impossible choices. The problem with that is when you waver in your decisions, choices will be made for you. Ignorance has no credence when it comes to the wicked; it only makes their job that much easier. As a result, decisions were made without full-disclosure that has left me with an ambiguous future. Trusting the immoral has shaped my life and buried my soul. A blessing in wolves' clothing, designed to steal my freewill and cast my existence into a slavery that will inevitably rule over the human race. Still, I seek hope, a slice of righteousness that cracks free and floats to the surface away from the discontent.

Even though my life is not my own and it belongs to the technology ravaging my mind and ransacking my body, I still hold out for the day I will exist again outside of its evolution. I dream of the moment my lips welcome the venom without the fear of dying. For me, the only way I will ever know the truth is to pick my poison, and his name is Alejandro Fernandez.

**prologue**

*One week ago...*

This time I would be strong. *Time to take your life back!* I kept chanting in my head as I drove to the office of Grayson Industries. Marshall Grayson requested that I meet him there. Convincing in his words, he found a way to entrench himself into my thoughts again. He was the only man who I had betrayed the agency for and the one who kept me yearning for more than an occasional rapturous kiss. Marshall kept me believing he would fill the loneliest places that haunted my soul. He dangled me over the flames of desire for his own profits and gain. He's a man who stole my breath with just a look or a touch, and found a way to rule over my deepest desires while torturing me with the unwavering control he had over me.

Reasons he chose me swirled feverishly around in my head. Marshall was a dynamic force to be reckoned with and he had a way of controlling every urge that swelled in my body. But I decided that I wanted more out of my life than settling on false hopes and temporary attention from him. So what if it took years to figure it out, I felt strong enough to walk away for good.

I parked in the underground garage of Marshall's building and took the elevator up to the thirteenth floor. It was the top floor, non-existent to most people, and was highly restricted. When the elevator doors rolled open, I was greeted by Marshall's assistant, an older woman with her gray hair pulled into a tight bun. "Lauren Matthews here to see Marshall Grayson."

"And the reason you are here?"

"Marshall asked me to meet with him," I huffed. She whipped her face up from her tablet, narrowing her eyes she responded.

"Well, Miss Matthews, *Mr. Grayson* will see you now."

I nodded and pushed through the doors to her left. I guess she didn't like that I called him by his first name.

"Lauren, thank you for meeting with me on such short notice." Marshall, catching me off-guard as his six-foot stature stood behind his desk chair. I heard the door click shut at the same time he tapped the heel of his hand against the top of his soft, black leather chair. He intentionally trailed his thick fingers down across the stitched edge and pushed the chair to spin as he sauntered from behind his desk. His potent blue eyes, darker than usual, were licked with impatience as he lingeringly sized me up. He leaned in and pressed his lips to my temple. I couldn't keep from curving into his contact. My insides twisted.

"Well, you said it was urgent." *Stay strong, Lauren ... don't let your desires control your mind.*

"I did say it was urgent, didn't I ... sit?" he asked as his hand caught my elbow.

"I'd rather stand," I answered, pulling out of his grasp. He was playing me; I could feel it. His fingers withdrew from my skin and every cell in my body took notice.

"Lauren, you know why I've asked you to come see me today." His tone was sharp enough to be thought of as playful if you didn't know him. But I knew him, he wasn't playing.

"My answer is still the same, Marshall. I need ... I need to move on." My breath caught on my words. He pulled off his suit jacket and loosened his dark purple tie.

"What do I need to do to change your mind? I want you to reconsider leaving me." His short, dusky brown hair brushed across his collar as he unfastened the top button on his white dress shirt and sat back against the front of his desk.

"You meant to say, leaving Grayson Industries, right?"

"Lauren," he growled as he pulled an overconfident smile across his face and locked his arms against his chest, a mannerism that has become a sign that he was going to work his angle.

Marshall knew how to play me and make me cave on my decisions. An undeniable look, chased by a slight cock of his head; a wink and I was lost ... twisted with a smirk or a flash of his charm and I was done. He knew how to take every decision I confidently made and tangle them into moments where I'd second guess my reasons. I wasn't stupid, and was trained by the best to avoid people like him ... but that's exactly what drew me to him ... the way he could make me *feel*.

"You can't do this to me. Not anymore. This time I really am done," I groused.

"Lauren," he mused as he uncrossed his ankles and pulled me into his embrace. His clean musky scent twisted my resolve into knots and the heat from his arms made every reason I was saying no dissolve with his touch. He brought his face next to mine; his breath warmed the edge of my ear as he exhaled. "I need you more than ever. I promise this will be the last time."

His lips scraped my skin as he mentioned how he couldn't do this without me. I fell into the same look he gave me when I first told him yes so many years ago. Gradually, almost unnoticeably, Marshall methodically interlaced himself into my life, controlling more of me than just my heart rate.

"There will never be a last time with you, Marshall," I whispered breathily.

He leaned back, making sure I looked at him; his steely eyes begged for me to falter in his expression.

"Haven't I been here for you? Taken care of you, given you what all the other men have failed to give?" His eyes were vacillating between mine; his jaw tightened as he lifted his fingers to catch some loose strands of my hair and delicately tucked them back. "Do you even know what you've done to me?" Marshall whispered. And that's where he got me. His words took every ounce of pain I had buried and churned it into the desire I'd ached to have with him. "I've kept you safe, Lauren, protected your heart from being hurt again. Isn't that what you wanted me to do?"

"I don't know if I can take this."

"Take what, Lauren?" Marshall said against my flesh.

I inhaled the aroma of his hair as it ticked across my jaw. Maybe this time he would take me further than my fantasies. Clinging to the hope I could be anything to him. He dragged his hands up around my waist. Never more between us than kissing, his intentions screamed for something much more intimate. Was the assignment so important that he was willing to take me further than ever before?

"I can't take this ... what you are doing to me." My breathing sped.

"Is it so wrong? Me *taking* ... you? Your body is telling me otherwise. If you don't like what I am doing, tell me and I'll stop," he whispered between the moments his lips encountered the swell of my breasts.

I couldn't hear anything over the thundering of my heart in my ears. No, I couldn't find my voice to answer him ... nothing rolled across my tongue except the heated moans he had created.

*I can't do this ... it is just going to rip me apart ... He will never love me more than what he can use me for.* He tickled one hand down my spine before his other seized the back of my neck. Catching the curve of my backside, he tucked me against his body. This kiss went beyond our tempestuous peck on the mouth. Rapacious and potent, his tongue swiped the sharp edge of my teeth before hungrily tangling with mine.

"I need to go," I breathed as I pulled away, rubbing my fingertips across my bottom lip. Hoping, praying that I could somehow stay strong enough to keep walking.

Worked up beyond the occasional flirtatious moments we've had, suddenly … it had become real, too real, at least to me. I had wanted it for too long, but now that it was happening, I couldn't seem to allow myself to make love to someone who fed my physical desires before my emotional needs.

I reached the door handle when Marshall's voice pervaded the room.

"Lauren, wait!" He caught me around my bicep and pulled me back into his chest. His nose pushed against the curve of my head; I felt him inhale every ounce of me and for that solitary moment I believed he wanted me. "Don't leave. I need your help … more than ever before."

His words broke me. If he only saw that he meant more to me than any job. God, for just once I had wished it wasn't about what I could do for him or what he could gain from using me … But he will never see it … he'll never see me as more than a means to an end. I pushed out of his arms and let the cold vacant moment wrap its poisonous verdict around my heart.

8

"Don't worry, Marshall, I'll do it," I deadpanned before my brain realized the commitment I had made. As I pulled open his door, I felt ... defeated. *Please, stop me, Marshall ... tell me it is more than the job.*

"Lauren?"

"Yes?" My breath caught on the way he said my name and a spark of hope returned in my gut.

"I'll call you tomorrow ... with details ... and you did the right thing; you'll see," he answered.

And just like that, all the conviction I worked so hard to embody ... became the dust that vanished in a gust of wind.

# one

My eyes snapped open and I gasped for any air I could steal. My knuckles ached, gleaming pasty white as the freezing air ravaged my drenched skin. My sodden hair clung to my neck, drowning me in a cold sweat; I knew deep in my body something wasn't right.

Today was going to be different; besides being born from the nightmares brought on by my inability to say no to Marshall, I just couldn't put my finger on it. It was as if some power in the universe was trying to tell me to stay home and for once, maybe I should have listened.

Fortunately, today was the first day of my two week long vacation. I had fourteen whole days away from the agency; it was just enough time to miss my job and yet short enough to ache for more. I guess if I had a social life I would look forward to the time off, like other CIA agents. But, I'm the type that would be bored by day three and unfortunately, Marshall knew that. That's why he manipulated me into helping him this one last time. Lately, I'd become disenchanted with Marshall and his company. It wasn't that I didn't like the money or the attention he paid me when the project was a success; it had become more personal than that. I was tired of the constant ache to be with him. I wanted to be more than the girl he would call when he wanted to test out some new state-of-the-art device. So, I told him that I was done testing nanotechnology and configuring ocular gear for him. I decided to make my life more about what I needed and less about the unanswered chills he created when he'd touch me. Marshall could look at me and I'd be putty in his hands. He knew how to get to me, more than any other person alive.

I reluctantly backed my car out of the garage and joined the rat-race heading for D.C. I hated dealing with assholes that couldn't drive and tourists that never took the time to learn about the Metro system. Why I ever agreed to help Marshall this one last time was beyond me.

In no time I was turning into a tiny parking lot across from a strip mall loaded with suburbanites shopping the Black Friday super sales. I pushed open the heavy glass door labeled Optometry Office and met Doctor Finway as he stepped out from an exam room. "Good morning, Lauren, thanks for coming down," he said as he combed his fingers through his salt and pepper colored hair. He was all business this morning. Usually I'd get a peck on the cheek, a slight hug, even a wink, but today … he was different.

"Good morning, Doctor," I answered. Pleasantries weren't my strong suit. I was the type that would rather get down to business. "I'm confused. Why do you have to measure my eyes again? I thought you'd just give me the lenses?" I asked, hoping to get the answer I was looking for. He pinched his lower lip between his thumb and index finger, lost in thought. I waited before the silence turned uncomfortable.

"I mean, it seems like a waste of time … re-measuring my eyes," I stated matter of factly.

"Marshall called me personally — mentioned something about explaining it to you later," he said before he tossed the folder on the counter and began rummaging around the drawer. This time I noticed there was nothing familiar in his motions. "You wouldn't be here if he didn't feel you were the right woman for the job," he continued as his steel blue eyes gleamed.

He dropped his retinoscope into the pocket of his lab coat and spun my chair in a half circle. "Alright, I'm just about done with you." His face vacant of any warmth, he winked his left eye. Sarcasm from him was something I would never take personally, even if there was a bit of truth to it. "Lauren, these lenses, they have capabilities that have never been seen before. They make the ones you used in Pakistan look like child's play," he bragged.

I straightened up just as my iPhone chimed with a text from Marshall:

> *Your next appointment is with Roger. 10am don't be late!*

Another awkward moment clung between us before Doctor Finway cleared his throat.

"Well then, let's talk about ocular pressure. No diving or airplanes for at least two days after the lenses are installed. *Really* important you get this. I don't want to explain to your family why you've lost your eyesight. Understand?"

Without waiting for a response, he snatched up my file from the counter and left the room. My nerves frayed, everything in my body screamed to leave. *What was the purpose of this?*

Suddenly, there were three short raps at the door before Doctor Finway came in carrying a small black steel box. *It seemed strange that they come in a steel box.*

"You concerned they'd burn up in a fire?" I teased, hoping to lighten his mood. He didn't laugh; he didn't even smile.

"No, Lauren, security is a priority. We don't want them to get into the wrong hands," he answered very businesslike, before he turned back and locked the door.

His thin fingers, almost feminine in structure, slid the steel cover off the box exposing a tiny keypad. I looked down, giving him the false security he needed out of courtesy. *What exactly are we dealing with here—wrong hands? Who else knows about these lenses?*

"Lauren, these lenses are different, very different. They link to your brain." He grabbed latex gloves and pulled them on. "Well, not in a literal sense." He reached up and tapped a bright circular light above my face. I watched as he lowered the lens into my eye. The chilling texture, a horrific shooting pain, an intense flash of light burned under my pinched lids. It felt as if the lens had fingers reaching beyond my eye. The pressure built fast, pushing and twisting, as if it was creating intricate webs connecting my mind to the lens. *I tried to remember what Doctor Finway had told me, but I couldn't—what the hell did I just agree to?*

The sickening pain faded as I began to see cast shadows change to outlines of colored images. Muffled sounds of the room quietly resumed. I breathed deep, trying to erase what had just happened.

"Next eye," Doctor Finway said as he pressed his fingertips to my shoulder. A look of concern draped his face. "I'm sorry, I know I should've told you what to expect. You ok? Do you need a minute?"

"No, I'm fine, let's get this over with," I lied.

Doctor Finway repeated the process with my left eye. I felt the same pluck at my brain. As fast as the pain came, it too disappeared. The contact lenses turned and clung to my corneas; suddenly small black words appeared imprinted on the face of Doctor Finway. It was strange; I wanted to blink a hundred times and clear my eyes, but nothing helped. The words were still burnt across my vision.

*PROCESSING PLEASE WAIT*

# two

"You ok?" Roger startled me. I was standing in his small lobby, preoccupied with trying to move the wicked flashing line that sat in the bottom of my right eye. His thin pale face held deep fret lines as his eyebrows fused together.

"Well, how do you think I am?" I quipped.

"How bad was it? I told Finway to take it easy on you."

"You're a sadistic fuck, you know that, Roger? Maybe next time try doing it on yourself."

"Well, come on Lauren, nobody does guinea pig better than you ..." An impish smile spread across his clean-shaven face.

My answer? I flipped him the bird.

I had met Roger at the CIA Training Academy over thirteen years ago. We had dated once, but the chemistry wasn't there. I was actually glad because we made better friends, anyway; he always felt more like a brother.

"I'm really excited about this project." His eyes widened behind his Elvis Costello-style glasses. He pulled me into a sideways hug against his scrawny frame, making me uncomfortable.

"I need to set you up with the rest of the components that go with those lenses. How do they feel?" His inquisitive nature filled the room.

I rubbed my eyes, hoping to stop the scratching sensation across my corneas that seemed to all but disappear when I didn't think about it.

"I feel them, but Doctor Finway said that in a couple of days I won't even know they're there."

"Well, he's right. I bet even later today that sensation will go away. Basically, Lauren, it's all in your mind." He pushed his thick black glasses back up the bridge of his nose.

I wanted to tell him where he could 'stick it' and that the scratching feelings in my eyes were most definitely real, but I decided to be the bigger person.

He propped himself on the sharp edge of his mahogany desk and motioned for me to sit in a chair opposite him, his rosy red lips pulled into a straight line as he looked at me. Roger wasn't much taller than me but thinner and always wore dark colored clothes in a futile attempt to appear younger than he was. I noticed that today his brown wavy hair, which never touched the tops of his ears before, seemed to cover them just enough.

"Do you mind if I take a look at the lenses?" he asked. His broad nose, ample enough to hold his glasses in place, flared after he spoke. I shook my head as he slid from his desk, took off his glasses and stared into my eyes. As long as I had known Roger, I never realized how dark brown his eyes were.

He shuffled back behind his desk, opened one of his drawers and pulled out a box that looked like a remote control. His bony fingers pushed the buttons and motorized sounds filled the room as the top of the box slid open.

"What's that?"

"It's a nanobiosensor, a prototype that I invented," he said as he stretched on a pair of latex gloves. He pinched a pair of tweezers between his fingers and picked up the tiny biosensor. "This little thing is going to help you control those lenses."

"Control the lenses from where?" I asked.

He stared at it and I watched as his thoughts carried him away. "Lauren, I don't want you to—you gotta remember—this isn't supposed to hurt." He blushed as he stumbled over his words.

"Just wait a damn minute. Where in the hell is that thing going?" I demanded. Instantly, I got the same anxious feeling as when I knew I had gotten myself into something too deep.

"I'll install it through your nasal passage." Concern usurped his expression.

"The hell you are! That thing is not going up my nose."

"Lauren, this is everything to me. It's going to change the world. It's going to revolutionize communication ... I've put my whole life into developing it," Roger baited me.

"What are we testing for with this prototype? I mean, what are you expecting from it?" I knew asking would buy me a little time and even if his answer was vague, he quite possibly could tell me something Marshall hadn't.

"Well depends, if you're asking from a military point of reference, it will revolutionize the way we handle war. Less equipment to carry means soldiers will be more efficient on the ground. Wicked fast processing, will give access to the internet, records, viable information quicker, which will lead to less lives lost. For the everyday-Joe, well, the prototype will replace every last piece of technology they fumble with on a daily basis. They will have everything thing they need, right there with them at all times. Realistically, this could replace every piece of hardware that exists in your home. Well, with the exception of your kitchen appliances." He let out a chuckle.

I can't say my curiosity wasn't piqued.

"Tell me what to expect?" I sat up rigid. "Will it do anything permanent to my body? Cause pain, what are the side effects? I'm done with surprises, Roger. I think the lenses Doctor Finway installed are surprise enough for one day," I spat.

"You'll be uncomfortable when I install it, but nothing like the lenses. You might get a little dizzy. You're going to notice stuff. Your vision will improve; you may feel stronger. Information will transfer between your consciousness and the nanobiosensor at an instantaneous rate." He was unemotional. "The thing is, Lauren; you'll need this device to have the lenses work properly."

"How long does the device have to stay in my head?" The muscles in my face began to twitch.

"It must be removed before the lenses." The words of Doctor Finway clung to my mind. *The lenses have to be in your eyes for a minimum of two weeks.* A thumping pulse in the pit of my stomach rekindled. Nothing about having these foreign objects in my body for one day, let alone fourteen, excited me.

"Lauren, which eye is dominant?" He pointed at my face.

I swallowed hard. "The right one has the blinking cursor."

He looked at the device; his eyes smoldered and his body reflected a new found confidence.

"Okay, are you ready for this, Lauren?" Roger asked as I closed my eyes and swallowed.

"Sure." The word shot out of my mouth. *At what point do I stop going along with this?* I was torn between my unrealistic loyalty to Marshall and my own self-preservation.

"I'm going to recline your head until it's lower than your feet. I'll count down from ten. You'll feel a warm liquid enter your nose and push against the back of your throat. It is very important that you do not swallow any of it. Oh, and you might feel like you have vertigo for about five minutes." He stood with his body at a slight camber over my right side; he pushed his glasses up, wedging them lopsided across his crumpled brow and counted down from ten … I did exactly what he told me to and he did exactly what he said he would do.

"Looks like we have lift-off! The biosensor is in place."

No sooner did Roger say that when the room started to spin and I couldn't keep my mind from twisting inside out. Uncontrollable in my reflexes, I felt every nerve jump at the chance to kick at my stomach and throw up whatever small drops of this thick, bitter fluid that snuck its way past my taste buds. Roger saw my face and how my body lurched, and grabbed the trashcan from next to his desk.

"I don't remember you mentioning torture as one of the side effects!"

"Sorry about that—I guess I just forgot," he mumbled. I shot him a nasty look.

He had to be embarrassed, or maybe he just felt guilty. Either way, he refocused his attention and began to run through the steps to make sure the device linked with the lenses.

We spent the next four hours going over the functions of the prototype. When the time was up, Roger stood there in front of me, eyes narrowed behind his glasses; he was focused and confident. I looked at him and at that moment I realized I was in the presence of a true genius.

"This is incredible, Roger."

"I know."

# three

I didn't remember driving to Marshall Grayson's house. The images of what happened at Roger's kept rolling over and over in my mind. I noticed the heavy grey sky influencing the clouds to drizzle and the uneasiness as it began to roll across the heavens. I remembered getting in the car. I even remembered the first couple of turns as I left Roger's office. After that—nothing—until I found myself idling in front of Marshall's massive, black wrought iron gate.

I pressed the button on the intercom a dry monotone voice spewed from the speaker at the same time. The overcast sky won the battle and rain fell from the dark gloomy clouds. Irritated by the drab asshole in the speaker box, I took a calculated breath and answered him before I turned on my windshield wipers and rolled up my window. I looked at the clock on my dash; it was already two thirty.

*Damn it, I'm totally late. Marshall's not going to be happy. Why in the hell do I even care? We never talked about expectations. Son of a bitch, I knew better than this … here I am once again, affected by Marshall.*

By the time I pulled up to the front of his house, I was seething. A man dressed in a black tuxedo with white gloves, holding a huge black umbrella, pulled open my door as the rain still poured down.

"Good afternoon, Miss Matthews," he said, obliviously properly trained in his manners.

I got out of my car and handed him my keys. Without waiting for the umbrella to keep me dry or answering his statement, I stomped up the slippery hand-chiseled marble steps and stormed toward Marshall's house. The heavy raindrops fell against the bushes and trees, causing their leaves to shimmy and shake glistening under the drops that rolled off their leaves. Details I'd never paid attention to before, yet seemed to resonate with me at this particular moment. A unique serenity began to swallow me with every step I took. My hair was damp enough to cling to my checks and my olive blouse was beginning to stick to my skin. By the time I was ready to knock, my wild anger had cooled off to a rumbling irritation.

The whole front entry to Marshall's house was custom-built of pure glass and aged metal. The two doors were fastened to the massive solid glass windows on either side by huge burly hinges. Ivy leaves created from patina copper were intricately woven into branches, intentionally designed to make the front doors look opaque. The entire entry was no doubt designed to remind his guests just how inadequate they truly were. Marshall was wealthy beyond any normal person's understanding. The ability to get whatever he wanted, when he wanted it, was his everyday reality. Shallow as it may seem, there was something magnetizing about it.

Ashton, Marshall's butler, was an average-sized man, not muscular or undernourished looking. He was perfectly groomed so he would never be set apart from the mechanics of the house—black suit and tie.

"Good afternoon, Ms. Matthews." His English accent catered to the persona of sophistication as he answered the door.

"Hi, Ashton," I replied.

He was always nice to me, even though I knew it was his job, and he never made me feel inadequate. I guess I just found a simple comfort with him, no matter how proper he seemed with me.

"Mr. Grayson will call on you shortly. Please come in and make yourself comfortable. May I get you something to drink?"

"Why, yes, water would be perfect, thank you," I answered, mimicking the timbre of his voice.

He held his hand out, indicating where he wanted me to sit. I passed by where he pointed and meandered my way to the library, the most comfortable place in Marshall's house and by far the most captivating. High ceilings above my head and pristine Persian rugs meticulously lay under my feet. The finest Italian leather chairs and ornate gold leaf floor lamps populated the room. Rich with dark browns, reds and blacks, his library was tinted with colors that weren't meddlesome as you escaped into your favorite book. Maybe that's why I was the most comfortable here. From floor to ceiling on every wall were shelves of hardbound books with no gaps for trinkets.

I caressed my fingers along the gilded spines, browsing and wondering what adventures waited within their pages when I noticed one that was different. As a matter of fact, all it had was a handwritten symbol and a number printed underneath. Instinctively, I caught the top of the book and pulled, allowing it to find its way into my hands. It was ancient, smaller than it looked on the shelf, and heavier than I expected. It was soft worn leather that gave way as I caressed it. I found my way into an oversized chair, sat down and was ready to read it when the pale yellow glow of the lamp dissolved into a dark gray.

"Ms. Matthews, your water," the butler said, extending the glass out to me.

"Thanks, Ashton." I took a sip and set it down on the table next to me.

"Mr. Grayson will see you now, in his study. Please follow me."

He held out his hand, expecting me to give him the book. I adjusted it to my left hand and grabbed his offer with my right. I was completely aware he wanted me to leave the book in the library, but there was something about this book and I wasn't about to give it back just yet. I followed him as he walked at a brisk pace down a huge hall decorated with large oil-on-canvas paintings of what I had to assume were past relatives. Dark brown mission-style doors peppered in between the paintings. I glanced at each one, wondering what stories were locked behind them. We stopped at the end of the hall in front of a pair of massive doors pulled shut. I wondered if the story I was about to encounter was as invoking as the one I wanted to read in the old tattered book.

Ashton, in his most precise service motion, pushed the double doors open. I floated forward and he closed them behind me. Marshall looked up from his computer, his gallant eyes danced and his smile caught me. Everything I was going to tell him vanished in that instant.

It was his deep blue eyes that harnessed your soul and pulled you into his world. Marshall knew the power he had and always used it to his advantage. He was older than me by several years and exuded confidence that always commanded a room. His words masterfully wrapped themselves around your heart and possessed the deepest, most private corners of your mind. His raw, unchallenged power was influential and seductive.

I stood there consciously trying to swallow in hopes of dampening the back of my throat. His dark brown hair tumbled across his eyes as he got up from his desk and came around to greet me. I froze, my heart pounded in my ears. Every ounce of restraint I owned was dissipating in his presence ... I was losing the battle in my body. He came toward me, his arms extended and I knew to deny him would be futile.

The unyielding electricity that shot through my body as the contour of our bodies molded to one another as he pulled me into his chest. I didn't want to let go, he smelled so intoxicating. "Lauren. I am pleased you are on board with this. How are you?" His warm breath penetrated my ear. I used to love how he dragged out the *au* in my name. Now it just made my stomach tie in knots.

"I'm doing okay," I lied. My body hijacked my mind, creating a memory from a week ago when he manipulated me into agreeing to this.

"Well, you look good for a woman that's been poked, pricked and prodded." He pulled away and looked into my eyes. "Are you okay?"

I nodded, completely casting off any frustration I had left. He always knew how to make moments all about him and what he needed; this time I had to make this moment about me. I pushed my weakened feelings aside, pulled up all the dignity I could muscle and let the words spew from the deepest part of my gut.

"I agreed to this last job … that's it. Had I known what you were going to put me through, I wouldn't be standing here right now. You never told me I'd have lenses thrust into my eyes, a computer configured in my head, and my nose filled with so much god awful fluid I gagged. Why?"

Marshall stood resolute, listening without interrupting. When I was finished, he turned and pulled me closer. His aroma swarmed and caught low in my stomach. Without saying a word, he led me to the dark brown suede sofa that faced his desk. I sat down as the swell of regret filled the empty space between my heart and stomach. It wasn't fair that I had no defense to his allure.

Calmly he strolled over to a bar tucked behind his desk and pulled out two small glasses, dropped in several ice cubes and filled them with Gran Patron Platinum. He scooped them up and stood in front of me, baiting me to take the drink. When I didn't take it, he swirled the glass again. Silently, I grabbed the shot and nodded waiting for him to answer me. He pushed his glass toward me, and then downed the liquid in his glass before he narrowed his eyes at me when I didn't follow his lead.

I watched his mannerisms change before me. He pulled his broad shoulders back and cocked his head slightly. A shit-eating grin came over his face. It was the same person he became when he was about to strong-arm one of his clients into agreeing to something.

"Lauren, my love, come on ... we both knew I could get you to do anything I needed, and without a lot of explanation. I *know* how you feel about me. Now, I can see where you might think I took advantage of my position, and I am sorry for that," he continued. "But in my defense, you decided to leave me and not come back. I couldn't have that. I needed some type of insurance, something to keep you active with Grayson Industries. Roger's invention became the perfect excuse." His words cut me like a shard of glass. My heart crumbled as my soul poured from the huge hole he created. I couldn't find any words to respond.

"I had them install the prototype in your head because I knew it would buy me two weeks. That's just enough time. Then you can be on your way to whatever life you want and I will have the assets I wanted. I didn't have to convince Finway or Roger; they knew I would take care of them, just as I plan on taking care of you." The words tumbled prolifically out of his mouth. I raised the glass of Patron to my lips and took a burning drink.

Betrayal scorched every brittle thread of trust I had left. The tenacity I once regarded as an asset became the deficit I blatantly marked myself. He used me knowing I would have done this for him.

It was Marshall who ruined me for anyone else. He might as well have torn my heart from my chest, stripped the air from my lungs and left me for dead. Being here, trying to be strong, was pointless ... he found my weakness for him and kept exploiting it.

I shot the rest of the tequila and took my empty glass to the bar. On the way out I snatched up the old book, an undersized payment for the enormous pain he caused me, and barreled down the long decorative hall. I heaved open the ornate front doors and told the man in the tuxedo, holding the massive black umbrella, to bring me my car.

I was reduced to a mangled heap of emotional leftovers. The logical part of me was done with the demands of Marshall and done with Grayson Industries for good; and yet, the emotional side couldn't stop visualizing Marshall chasing after me; taking me in his arms and begging me for forgiveness. I struggled to get away as he fervently took hold of my face and finished what he started in his office days ago. The cold rain falling hard between us as it rolled and caressed down the curve of his exposed skin. He looked deep into my eyes, drawing me in as his soft lips drowned mine. His tongue sweeping vigorously through my mouth with an uncompromising fury causing my knees to weaken, igniting trimmers down my spine. Nothing stopped me from giving in to his unyielding kiss. When I opened my eyes, my car had been pulled around. The rain had slowed to a mist and just like that, so did my fantasy. It was nothing but an empty delusion.

My eyes burned, stinging with the moisture that welled in the corners and ran down my cheeks. I brushed the wetness away with the backside of my hand and remembered why I'd left. I thundered down the slippery marble stairs, hurried into my car and drove away.

**four**

I couldn't explain the unabashed hate that bubbled for Marshall. It ate away at the most vulnerable part of my heart. My tears fell fast. Before I could wipe the old ones away, new ones would form; each tear being more influential than the last. I didn't appreciate the fact that Marshall had me crying. I'm not a crier ... it's just not conducive to my line of work. My problem—I'm fiercely loyal and it was completely fucked to be treated so horribly by someone I emphatically trusted. Lesson learned—I will never trust like that again ...

I approached the wrought iron gate when the cursor that obstructed the lower part of my right eye began to flicker. It made me wonder if it was possible to contact Roger. Even if he didn't have the prototype in his head, there had to be a way to contact him ... I needed to talk to him. Roger had a way of reasoning with me when I was frustrated by Marshall. I drove a couple of miles past Marshall's property before I pulled into a well-hidden turnout on the side of the road. I turned off the key and sat there for a moment, feeling edgy and compromised. I clung to the idea that there had to be some way to contact Roger, even through his iPhone. I mumbled *Roger Clarke* and his file popped open, filling my entire vision. Anything I wanted to know was there plain as day. His full name, the last four digits of his social security number, education, previous addresses, work history, family history, medical history, people he associated with — everything. To be honest, it was a bit creepy. I forced my eyes to focus and scanned the file, looking for any way to contact him. Finally, down at the bottom on the right side, I noticed a phone icon. I focused on it and thought, *call Roger.* Suddenly the icon turned bright green and a small rectangular graphic equalizer surfaced on the screen as a phone rang impatiently in my ear. *Holy shit!*

"*Hello? This is Roger.*" His voice was calm, eerily calm. I didn't answer immediately. A low frequency hum and his voice was all I heard in my head.

"*Hello? Hello … Lauren?*" Roger asked as I watched the lines on the screen record his voice.

"Yeah, it's me," I answered in a whisper after a long pause. "*Lauren! Are you ok?*"

"Yeah, I guess so. Why? What's going on?" I asked.

"*I want you to stay where you are,*" he demanded.

"What's going on, Rog?"

"*We don't have time. Listen, I need you to stay where you are. I will call you back and tell*" — his voice cut off … silence.

The phone icon went dark and the lines on the graphic equalizer disappeared.

The words CONNECTION TERMINATED flashed red once across my eyes … something was wrong. Without thinking, I pushed open the car door, stepped out into the dampened air and tried to contact him again. Pacing back and forth, I could feel the thick air pass through my hair and moisten my skin; I was determined to hear his voice. There was so much I needed to know. Did he really betray our friendship? *He wouldn't!* There was no way he would be a part of Marshall's plan. He wouldn't manipulate me like that. I stared at the blinking cursor and screamed his name, but nothing; I couldn't reconnect with him.

Moment after painstaking moment taunted me. Time was moving too fast, cluttering my thoughts and slowing every attempt to reach Roger. Finally, his information appeared just as it did earlier; my heart pounded heavily in my chest. At last, I would get a chance to talk to him and find out what was going on. Relief spread across my mind but was stilted when a big red word blinked in a diagonal line across his information—DECEASED.

Words spun and images were plastered across my vision; my stomach muscles tighten and I stiffened as my body excreted the pain that poisoned my mind. *Was this real? Not Roger, not him. I couldn't lose him; not this way.* I couldn't believe what I read. Suddenly, I couldn't discern what was reality and what wasn't. I heard my phone chime with a text. My eyes clouded and I could barely see as I swam in the air to my car. I needed to find my phone, but it was nowhere. The more time it took to find it, the more my mind created images of Roger's death.

Finally, I swung my upper body toward the passenger's side; looking in between the seats, I spotted it. As tears clustered in my eyes, I slid my finger across the screen, scanning my previous calls. Vicious confusion clouded my mind and I couldn't think of the last time I had called him. Finally, I found his number, but it seemed to ring forever.

*Come on, pick up the phone. Come on, Rog.*

"Hi, this is Roger, leave me a message." — and then there was a beep. I pressed it hard against my ear as tears poured down my cheeks, confirmation of my worst fears.

Roger was dead.

I was snapped from my heartbreak by the phone ringing loud against my ear. I choked a short breath and looked to see who it was. NO DATA flashed across the screen. I pressed the talk button on the phone and listened.

"Lauren? — Hello? — this is George, Doctor George Finway — is this Lauren?" his voice rushed to get an answer.

Suddenly Doctor Finway's information filled my eyes, just like Roger's had.

"Lauren — listen to me very carefully, I don't have much time. You need to get out of town. Do you hear me?" I couldn't tell if I heard him on my phone or in my head.

"Get away, and do not trust anyone. Don't tell anyone where you are—understand—nobody!" He forced the words out. "I'll try and contac—"

Suddenly, horrific sounds echoed through my head. I heard him begging for his life, sobbing. My hands shook and the phone dropped from my ear, but his heinous torture didn't stop. Every thud, yelp, gasp, and tear created graphic images in my mind. They were coming from my inside my head; Sounds etched in every fiber of my being before dead silence and the big red word DECEASED filled my vision.

This exact moment, where death owned more than anything life could barter, my mind surged and was out of control. My body jerked as the acidic pain of death rotted in my trachea. Warped visions of Finway's murder embroiled my whole body from my skin to my soul; I had experienced his murder.

I snatched my phone from the floor of the car and tossed it across to the passenger's side, the old book that I had taken from Marshall's library caught my eye as it sat awry on the seat. I reached over and grabbed it with my fingertips; a slight gap appeared half way through the pile of pages. I balanced the book in my hand and re-examined it again, running my index finger across the tiny gap. I gently pulled the pages apart with my thumb. A small single sheet of paper was purposely taped to the left side of the book.

I looked at the words and recognized the handwriting immediately—It was Roger's. I placed my hand on the paper, wanting to feel his words speak to me. I tried to decipher the notes he had scribbled in countless directions, skimming what he wrote. My heart tumbled into my gut and the wind that kept me alive vanished all together. Peering up at me from the bottom of the page were five names, four I was quite familiar with and one I didn't know at all.

1. Roger Clarke ✓ 2. Marshall Grayson ✓ 3. George Finway ✓ 4. Sam Wilkins ✓ 5. Lauren Matthews.

Every name had a check mark behind it but with the exception of mine. *What did that mean?* I read what Roger had written below the five names. The deepest betrayal I have *ever* experienced was confirmed by four affirming words.

*Prototypes installed and functional.*

Just when I didn't think my life could get any worse, a pitch black limousine pulled up behind my car. I glanced in the rear-view mirror and realized there was no time to escape. I ripped the paper from the book and shoved it into my back pocket before hurling the book onto the floor. I grabbed my cell phone and shoved it into my front pocket. I should have known that Marshall would find me.

I watched the driver's reflection in my rear-view mirror as he stepped out of the limo and lumbered up to my car. I knew it was Marshall's chauffeur, the perfect black suit and small captain's hat gave him away. His huge knuckle rapped on my window, motioning me to roll it down. I let it go a quarter of the way, peeking up to see him. I sat there waiting

35

for him to speak, trying not to look like a deer in the headlights.

"Ms. Matthews, Mr. Grayson would like me to bring you to the house."

"Well, what if I say no?"

"Ms. Matthews, you know he won't take no for an answer." He dropped his hand to the front edge of his jacket and pulled it back; there tucked in a shoulder holster was a semi-automatic handgun. It was just enough evidence to convince me there was no way I was going to get away from Marshall or his massive goon. I nodded and closed my window. I leaned over the passenger's seat and wiggled my way to reach the old book I so carelessly threw to the floor. With the old book in one hand and my keys in the other, I stepped out and locked my door.

I slipped into the limo and positioned myself in the far corner. I kept my hands busy by flipping pages of the ancient book back and forth. My mind shuffled images of what was going to happen when I got to Marshall's house. Suddenly the name *Sam Wilkins* flashed across my thoughts. The cursor in the bottom of my eye flickered and data materialize. I shuttered. Anticipating another huge red word blinking across the file, but when the information appeared I gasped. Somehow in my mind I figured Sam was a man, I didn't expect to see a woman's picture embedded amongst the file. The details of the image left much to be desired but the way her long red hair cascaded and pressed on her shoulders, I could tell she was beautiful. I skimmed down through her information and found the same phone icon that Doctor Finway and Roger had in their files. I focused on it. It turned bright green and again the graphic equalizer appeared. It was a long shot, but this could be my one chance to contact her and maybe the only way I was going to save my life.

The ringing in my head became impatient as each ring quickly pursued the next. We were through the gate and on the driveway leading to Marshall's. I knew I was running out of time; I was anxious to talk to her.

"Who's there?" Sam asked after she answered the ringing in my ears.

I focused on communicating with her in my thoughts, hoping she was able to hear me. *"You don't know me, my name's Lauren Matthews and I've got some bad news."*

"I'm sorry, but you must be mistaken I'm —"

I focused and projected my thoughts, interrupting her before she could hang up. *"No wait, Roger and George are dead! I'm in Marshall's limo and I think he is going to kill me. You're the only person I think I can trust."*

All the lines on the graphic equalizer that vibrantly moved as she spoke dropped flat. She was silent.

"Samantha — please," I whispered.

"Where are you now?" she questioned. I forced myself to focus and send the last part of my message.

*"I'm on the way up to his house; I don't have much time. I know about the prototype embedded in your head."*

I waited for a slight moment before I continued. *"You, Marshall and I are the only ones left. I'm the next one to be killed. Please, I need your help."*

The limousine came to an abrupt halt and I adjusted my sight to what was happening outside the car. Sam must have severed our connection because all of a sudden I was looking out with both eyes. The door quickly swung open and I knew I was going to face Marshall—alone.

I noticed the sun had already set and the stars were beginning to shine. I saw a slight glow in the sky. The moon must be hiding behind the dark clouds pasted randomly in the heavens. The perfect indication it's been a long day.

My eyes stung as they adjusted to the lights that lit the way to Marshall's huge marble steps. I tried to remember the last time I was here at night. I scoured my memories, but found nothing. Environments change in the dark, things disappear in different lighting. I thought about the advantage I'd have if I had a way to record what I was seeing. Immediately a small camera icon appeared in the upper left hand corner of my eye. Teeny numbers rolled over as the recording started with a small graphic equalizer that showed the inflection of the sounds around me. I followed the same tuxedo man I had ignored hours earlier today. He stopped and directed me to a sidewalk that wrapped symmetrically around to the side of the house. Now he was following closely behind me. I made sure I scanned the landscape, carefully recording it, just in case I needed to escape.

The door on the side of the house was unimpressive, a plain white metal with a numbered keypad located just above the doorknob. I felt the man's arm brush past me and push several numbers on the keypad.

The door popped unlocked and he pulled it open before he shoved me through and slammed the door. I turned around and saw I was alone.

The room was small, a dungeon with white walls. It had no character, no color. When an unmarked door on the other side of the room swung open, my heart leapt into my throat. My pulse hammered fiercely through my veins as I looked at him. I couldn't tell if it was from fear or passion. Maybe a little of both. My eyes recorded Marshall from his feet to his head, stalling at his eyes. He slowly entered the cold sterile room; the door shut firmly behind him.

"Are you okay, Lauren?" he asked in a low solemn tone. His intrinsic steely eyes lulled across my body. I straightened up and deflected the trance he knowingly could put me under. It was time to embody the years of experience and training to disconnect from him.

"I'm fine." I turned away, dragging my confidence behind me. Marshall swiftly caught my forearm and swung me around; anger smoldered in his eyes.

"I want to know what you've done!" he barked, "ever since you left my house, people have been dying! What do you know?" He clutched my arm tighter, but I was able to jerk out of his grasp.

"I was about to ask you the same question!"

He took a step toward me, but I shuffled back. Instantly, Marshall's strained eyes filled with worry, his body saddled with hesitancy.

"You? Wait … you don't think it was me?"

"I don't know what to believe!" I barked, pulling my face out of his clutch. I shuffled backward until I was against the wall and had nowhere else to go. I closed my eyes, pushing my fears from my mind.

"What was my mission?" I demanded.

"Test the prototype," he said shaking his head. I glared deep into his eyes and asked again.

"Bullshit, Marshall! What in the hell was my mission?"

Silence filled the space between us; pushing back with his words, he answered.

"Does it matter now? It won't change anything … it won't bring them back."

I grabbed the words he spat at me and masterfully warped them into the confidence I needed to keep pressing.

"I don't care, I want to know what was I suppose to do. What was my mission? You owe me that, Marshall. I haven't asked for anything!" I pushed my body forward as my breath forced its way into my lungs. I felt like I was standing over him even though he towered above me. He dropped his eyes from my glare and began to speak.

"It was supposed to be simple, Lauren. We were going to fly to California, spend a couple of days and be back in D.C. before anyone knew we were gone. You would've been our person on the inside. Roger would remain here in D.C. and be the one to deliver the intelligence we needed to make the switch. I was going to be the one to keep—" he paused, "well, let's just say some *very* influential people at bay." He seemed to glow as he spoke. "George would be at the airport—in case we encountered any problems." He stopped and looked at me.

I focused on his eyes, and in my head I named all the people he rambled off in his explanation. He had only named four of the five on the list.

"What about Sam? What was she suppose to do?"

He gave me a puzzled look, like he didn't understand.

"Sam? Sam who?" he questioned.

I took a deep deliberate breath and repeated, "Samantha Wilkins."

My head started to shuffle images as I tried to put together my own thoughts. *Her name was on that sheet of paper taped into the old book from his library. She knew who Marshall was when I called her. Was Roger double-dealing between Marshall and Sam? What have I done? She knows that I'm here. She has the prototype in her head. She will have complete information on all of us. If Marshall is as innocent as he leads on, I might have just signed away both of our lives!*

My face must have read like a horror story. Before I could bring my mind back into the little white room, Marshall grabbed my arms and shook me.

"Lauren, what do you know? You need to tell me now," he demanded.

"I don't know; she was in the list of names, people who have the proto — she had a checkmark by her name," I babbled.

He pulled me to the chairs, sat me down and looked straight into my eyes, like he was willing the information from my mind.

"What list of names … Lauren, what list of names?" I melted at once; the tables had turned; now I was answering the questions he needed to know.

"Roger had a list of names … people who had the prototype implanted in their heads." The words poured out of me; I was a sieve and he knew it. He knew he still held a power over me that flared when I was weak.

"We're *all* on it … even you!" I said. He shifted and knelt in front of me.

"Where's this list?" he asked softly. When I didn't answer, he repeated his question, narrowing his eyes.

"Where's the list?"

There was no way I was going to tell him what else was on the paper. If he knew Roger had extensive notes on the capabilities of the prototype, he would've sold the technology already. There was no way I could let Roger's notes ever be seen by anyone.

"It's gone ... I burnt it ... when I found out Roger was murdered. I followed protocol for if we had evidence that we didn't want found," I methodically lied.

As shocked as I was about his reaction, that little piece of paper would be my lifeline and I sure wasn't ready to give it up that easily. I still didn't know if I could trust anyone, especially Marshall.

He stood planted and determinately in front of me. "My driver will take you to your car." At this point he had lifted me from the chair with nominal effort and continued speaking. "Go home and get some rest." I tried to interrupt, but he wouldn't have it. "I am taking you to the airport in the morning. Pack for California. You need to get out of town for a couple of weeks, just long enough for the dust to settle. When I've taken care of the issues here, I'll meet you in California."

I shook my head and allowed him to pull me to the door. It was important that Marshall didn't know I had Roger's paper in my back pocket or a video recording of him in my head. Just like Doctor Finway said in his last words to me. *Don't trust anyone.*

**five**

The limousine pulled away without waiting for me to fumble for my keys. Fortunately, working a car lock open in the dark was just another pitiful challenge I mastered years ago. I pulled the door opened, slid in and had the car running in no time. It felt like eons ago when I was in the car driving to escape Marshall's house. Looking down at my speedometer out of habit, I saw that my eye was still recording. I couldn't believe how fast I became accustomed to the graphics that sat in the corners of my vision. Mumbling *stop recording* caused it to disappear. I just wanted to get home, lock my door and isolate myself in my room so I could pull the small paper from my pocket. It was necessary to understand what Roger had written on that page.

Twenty-five minutes later I was home. Making my way to the kitchen, I grabbed a glass of water, pulled my laptop off my dining room table and headed to my bedroom. I reached into my back pocket, took a deep breath and pulled out the paper I had crumpled earlier. I pushed it flat on my desk and studied the letters and numbers that made up words.

I kept scanning the paper, intrigued by what Roger scribbled on the paper. If this is true, he was the first person with this thing implanted in his head. I kept reading:

Electrodes enhance body strength, for how long? Physical Strength + mental Access = total control. Mandatory adjustment to access before other subjects tested.

That line plucked at my thoughts. *What was he doing? Did he make an adjustment before I had my biosensor implanted?*

I concentrated on the file pathway. Instantly, it popped up and blocked my vision. *The adjustment was never made, but why?* As I dug deeper into the encrypted file, a map of the United States popped up; little pinprick spots lit up covering the map with heavy concentrations on both coasts and along the borders of Canada and Mexico. *What was I seeing? What did these bright tiny lights symbolize?* I focused on a random pinprick and a textbox burst open with some person's information.

JONATHAN CAMERON REYES
SS#:547-330-2547
5'11"/EYES:BRN/HAIR:BRN
LOC:BALT.MD/C.O.D:CANCER
10/18/1965 – 12/17/2019

*Who is this?* My eyes scanned his information, frozen on the dates of his life span. It was strange; whoever input this data projected the date of his death six years into the future.

Terror plucked at my soul as I focused on another spot on the map; my heart thundered in my chest as the information scorched my vision.

GEORGE EUGENE FINWAY, M.D.
SS#:320-099-5666
6'2"/EYES:BLUE/HAIR:BLK
LOC:WASH.DC/C.O.D:SUICIDE
04/15/1959-11/30/2013

It was today's date. A cold rush shivered down my spine. The cause of death was registered as a suicide. It was no suicide. Doctor Finway was murdered; I heard it with my own ears.

My chest tightened with every thunderous pump of my heart. I could feel that there was something ominous, something ... very dangerous about what I was seeing.

I zoomed in on the file name at the top of the map — *Persons of Interest.*

*What the hell was this ... and what if I was one?*

I scanned the pinpricks near the D.C. area and whispered, "Lauren Jean Matthews."

My eyes burning from not blinking as I struggled to read the words in the textbox.

LAUREN JEAN MATTHEWS
SS#:654-23-1970
5'7"/EYES:GREEN/HAIR:BLN
4/23/1978-12/06/2013
LOC:WASH.DC/C.O.D:APHIXIATION

It was that simple; in seven days I would be dead.

I thought about Marshall and a textbox with his name popped up from the D.C. area, cascading over mine. His textbox was different; under his name was an image of a locked padlock and the words "ACCESS DENIED," in red capital letters.

"What?" I questioned aloud.

Next, I mumbled Roger Clarke. His textbox appeared and oddly enough his also had a locked padlock image and the red flashing words, "ACCESS DENIED". I wish I could find out what he had to protect so fervently, even in his death? I needed to get out of my head and into something separate from myself, so I grabbed my laptop and carelessly set it at the foot of my bed. Maybe I'll find something that will unlock the maze that's tangled my thoughts. I started typing Roger's full name when an instant message appeared on my computer screen. It was my mother, Carolyn Jean Wilson. A person whose attempt to understand social media went no further than an abandoned Facebook page and AOL's instant message account. She is a real estate lawyer that knows nothing about my life with the CIA. I keep waiting for the day when she figures out that I don't sell computers.

*Hey sweetie, miss U!*

*Are you dating anyone yet?*

*Saw U online.*

**_Tried to call—your phone is disconnected._**

**_What's wrong? Do you need $? <3_**

I visualized her and how she always looked when she worried. Her green eyes peppered with specks of dark brown would water and shrink. The laugh lines that outlined her thin lips would weigh heavy and pull down her smile. The crease that was permanently carved between her eyebrows would deepen and she would anxiously pull back her shoulder length, ash-brown hair and continually tuck it behind her ears. My mom had always been that easy to read.

I will never forget the day she had called to me from downstairs.

_"Lauren, your father and I have to speak to you." She had forced out the words as her teeth had caught her lower lip._

_I had followed her to the dining room where my father had been sitting with his hands clasped strongly in front of him and he had been staring down at the floor. When he looked up at me, I remember seeing a broken man. I'll never forget how his dark hazel eyes had been sunken and swollen with red unforgiving puffy circles. His long thin eyelashes had been clumped together with the remnants of his tears. His cheeks were gaunt and his pale face had hung hopelessly._

_"Hi, honey bunny," he said in a low pathetic voice._

*I didn't know whether I should have hugged him or should have run away. Mom had put her hand on the small of my back and made sure I sat down at the table. I remembered obeying and she had followed.*

*"Honey," she said as she looked in my eyes before she continued, "Your father is going to ... we've decided to ... I need —"*

*She had been struggling to try to find the best way to tell me that she and dad had decided to get a divorce. I had never seen my mom fumble her words like that before.*

*My dad looked at me from across the table.*

*"I'm sorry, Lauren. Mom and I just couldn't make it work." Tears filled his eyes and ran down his cheeks.*

*I couldn't have helped myself, I had followed him in his pain. This had been the only time in my entire life I had ever seen my father cry. I had glanced over to my mom; tears were streaming down her cheeks. My heart desperately hammered in my chest, before it dropped into my gut, and I felt like I was going to heave. That had been the first time in my life I felt defeated, annihilated, and alone. Sadly enough, it wouldn't be the last.*

Another sentence came up from my mother as it chimed the familiar tone ripping me from my painful memories.

**Lauren, I know you're online, answer me!**

I typed back as fast as I could.

**Hi mom, I am fine!**

49

*I miss U too. I MIGHT be coming out see U soon.*

*I have some work I have to do first.*

*I will call U, K <3 me*

I pressed the send button on the screen and a short moment later she wrote back.

*Get your phone checked — call me tomorrow!*

*Love U <3 Mom*

I refocused and finished typing Roger Clarke on my laptop when I remembered that my pinprick textbox was still open. I was going to be killed in cold blood in seven days. I peered at the clock at the bottom of the screen, 12:28am. Actually, I was going to be dead in six.

 The stress of the day won the war between the fears of my death and trying to break Roger's access code; my eyes shut heavy and they didn't rebound open. I remembered the conversation I had with Marshall earlier in the day.

*You need to pack for California; I will pick you up in the morning and when I have taken care of the issues here in D.C., I'll join you.*

His words floated into my head as I drifted off.

*I was floating in dilapidated dinghy on a raging sea. Torrent waves thrashing me back and forth, the water flooding over the sides; I was suffocating. Drowning in the fear of my death, I couldn't breathe. I couldn't open my eyes, I couldn't scream out to save my life. I was dying ... little by little I was slipping away. Suddenly, a faint voice came at me from the middle of nowhere ..."Lauren, come to me, I will save you ... don't be afraid. Open your eyes." I struggled to see, opening my eyes as wide as I could, I looked out across the stormy sea and saw Marshall walking toward the boat, his feet cresting the sea, water licking at his ankles, his hands were spread wide. "I can't breathe, I am suffocating, I can't ... I need help ... I'm dying, Marshall, I'm dying." I screamed at him as I pulled at my throat. "You aren't dying, you are living," Marshall answered as he stood at the edge of my boat still holding his hands out to me. "I'm dead! That's it Marshall, you are here to take me to hell!"*

"Lauren, you're not dead. You're having a nightmare … Lauren, wake up!" I heard Marshall say as his body disappeared from the sea. I opened my eyes, gasping for air, breathing again, air burning as it filled my lungs.

"Lauren … You are here, at home," Marshall assured me, holding my face in his hands.

"I was dying!"

"Well, you didn't die … and we need to go. I need to get you to California. Where are your bags?" he asked looking around.

"Um—well—I'll pack now, just enough for a week, right?" I asked him. I was still discombobulated from my nightmare.

I shuffled out of my bed, realizing I was in the same clothes I wore yesterday; I didn't have time to be embarrassed. I knew the best thing I could do was to collect up and pack some essentials, including the paper that held Roger's notes about the computer imbedded in my head. I looked over to the desk where I remembered flattening it out last night and I froze in my tracks, it wasn't there. I tried to think about moving it last night but I couldn't remember taking the paper from my desk. I needed to make sure I had that paper. I needed it with me in California.

"Are you okay, Lauren?" Marshall asked.

"Yeah, I just need to find something I had with me when I came home last night." After the words left my mouth, I regretted them.

"Are you looking for this?" He held up the same paper I took from the old book in his library, the paper that held the file pathway that granted access the encrypted government file that nobody, not even Marshall, should have access to. Yes, the same paper I told Marshall that I burned, that's what I was looking for. Our eyes met, and I knew he was furious.

"Lauren, why did you lie to me? Why wouldn't you tell me the truth?—you never burnt this." He was angry; his eyes narrowed and darkened. He wasn't the same man from my dreams.

I had to think carefully before I spoke. Now more than ever, I had to make sure I said the right words. I took a huge gulp of air and tried to remain calm.

"Marshall, you can't honestly tell me that you thought that I'd burned that paper—"

"Good or bad, you should have come to me—I could've helped you—I could have protected you! Now I have—" He stopped mid sentence.

I was going to see the side of him that I've only heard about. I've always been everything he has asked me to be ... but right now, I had to take the chance of him either killing me or letting me go, so I took my chances and attacked him head on.

"Now what Marshall?—just because I didn't come to you with this information what are you going to do?—you gonna take me out? All the years mean nothing to you? My loyalty is nothing to you?" I figured I better get to point as quickly as possible. "Roger, Doctor Finway; they're both dead, Marshall! Which one of us is next? Four other people already had it in their heads. Why?"

He put the paper down on my desk. His demeanor changed as he turned his back to me and started to talk as if I wasn't in the room.

"This is useless ... it's not going to be worth it. I need her to go to California ... she needs to finish the job! No, wait ... he's paid a lot of money up front for it and he wants to make sure it's viable before the transfer."

*Job? Viable?* "Transfer What?" I interrupted and broke his concentration.

"Disconnect." I heard him mumbled under his breath.

I stood toe to toe with him, right in his face; I had reached the end of my rope. I wanted answers.

"What job? Who were you talking to? What do you mean viable? Start answering me. You're in my house and I ..." It had suddenly clicked that I never let him in and I locked up tighter than a drum before I went to bed. "Wait, how did you get in?"

"Lauren, you need to settle down ... I'm willing to tell you what you *need* to know, but you work for me and with that comes the responsibilities. I need you in California." He was holding my arms right

54

below my shoulders, looking me square in the eyes as he wrapped his words in a deliberate tone. "Settle down ... I'll tell you what you *want* to hear."

I pulled out of his grasp.

"I want the truth, Marshall!" I howled.

"Fine, the truth," he sighed before continuing, "Roger and I entered into a contract with a private company that specializes in data storage and replication of software for a clandestine sect of our government." His eyes widened as he kept talking, "Roger was the brains behind the nanobiotechnology and I was the capital. We made a perfect team. He created it without anyone knowing about it, not even you. When it came time to reveal it, we couldn't risk using the computer in Roger's head for obvious reasons. And I couldn't compromise my position in the negotiations. Sam and Finway were no-goes from the start. So we had to make the next logical choice, and that was you. I could've let the prototype go to Russia, North Korea or whoever was willing to pay our price," he chastised, showing me that he was in charge.

"Basically, Marshall, what you're telling me is that you manipulated me mentally and physically so you could sell me to your highest bidder? —you son of a bitch! Obviously I was completely wrong about you—but Roger, he wouldn't do that. He has morals. He wouldn't be so vile."

I stood up and leaned forward. He shifted into a defensive stance.

"You're wrong about Roger, Lauren. He was the one who suggested you because you're fiercely loyal. I was the one who questioned him about your abilities. Roger reassured me, he said, *"Lauren has the perfect mind for this, and that if anyone could handle the psychological component of the prototype, she could."* He relaxed, as I stood there again frozen as my mind worked to catch up to my reactions.

"The page you found in the old book at my library, Roger put it there. He knew you would find it … it was the only way he was able to test the prototype objectively; as long as you thought you weren't suppose to see it, he would be able to collect data on your ability to interact with the prototype and how the prototype responded to you and your commands."

I cradled my head in my hands between my knees. Everything was so convoluted I couldn't hear him speak. I couldn't register what he was telling me. Moreover, I couldn't trust him.

Almost broken, I questioned him, "Who's in California?"

"The buyer — that's all you need to know."

I took a long deep breath knowing I couldn't accept his answer. "What's to stop our government from finding and killing you for the technology?"

There was an awkward pause between us. I lifted my head and peered into his eyes, waiting for him to answer me.

"You … they aren't going to kill us because they need Roger's research. As long as you are around, we will live ... they aren't going to kill the people who keep the prototype evolving."

I stood there trying to wrap my brain around all of the information. "So as long as you keep developing *upgrades* to the computer in my head, they won't come and kill you."

He turned and looked at me and mumbled, "Yeah, something like that."

"Well how do you suppose you're going to do that if Roger's dead?"

He stared into my eyes, and I could tell he didn't want to answer me. There was a long period of silence between us.

"Who were you talking to?" I demanded, hoping he would say Roger. He started to say something when he stopped. I could see on his face that something was terribly wrong. He looked at me and then peered out the window. Without warning he leapt at me, his body pinned me to the bed before rolling us both down onto the floor. His gun cut and pressed into my stomach. He rose slightly and in seconds drew his gun.

"Stay down here and don't move! I am going to check the house; I'll be back." He carefully slid his body off of mine; while crouching he scurried across to my bedroom door. "Don't move," he repeated in a whisper before turning and leaving the room.

There was no way in hell I was going to stay here if someone was breaking into my house. I stretched my hand up to my nightstand and slowly pulled the drawer open. I reached in, groping for my loaded revolver. I was not the type to wait around for danger to find me.

I crawled to my bedroom window, leaned against the wall, and shimmied up to look out into my backyard. I peeked out and saw three quarters of my yard. The other quarter of my yard I couldn't see, dictating to me what I had to do. I crawled on my belly to the bedroom door and scurried down the hall, stealthy as possible. Seconds later I pushed up against the wall in my living room. My french doors were sprung wide open to my side yard patio. I peered around the corner and saw two people talking and the only one I recognized was Marshall.

I noticed that he didn't have his gun drawn or pointed at the person. In fact, it seemed they were in a friendly conversation. His body blocked my vision and for a moment my heart leapt in my chest, thinking it was Roger. Consequently, once Marshall shifted to one side, I caught a glimpse of the person, a woman; someone I had only met in my head. Her long red hair blazed in the sunlight and her facial expressions were strong and forceful. It was Samantha Wilkins. I leaned closer to hear their conversation.

"Marshall, she might compromise the exchange now that you told her so much!" Her left hand split the air pushing it toward him while using the backside of her other to pop him in the chest.

"Don't worry, she doesn't know all the details." He grabbed her hands and pulled her toward him.

"What details did you leave out? Because from what I heard —"

"Sweetheart, don't worry, after we get what we want, we'll be long gone, and it will be just you and me." He slowly bent forward and kissed her.

I watched as his mouth curved to bury hers. Every moment I had pushed my lips against his filled the hollow space in my heart. His hands anchored strong into her back just before he reached feverishly down to her rear, thrusting her hips against him; she let out a slight whimper. Was he giving her what I achingly craved for so many years? Every moment of betrayal thundered through my body.

"Haven't I been here for you? Taken care of you, given you what all the other men have failed?" Marshall whispered across her cheek.

I recognized those words, they were the same ones he said when using me. My blood boiled as I watched her push her hands up into his hair and give him back every ounce of desire. The pit in my stomach tore open, spilling any hope for us. Instead of desolation filling my soul, it seethed with anger. *Marshall had lied to me about everything.*

I hurried to the garage, yanked the keys from the hook in the wall and noticed that my garage door had been left wide open. *That's the way Marshall got into my house.* I slipped into my car and put the gun on the passengers' seat as I backed out. I had no idea where I was going. I just knew I needed to get out of there. I left without anything; no bag packed for California, no tickets, and no money.

The images of Marshall and Sam kissing exploded through my mind, causing everything in my soul to become tainted. Every job I did for him, every moment I ached for him to want me ... all were lies painted by his deception. I just needed to get the hell out of there, deal with situations as they came up. Unexpectedly, I felt my phone vibrated in my front pocket. I didn't want to look at it; I didn't want to see that Marshall had discovered I was gone. I didn't want to hear any more of his devious lies. Then, again, I was a slave to technology ... and the urge to see if it was him out-weighted my stubbornness. I glanced at it and noticed it was my dad calling. Wouldn't you know it ... He must have a built-in daughter distraught detector. It never seemed to fail that in a crisis of emotional upheaval, he'd call me. I answered it as cheerful as I could.

"Hi, Dad."

"Hey, Honey Bunny." *He always called me that.* "I talked to your mom last night and she mentioned you were coming home to see us."

My mom could never keep information to herself. There is no way I would ever tell her what I truly do for a living. If she knew I was a field agent for the CIA, she would probably inadvertently post it on her debunk Facebook page or forward it to her entire email list. I know better than that, so for all intents and purposes, I worked for a company that sells computers and instructional software to the government.

My dad, on the other hand, knows I work for the CIA. However, thinks I sit at a desk decoding and deciphering messages all day; he doesn't know that I am a field agent. "Dad, I told her that I *might* be coming to California. I have some work I have to do. I'll call you if I'm coming, I promise." I was glad to hear his voice but at the same time it caused me to feel homesick. I missed my family.

"Okay, Hon, well, I love you, and don't forget to call me!"

"I will. Love you, too! Bye." I tapped my phone off and I kept driving as my mind throttled back to Marshall and how I got involved with him beyond the CIA.

A file popped up, robbing my vision. It was very unnerving to have shit pop up without so much as a warning. Fortunately I was at a stop sign. Marshall's picture appeared and the phone receiver icon glowed bright green. *Mental note ... shit popping up in your line of vision is a bad thing when driving.* I wonder if that was something Roger was working on before he die — was murdered.

"What do you want?" I spouted.

"*I want you to come back to the house. Where are you? I told you to stay in the room.*"

His voice echoed loud through my head.

"I am not coming back; you are nothing more than a fucking liar. I am done being used by you, Marshall. Done. God, I don't even know why I trusted you. All I had done was trust you and you've done nothing but lie to me from the very beginning."

*"Lauren, what are you talking about? You need to get back here. You're bags are still here with your laptop."*

"Marshall, you are the biggest asshole I know; you lied to me about Sam. I saw you with her in my side yard. Didn't you think I would come looking for you?" I asked combatively.

He was silent for a long, excruciating minute.

*"Lauren, don't make me play my hand,"* he stated resolvedly. A chill scurried across my skin.

"What are you talking about, Marshall?" My question lingered in my head.

*"Isn't your mother in San Francisco?"* His words were like spears of ice running through my veins. I stared at the equalizer in my eye as it recorded his words. The one fear that all agents have is a threat against their family. I had no choice.

A moment of silence grew between us.

"Fine."

*"Good, drive safely,"* he replied.

The file disappeared and I had my vision back in my right eye. I flipped a U-turn and headed back to my house. And like that ... I hated him. I hated his ice-drenched words that dragged me back to him, hated the fear he sparked in my heart for my family, and I hated that he still had enough control to make me come back to him. When I pulled my car into my garage, Marshall was waiting with Sam by his side. My blood boiled through my veins ... it wasn't enough that he threatened my family, now he thinks I'm going to be okay with that woman in my house?

I grabbed the revolver that openly sat on the passenger's seat and slid it into my waistband, wedging it in the small of my back as I got out of my car.

"Glad you're back, Lauren," he said.

"You made it quite clear I had no choice," I countered.

"You always have a choice," he said with an arrogant smirk.

"Well, maybe in your world, but it my world I value people's lives." I slammed the car door and walked past him and Sam, the biggest mistake he's made, as I entered my kitchen. I was done bantering with him. They followed behind me.

"Lauren, I want to finish our conversation. I'll hold this for you." I felt him snatch the revolver from the band of my jeans. I swung around and grabbed his wrist, our eyes met.

"Lauren, let go of my wrist."

My hand tightened.

"I want my gun back, Marshall," I leered.

"I'm not an imbecile, Lauren. I'm not giving the gun back to you, and you aren't in any position to try and negotiate conditions with me." His hands flexed tighter around the handle. I squeezed a little tighter before I let go of his wrist. I wanted him to know that he had no control over me.

"I've been more than patient with you. Where's your safe?"

Without answering him, I lead him to my room where I had left my half-packed bag at the foot of the bed, next to my laptop. I went straight to the safe, looked around and took advantage of feeding the combination into the silent keypad when he looked away. I opened it just enough so he could slip the gun in before I closed it.

"Okay ... now let's talk," he snarled.

I didn't respond; instead, I stood up pushing my shoulders back and slipped past him down the hall and into my living room. His loud footsteps echoed, letting me know that he was only a couple of strides behind me.

I paced around the corner and was taken aback. Sam was standing, facing an Ansel Adams photo of Yosemite that hung on my wall. She was intently staring before she turned and watched me enter the room. She was strikingly beautiful. Her long cascading hair was a deep fire red that perfectly framed her color-lavished face. Her light green eyes swallowed me with every blink of her thick long eyelashes. I hated her for being so beautiful; I just wanted to rip out her throat. Painfully, I could see exactly why Marshall was so taken by her.

"You must be Lauren," she said in a deep breathy voice.

"Of course, she'd have a sexy voice too," I mumbled to myself.

Her hips hung in the air and her body brushed the space she occupied as she swayed toward me. Her five-foot-seven voluptuously curvy figure represented the type of body most women would kill for. She held out her hand, expecting me to reach for it. I grabbed her hand and forced her close to me.

"Who do you work for?" I asked.

Her eyes narrowed as she gently loosened my fingers from her hand and pulled away, meeting my eyes as she spoke.

"I work for Marshall." Sam tossed me a gutsy smile.

"Are you sure of that? Because up until this morning I worked for Marshall, too," I groused, hoping that she'd contemplate my words.

"You still work for me, Lauren. You will always work for me," Marshall interrupted as he came into the room, striding with his shoulders back and his hands brushing across his pants. I looked at him and all I felt was repulsed. I knew better than to wager a bet in his psychological bullshit game. I still didn't know if he had someone at my mom's house waiting to hurt her.

"I don't know about that, Marshall. I used to think that Roger and I meant something to you, but after today, I realize we were just pawns, played so you can keep pursuing this fucked up idea about selling this technology," I snarled.

"Pawns? Is that what you think? You have no idea what I'm pursuing, and right now that is beside the point. I need *you* to fly to California and meet with the buyer," he insisted.

"Well that's exactly my point. If you were involved in or pursuing something greater than your own damn ego, you'd know that Doctor Finway said

I can't fly or dive for the first two days after the lenses were installed in my eyes. So unless you want to ruin your investment, I am here until tomorrow." I got up, casting a fake smile at Sam before heading to my room.

I had to finish packing for California. My whole life seemed to be wrapped up in *have to's*. No matter the side of the coin, be it pain or anger I felt for Marshall and Sam, I knew there was no way I could avoid going. I hadn't been willing to risk testing Marshall's follow through … besides, my mom's life had depended on it.

**seven**

My duffle bag sat packed at the foot of the bed, ready to go. Marshall softly rapped on my bedroom door as he opened it.

"Sam just left," he said, shutting the door behind him.

"I don't really care," I muttered under my breath. I hated her on so many levels, but mainly for being so beautiful. "Give me the details I need to know for my trip to California." I briskly crossed past him, waiting for his answer as I forced a couple extra things in my duffle bag.

"I have you on a flight leaving National Airport tomorrow at ten forty-five." He handed me the ticket with a new driver's license. I tossed it on my nightstand, unopened and continued to shove things into my bag.

"You should arrive at SFO around one in the afternoon. I booked you on a nonstop flight." I didn't respond. "I need to give you instructions. What you're going to do once you're in San Francisco." His hand wrapped around my arm, gripping me like I was a child being scolded. I yanked away as I spun around. Hell would freeze over before he'd get a chance to manhandle me. "Lauren, I have to upload the file," he insisted.

"Just give me the file."

"I can't physically hand it to you. It's up here," he hissed as he tapped his finger against his temple.

"How do you plan on me getting it then?"

"It's a wireless transmission. The lenses are encoded with patterns programmed to recognize and sync with each other. I have to look into your eyes."

"What? You're telling me Roger invents this world-altering prototype; and in order to share files, you have to stare into my eyes?" Sarcasm dripped from my words. This was an all around bad idea.

I started to feel the ebb and flow of the unchallenged power someone else had over the prototype in my head. *What's to stop him from sending me a corrupt file or a virus to destroy my mind? Or worse my heart forgets what my mind has stockpiled against him?*

"Wait a minute, Marshall. You're telling me that just by staring into my eyes, you'll be able to download a file into my head? I'm not comfortable with that." I had to think of my safety now that Roger was gone.

"There has to be another option. Can't you download it onto my laptop and then I will upload it to this thing in my head?"

I had to protect myself ... Those were my conditions! He stood there silent and motionless like he was almost considering it.

"Nope, that's not going to work. It's too risky. I don't want it downloaded to any computers outside of our devices."

There was no way in hell that I was going to let Marshall, or anyone, download anything into my head. I had to think fast, I had to come up with something that would show him that I had options too. That's when the idea to call Sam popped into my head.

"Fine," I hissed, "You leave me no other choice." I stood firm, readying myself for what I was about to do.

"Call Samantha Wilkins," I said loud and clear for Marshall to hear. I focused on the icon with the phone receiver. It was ringing in my head as I watched the graphic equalizer bounce with every sound.

"*Hello, Lauren,*" the sultry voice answered.

"Hi, Samantha, I am here with Marshall and —"

"Lauren, you are playing a very dangerous game," Marshall yelled. "Whatever's going on in your head, Lauren, you'd better think twice before you do something you are going to regret," Marshall threatened. I was getting under his skin.

I continued to talk to Sam. "I think you should know, while you were making future plans with him —"

"Disconnect, Lauren, do it now!" Marshall interrupted. His body pulsated with rage. I pushed the fear down in my gut. I wasn't going to let him download anything in my head.

"Sam, you should be aware, Marshall's been pushing for me to take our relationship farther. But I would have never considered sex with him if I had known about you," I said loud and clear.

I disconnected from Samantha, hoping what I said would bring her to my house. She seemed like the type of woman that would fight to save what belonged to her, Marshall being no exception.

When I looked over at Marshall, his body was trembling and his eyes were thick with revenge. He came at me and caught me around my forearms, caging my arms to my sides. He was livid, his breathing ragged.

"You just couldn't leave it alone." He shoved me and I stumbled back, losing my balance, my heel caught on the area rug and I fell backward cracking my head against the edge of my nightstand. The room swirled in my eyes as I lay there a moment before everything faded out to pitch black ... I *was* going to die today after all. My sporadic breathing in my ears became nothing more than shallow huffs as I struggled to stay conscious, then everything was gone ... yeah, I was dead.

I opened my eyes to complete nothingness. There wasn't even a beam of light from anywhere. Could it be that the prototype had malfunctioned and left me blind to the world, or could this quite possibly be my purgatory? Bewildered, I lifted my head and tried to gain my bearings. Slowly I began to see the faded bright colors of words blinking in my lower line of vision. The last thing I remembered was Marshall coming at me and now I lay here in my bed with the words **FILE DOWNLOAD COMPLETE** crowding my right eye.

"What the hell!" I tried to scream but my sternum hurt so badly, like someone had swung a sledgehammer a million times against my chest and stomach. The shooting pain radiating through my diaphragm was paralyzing. Maybe death would have been easier than this. I bit my bottom lip hoping the pain would subside in my chest. It didn't; I pressed my hands as hard as I could against my sternum and got up from the bed to leave.

Hobbling across my room with my chest feeling like it was going to crumble under my hands, I pulled open my bedroom door and instantly met Samantha face to face. She was furious. We both stared at each other; circling like worked up boxers, our hands clutched in fists ready to fight, waiting for the other one to blink.

"Who the hell downloaded the file into my head?" I demanded. My fists still primed to fight, I made sure to keep at a good striking distance.

"I did," she answered. Her eyes glowed with satisfaction as we continued to circle around in a dance of wills.

"How do I know you're telling the truth?" I snarled.

"You don't," she answered

"Where in the hell is Marshall?" I retaliated.

"It doesn't matter. He told me what you did. What were you thinking? You're lucky he didn't kill you. I would've killed you!"

"He's already tried to kill me! He made it perfectly clear he'll harm my mother. So go ahead and try it." I released my fists and motioned her to start something. She just looked at me and dropped her hands. A moment marked by anger, fear and pain dissipated in her stance. She was giving up. Surrendering to what I stood for. Maybe through all of the bullshit, she was starting to see the light.

"Marshall wants me to see if you can access the file. If you have any questions—"

"I don't need your help to do my job," I interrupted. I dropped my hands; the pain in my chest swelled fast. "Aahh," I groused.

"Are you okay?" Sam took a step closer to me.

"I'm fine. Keep your fucking hands off me." I pushed her away as I straightened up.

"Well, Lauren, after what you did, I could give a rat's ass about helping you."

"And your threat is supposed to be helpful or convincing?"

"Hey, all I need to do is make sure the file transferred so."

I stood frozen where I was, thinking about her words and the empty threats she spewed at me just mere seconds ago. She rolled her eyes and pointed to the bed.

"Would you prefer the chair?" she asked as she collected my desk chair and rolled it over to the bed.

"Either one you're the most comfortable with." What the hell was I supposed to do? If I didn't find out what she downloaded, I was going to be screwed anyway. I walked over and pressed both hands against my sternum before I slowly sat on the bed.

She rolled my desk chair in front of me and spoke in her sexy, breathy tone. "Pull up the folder labeled, m-t-c-c-d, delivery date and location."

"Why should I trust you?" I asked.

"Because right now, I'm all you've got," she answered.

There was at least one thing I remembered Roger telling me. Nobody could access the files in my head unless they could mimic my vocal tones and patterns. That was one of the security protocols he designed for the device. Even if someone downloaded an unknown file into my head, they couldn't access it or open it. *Nice job, Roger.* A pang of sadness filled my heart. Even though I wanted to soak in the pain of Roger's death, I had to figure out what Marshall's plans were.

"Are you going to California with Marshall?" I asked pulling my hair back from my face and smiling as pleasant as I could. I didn't want her in my head … and I was willing to do about anything to avoid it.

"No, now that Roger's gotten himself killed, I have to do his job." I felt my body flinch and my mouth fall open. I wasn't ready for her callous, cold hearted words.

"Can't you do the job in California? Wouldn't Marshall want you to meet with the buyer? You seem to be pretty knowledgeable about it."

"I am not that involved Lauren; I just know how these types of deals go. I worked for—" She stopped and cleared her throat. "I know these people and what they want." She tried to correct her words a little too late.

"Who are they? What do they want to do with Roger's technology?" I pressed just enough, hoping she would volunteer some information.

"They are people that don't have time to play games." She spoke cautiously, keeping her words vague as she stiffened. "They want the technology that Roger invented and the rights to all of the future software upgrades," she volunteered in a whisper.

"Who am I supposed to meet?" I asked.

She rubbed her hands up and down her thighs, clearing the perspiration that pushed from her pores as she looked around.

"You're meeting with the president of Spartacus Industries. Marshall's meeting with their competition and I am the one that will upload the pass code to the company who wants it the most."

"Name? Give me a name!" I demanded. The more I procrastinated opening the file, the better sense I would have of its contents. She hesitated for a moment and then began to talk.

"His name is Alejandro, and his company is in— well, let's just say—it takes technology, modifies it then advances it way beyond our conceivable potential. He is a very powerful and very hazardous man."

Her words sat heavy in my gut. It was inevitable that once the technology was sold to Alejandro, his company will choose to do whatever they want with it, including selling it to our country's worst enemies. I had become nothing more than Marshall's whore and he was nothing more than my pimp.

I needed more information on this Alejandro and what he was planning on doing with the prototype technology. I decided to open the file Sam downloaded into my head.

"What was the file name again?"

She rumbled it off like it was a phone number. The file opened my entire focus was on the information that filled my eyes. It was all about Spartacus Industries' history, their mission statement and high-level management names with contact information. I immediately saw Alejandro's name and I focused on it. His file filled my eyes. Captivated by his life, I forgot Samantha was in the room.

"File minimize," I muttered.

"What, you're not crazy? No brain eating virus?" Sam's sarcasm was thick.

"No."

"Ok — well give me a minute — let me pull up the file." Her expression preoccupied by her eyes dancing back and forth. A few minutes passed when she started to talk.

"Ok, now let me see — "

"What are you doing?"

She held up her hand with her pointer finger across her lips, her eyes widened as her face owned the flush that rose against her cheek bones.

"Hi, Marshall—yeah the file is downloaded; she's awake and I was able to test that the file transferred completely—no—yeah, ok, see you, What time again?—Ok, good. Bye." Her attention focused on me again.

"Well, let's get this done." Samantha seemed to be a little warmer to me; as if we were friends, only I knew better. Being in my line of work you learn how quickly people could turn on you if you had something they needed. "Lauren, make sure you pull up the file on Spartacus Industries and study it. We can't afford any mistakes. Marshall will be following you to San Francisco, no matter what he tries to tell you. He is booked on the next flight out after yours." The warmth in her voice continued.

"What is this?" I questioned. She didn't answer, and instead continued to instruct me.

"You need to read and reread the document labeled *mission* before you touch down at SFO. Use your time wisely. You will only get one chance at this!" A scowl broke across her face as she spoke. Preoccupied, she turned and scampered out; finally, I was alone.

Out the front window I noticed the only light outside was the glare from the crescent moon and the dusting of stars in the sky. Even though I was passed out half the day, my body still reacted to the pull of the moon. I was tired and the muscles across my chest ached. I slipped into the shower, let the hot water slide and dance across my skin, relaxing me enough to feel the stress dissipate through my skin. I pulled the towel across my skin before I put on my favorite pair of pajamas and decided to make my way to the kitchen for a glass of water. Alone, exhausted and ready to call it a night, I surely wasn't expecting to hear footsteps creeping up behind me. I spun around and found Marshall entering my kitchen with Sam trailing. Her eyes, focused on me and her eyebrows raised as she mouthed, *read the document labeled mission* behind Marshall's back. I nodded.

"Marshall, call me when you have her in the air," Samantha breathed and walked out, making sure not to acknowledge me as she left. I turned with my glass of water, not looking at Marshall and headed toward my room and wordlessly pointed to the guest bedroom as I passed it. I heard the door close before I shut my bedroom door and locked it behind me. I crawled into bed … I was mentally spent and physically done and I just wanted to get a good night's sleep.

Of course, I didn't sleep well. Thoughts of California pushed their way into my subconscious. My alarm clock belched an awful sound at five am causing me to spring up. Pain shot through the back of my head and down into my stomach. I couldn't let the pain slow me down today. Of all days, today I had to be at the airport by seven thirty. I fumbled for the lamp next to my bed as it lit the room just enough to see where I had to go. I flipped the covers off, slipped into my robe and headed to the kitchen.

The guest bedroom's door was pushed opened enough to see if Marshall had spent the night. The bed was made and the only evidence that anyone was even in the room was the small black duffle bag that sat at the end of the bed. I followed the aroma of French Roast coffee that wafted from the kitchen, feeding my addiction to caffeine first thing in the morning.

"Good morning," Marshall said in a more than acceptable chipper voice. I noticed his hair was wet and combed tame. Damn him, he must've showered while I was asleep. His dark blue t-shirt showed off his muscular back while the edges of his sleeves hugged tight to his biceps. His denim jeans tugged at his backside and pulled at his thighs, bunching just enough at his ankles. I knew he was bad for me, a poisonous strike from a dangerous snake. But there was that miniscule part of me, the crumb that tainted my whole body that believed I could wake up to him every morning, make all my fantasies a reality. Reality is what I needed. He was the reason I was hurting and I didn't want to forget that—ever.

"Morning," I managed to mumble. I reached past him and grabbed a coffee mug from the cabinet.

"I found some eggs and bread. I thought you would want to eat something before we rushed off to the airport." After filling my coffee cup, I went into the dining room and cleared some of the papers that took possession over my table before sitting down and sipping my coffee. I think he got the feeling that I wasn't happy with him. His voice rose from the kitchen.

"How do you like your eggs?"

"Over easy," I huffed. *Funny how forced my statement seemed since there was nothing easy about today.*

"How about over hard? The yolk broke," he called.

"Fine." *That was more like it anyway.*

Marshall breezed out of the kitchen with a plate in each hand. He busied himself as if he was a waiter, sliding the plate down in front of me, before pulling a couple napkins and forks out of his back pocket. He straddled the chair across from me and lowered himself in front of his breakfast.

"Lauren, the client you're meeting in California is very important to me. His company represents the future of my business — of *our* business." He swung his fork in a circular motion toward me. "I need to know if you are going to follow through with this." He looked at me, his eyes drew narrow. Demands pressed at my chest and my answer swelled from my throat.

"Marshall, I have no idea what you want me to do. All I know is that you're sending me to California, and you've set up meetings with some buyer. I know he's interested in the technology in my head. I know you've threatened my mother's life and

I know you've left me no choice. I have to do this for you. That's all I know."

He rolled his eyes as he pulled his lips into a slight haughty frown.

"His name is Alejandro, I met him back in 2002, when his business was new and he was young. He had this idea that he'd be able to change the world, but the world ... well, it got the better of him. From that point on he has done what he wants to whomever he wants, when he wants. Lauren, he'll take Roger's work and transform it. Just think, there will be a day when everyone will have this biotechnology in their head and it will be because we didn't give up. It's exactly what Roger would have wanted us to do." His eyes gleamed.

"Marshall, I'm not a fucking idiot, let's just call a spade a spade. You are selling it to him because he is going to pay you a shit load of money for the product." I stood up from the table and continued. "Tell me you took care of us. You, know, the three of us that still has the prototype in our bodies. You at least took care of that, right?"

"Yes, I did. Alejandro will have exclusive rights to all of the technology and software upgrades ... except for the five ... ummm, well, the three prototypes that are activated and in use. Lauren, we will have hardware and software upgrades for life." His words were like poison being thrust through my veins. *Life?*

"I'm going to fly to California next week," Marshall droned before he shoveled another cluster of scrambled eggs off his plate. I remembered what Sam told me about Marshall being on the flight right after mine. I was skeptical and didn't trust either of them completely. I snatched both of our plates and took them to the sink before I walked back and confronted him.

"What day *are* you coming to California? I'll need your flight information. I assume I'll be picking you up." He looked at me and without missing a beat he answered.

"Alejandro's sending a car—don't worry about me. He's sending one for you, too." I watched his eyes and searched for a hidden answer he didn't want to give.

"Wait, I called my mom and told her to come pick me up. It's been too long since I've seen her." He didn't look too comfortable with my choice, but I guess he decided to pick his battles with me today. He broke off, pulled his cell phone from his belt and made a call.

I took advantage of him being occupied to grab my bag from my bedroom and finish packing some essentials in my carryon. By the time I grabbed the tickets with the new driver's license and put my bags by the front door, Marshall was off the phone and ready to head out.

**eight**

We arrived at National Airport by seven thirty. I was already irritated by the fact that Marshall wanted me to be stuck waiting three hours before I could board my flight. I fumbled for my tickets and drivers license and handed them to the ticket agent.

"Did you enjoy your stay in our nation's capital, Miss Turnbuckle?" The words that squeaked from her mouth were something I was not mentally prepared to hear. It was only when I looked up at her did I realize that she was addressing me.

Caught off guard, I answered her question. "Oh—um, yeah I did. Thanks for asking."

"You must be excited to get home to California," she said rhetorically and continued, "well, I would like to thank you for flying with us on Northwest Airlines." She handed me my ticket and smiled. I smiled back. I didn't want to spend any more time dealing with this ... I just wanted to be done.

After I collected my carryon and laptop and pushed on my shoes, I rushed to my gate. Once I arrived in the waiting area, I pulled out my phone and glanced at the time—over two hours to kill I was determined to look at the situation as the cup was half full; I leaned up against the wall opposite my gate and dialed my mom. She answered after two rings. I spent the first couple of minutes warding off her worried relationship questions before enduring an exhausting one-way conversation about her job, computer problems, my social life, and all the things she wanted to do while I was back home. I managed to get a couple of words in edgewise though and tell her I needed to cut it short and call my dad. Needless to say, after the short conversation with my dad, I was officially homesick. Considering I haven't been back to California in over a couple of years ... it makes me ache for brisk summer days and foggy mornings. It totally sucked that both conversations only burnt up thirty minutes and caused me to crave seafood.

It wasn't until the information on the flight board started flashing that the conversation I had with the ticket agent popped back into my head. *Did you enjoy your stay in our nation's capital, Miss Turnbuckle? — Turnbuckle? You must be excited to get home — home? — my ticket — where is my ticket?* Finding it in the side pocket of my carryon, I pulled it out and flipped it over. The license, heavier than the ticket, slid out.

*CALIFORNIA DRIVER LICENSE*
*MARTHA ALLISON TURNBUCKLE*
*2901 VALLEJO STREET*
*SAN FRANCISCO, CA 94123*

I pulled out the ticket Marshall gave me and looked at it. It was a one-way flight to San Francisco. My heart climbed into my throat. *What was he planning?* Millions of thoughts ran through my head, but only one stuck ... he didn't expect me to come back. A one-way ticket meant one of two things. Either he was thinking I would be killed or he expected me to stay on the west coast. Neither option was okay with me.

I got up and paced over to the other side of the crowded gate and focused on the blinking cursor in my peripheral vision. It was truly amazing how I didn't even see the cursor anymore. I mumbled "Call Samantha Wilkins." Suddenly her file came up and the phone icon lit green. It started to ring and like always, the graphic equalizer appeared as it recorded the tones. She answered after the third ring.

*"Hi Lauren, is everything ok?"* I could hear a hint of concern.

"No, everything is not ok," I whispered. "I am standing here in the airport looking at my ticket, and—" I stopped before I gave to much information.

*"What is it Lauren?"*

I looked around the airport to make sure I didn't look too crazy talking to myself.

"Tell me what Marshall's plans are—*for me*," I demanded.

*"What do you mean?"* Her voice rang in my head.

"Come on, Sam, he must've told you what is going to happen to me in California. I'm tired of being treated like an idiot!" My face flushed hot and my ears burned warm.

*"Calm down, what's going on – what happened?"*

"Marshall gave me a one-way ticket to San Francisco and a California issued license." There was a long silence on the other end of the connection.

*"I am sorry, Lauren, I don't know what to say, you need to talk to Marshall,"* she said before our connection was gone.

I was confused; one minute she wanted to help me and then the next she was convoluted and cold. I was truly at a loss. The only thing she had been adamant about was reading the mission file she downloaded in my head. Without wasting any more time, I opened the file and scanned it until I saw a tab labeled mission. I focused on it and let the information wash over me. I wanted the information on the page to talk to me as I read the first line.

THE OBJECTIVE OF THIS MISSION IS TO ACCESS SPARTACUS INDUSTRIES MAINFRAME COMPUTER, PENETRATE THEIR ENCRYPTION SYSTEM AND DOWNLOAD THE FILE LABELED: VISIONARY INSPIRATION SF/2013.

I flinched as a voice interrupted my concentration.

"Good morning, ladies and gentleman. At this time we would like to start pre-boarding ..." I minimized the file and grabbed my carryon. Out of the corner of my eye I spotted the Washington Times on the table. Scooping up the newspaper, I slid it under my arm. After the ticket agent scanned my boarding pass, I walked down the ramp and boarded the plane.

When I reached my seat in first class, I stuffed the newspaper in the front pouch and handed my bag to the stewardess. The one thing Marshall always did right was get first class tickets when I had to fly. He always traveled that way and he made sure I did, too. I slipped into my oversized chair and pulled down the footrest. I wanted to relax, but the file that I had minimized called to me. "Maximize file," I muttered under my breath. It came up and I surfed through the words until I got to the place I left off and began to read again.

ONCE YOU'VE PROCURED THE FILE
DESTROY ITS EXISTENCE ON SI'S
MAINFRAME. LEAVE <u>NO</u> EVIDENCE.
*** IF COMPROMISED IN <u>ANY WAY</u>
ABORT MISSION*** FIND A <u>CLEAN</u>
HOUSE AND INITIATE CONTACT.
THIS MISSION IS NOT TO BE TAKEN
CASUALLY. YOUR LIFE <u>IS</u> IN DANGER.

I stopped; I had to back up and process what I just read. Not the part about my life being in danger, that comes with the job, but the part that I have to destroy the file on the mainframe computer at SI. My expectation for this *mission* was unclear. Now I was taking a file from this Alejandro guy instead of leaving one.

I was bemused by all of the conversations I had with Marshall. He had told me that he was selling the technology to Alejandro. I had to go to California to demonstrate its abilities. Alejandro would modify the computer and sell it off. He had told me that Roger's computer would be in everyone's head. It didn't add up. *What was Marshall not telling me?* Then the conversations I had with Samantha came back to me.

All the images came crashing down, suffocating me in the memories of her actions, replicating in my mind what she must have done. She was the one that downloaded the file in my head before Marshall came to see me. She was always secretive when the three of us were together. Come to think of it, since she downloaded the file into my head, the three of us hadn't been together at the same time. She added the mission document and ordered my ticket and driver license. *What other data did she tamper with in that file? How much of this does Marshall know?*

The words of Doctor Finway raged in my head … *don't trust anyone.* Who am I going to turn to? I can't trust anyone now. Marshall had threatened my family and every word out of Sam's mouth has been a lie. I pulled the newspaper from the pouch in front of me and opened it to the obituaries. There it was, third entry down on the left side. *Roger Fredrick Clarke.* I didn't read any further. I couldn't bring myself to have the pain of his death invade my soul again.

"He's dead; Roger's gone," I sobbed out loud, finally grasping that he was never coming back; I will never see him again. My heart was invaded, striped and ripped apart. My mind began to spiral down into a dark lonesome place, a place I had been carefully avoiding since the day I heard him murdered.

"Miss, are you okay? Is there something I can do to help you?" A shallow voice consoled me.

There was something familiar about that voice. Somehow, some way, I knew that voice. I felt a deep, warm sense of safety and familiarity before I even saw who it was. I looked across the aisle and our eyes met. I couldn't believe who I saw. It couldn't be—I heard him die ... he was dead. I just read the evidence that filled a space in the obituaries was incorrect; I had to be crazy. I blinked several times, pushing my hands to my eyes, rubbing the irrational thoughts that he could even be on the flight. When I looked at him ... he was real.

"Roger!" I screamed as I bolted at him and wrapped my arms around his neck. I didn't want to let go, I didn't want anything to take away the comfort I had just found. I was afraid he wasn't real. A cruel hallucination I didn't understand.

"Hey, ouch—your squeezing me, I—can't—breathe," he complained with a smile.

*This has to be a dream, I know I'm dreaming!*

"How? —You're alive—when? Oh my God, I am so glad you're here. I am so—" I couldn't find the words fast enough. My body went limp and I broke down and wept in his arms. It was Roger in the flesh and blood.

His arms released me and let my feet touch the floor, but I wasn't ready to let go. I felt a hand that didn't belong to either of us rub my back and a voice I didn't recognize spoke.

"We are getting ready for takeoff. I have to ask you both to please find your seats." I was in shock; he was with me on this flight, alive.

"Lauren, you never came to my office the next day. I had to assume you were in trouble."

"Well, I was in trouble; I tried to connect with you but the computer said you were — I just took care of myself." I heard my voice go low and dry.

Roger was sitting across the aisle from me. I just wanted to hear him speak. I wanted to be comfortable again, I needed that. He leaned toward me. "Lauren, I'm sorry you had to go through that. I didn't have enough time to warn you. I had to die to save my life."

I leaned into him as he spoke and it was like I never lost him.

"Why? What happened?"

"Someone wants me dead. They even hired an assassin to do it; but I beat him to the punch, he found me dead. I heard the guy talking to someone on his phone, saying he finished me off." Goosebumps broached my skin.

"Who do you think it is?" People's faces began to flash in my head.

"I don't know. I can't worry about it, we don't have much time before arriving in California and we have a lot to catch up on."

As always, he was good at changing the subject and I just went along.

The plane pulled from the runway, pressure pushed heavy on my body. The nose of the jet heightened and we were in the air, a huge sense of relief washed over my body.

"Roger, do you know a woman named Samantha?" I asked.

He thought for a moment before he answered me.

"Yeah, I do. She was someone that Marshall brought in to help with the job." He sounded tired.

"You don't sound like you are too enthusiastic about her," I answered quickly.

"No it's not that, we need to spend the limited time we have getting you ready for the meeting with the buyer in California," he growled.

"Roger you need to know, I think Samantha downloaded different plans in my head. Marshall talked about selling this to a guy named Alejandro." He looked down at his hands. I noticed a small surge of energy jolt his body when I said Alejandro. "The document I read said I had to download a file off SI's mainframe then destroy any evidence that it ever existed on their computer." He stared in my eyes catching up with what I just said.

"Lauren, do you mind if I access the file?" he asked as his voice pressed the sober words at me.

"I don't mind, but how? Where are you going to do this?" I asked. He thought for a moment before he answered me.

"When I created the prototype, I installed an encrypted Wi-Fi connection. It will basically let us to transfer files over a short distance. I'm going to go to the lavatory, meet me there." He unbuckled his seatbelt and carefully sauntered down the aisle.

I watched which door he entered and then followed him a couple of minutes later. I looked around and noticed nobody paid attention to us. I lightly knocked on the first class lavatory door.

Roger spoke first.

"This is what I'm going to do. I have a program on my prototype that allows me to take control and access the file in your head. I'm going to read what she installed. I have the original file in my head so if they are different, I can tell."

*Holy shit, was I really going to let him have complete control of my head?*

"Wait, Roger. Is there a way we could transfer the file? No offense, but I have had too many people in my head lately. I would prefer if you just downloaded it onto your comp- prototype," I stated, trying to be diplomatic.

"Sure, but it will take a little longer being that we are up twenty-five thousand feet. You might want to make yourself comfortable," he answered. I hopped onto the tiny counter and waited.

"It might take up to ten minutes. Ok?" he confirmed.

"Yeah—Okay," I answered as I accessed the file.

He was right; it took the whole ten minutes to download. I guess Wi-Fi just isn't the same in the stratosphere. It could have been all the images and documents, which was a pretty immense file. I was a little uncomfortable sitting on the small counter when the temperature in the crowded lavatory was smothering. I could feel my skin become sultry and sweat beads collected around my hairline and back of my neck. I was grateful he was alive and with me.

*File Transfer Complete* appeared across my vision at the same time Roger broke the trance between us. He was exceedingly superior when he navigated through his computer; I felt odd trying to keep up and understand what he was doing. Maybe allowing him to access my head would have worked better.

"Sorry, Lauren, but I want to compare the files. If I'm able to figure out the difference, we can plan our next step. Head back to your seat; I'll follow you in a couple of minutes, so it doesn't look like you just joined the mile high club," Roger said, bemused. Even through all of this, he was able to bring a smile to my face.

I punched him before I unlocked the lavatory door and slowly swung it open. I was embarrassed to notice a person waiting for the restroom. Lucky enough the door next to mine opened at the same time and the person waiting chose the other lavatory instead of mine.

Roger came back a couple of minutes later, just like he said and sat across the aisle from me. He twitched his head, asking me to lean in. We stretched to meet in the middle without leaving our seats.

"Lauren, I looked over the file and found the document that Sam uploaded. It is not part of the original. It was created yesterday at five forty-five pm. All of the original documents and files are dated November fifteenth, two thousand thirteen. That means she embedded the document for you to see after Marshall gave her the file." His brow furrowed.

"That means, she has to be working for someone else or Marshall *is* changing his plans without telling me," I responded.

We sat for a minute, looking at each other but not seeing each other. Our minds in deep thought, almost like we were competing to see who could figure out the missing pieces of this mind-boggling puzzle first.

He convinced the man next to me to change seats. Roger always had an attentive manor. I was relieved our conversation would be a little more private, and I had to admit my neck did feel better.

"You know Doctor Finway's dead, right?" I blurted out, hoping he could tell me that Finway faked his death too. Roger's face turned white and twisted in anguish. I guess he really was dead.

"I saw it on the news. It was my fault. If I didn't push him into helping me, he wouldn't have killed himself." He looked down.

I could see his entire demeanor change. He suddenly became very heavy and his shoulders rounded. I had to stop him from his guilt-looming thoughts. I interrupted his meltdown.

"Roger, he didn't kill himself, he was murdered." He looked up at me, his eyes shallow and wet. "I was on the phone with him and this thing in my head recorded it." I was taken aback at how matter of fact these words came out of my mouth. It felt like he was murdered eons ago; however, it had been less than forty-eight hours.

"I didn't know that. I'm sorry. I wish I could have been there for you. I'm so sorry." His voice filled with warmth that wrapped completely around my heart, cradling it in true remorse.

"I know this might be the wrong time to ask, but I would like to access that file." He was delicate, almost apologetic.

"Right now? I don't know, Roger," I retorted.

"No worries, I'm sorry I even asked. It was insensitive of me." Roger shifted in his seat. The horrific yells and sounds of his murder were too fresh in my mind. I feared reliving the experience might tilt my mind into being unhinged forever. I was always able to compartmentalize parts of my mind; today I didn't have the propensity. I wasn't ready to take a chance.

We were two and a half hours into the flight and we still didn't know who killed Doctor Finway or who Samantha worked for. Roger and I needed to originate a plan of action before we landed. One thing we both agreed upon was that we weren't telling *anyone* he was alive. Because of the enormity of the file, we decided to split it up and we each took a section. I studied all of the personnel files and he scrutinized all of the intelligence collected on Spartacus Industries. I was scanning the file of Terence Cummings, a researcher and developer for SI. I expected to see a stereotypical geeky guy like Roger; instead I saw a gorgeous African American man with thick long dreadlocks and a body the size of a lineman in the NFL.

Terence Cummings was the person who tied Sam to Spartacus Industries. He was the one assigned to modify Roger's prototype. Samantha Wilkins was listed as a reference and the person he requested to work with him on the project. In his statement he requests Sam because of her background in computer programming and software development. He mentions that she's been a loyal employee for over ten years. *Why would Sam tell me that I needed to destroy the file on the mainframe computer at SI? If she works for Alejandro's company, why would she want to ruin it? Unless she read the file and was as disturbed as I was about Roger's prototype being used on innocent people.* Suddenly I heard Roger's voice in my head.

*"She works for both the CIA and Alejandro!"* he said.

I minimized Terence's file.

*"How would you know?"* I asked.

*"Because I found the information she left in her file,"* Roger answered.

I scanned the information and there it was; she started working for the CIA around the same time I did. I read further down and noticed the last entry 2013 Domestic- MindWarp? What was that? I clicked on it, hoping it would open to the information about the operation. No luck, it led me to a restricted page. Now we knew what Roger had to do; he needed to find and crack the security codes for the MindWarp file. It had to be the file that contained the reason why she was acting as a double agent.

Roger scoured page after page, looking for anything that would give us a hint to Sam's main objective while I scanned all the information in her file. I couldn't find anything on her relationship with Marshall or Alejandro and Spartacus Industries, and Roger didn't have any luck breaching the codes.

Terence Cummings' file sat minimized in my eye for a solid couple of hours until I put it together that Terence just may be our way into SI. "Hey, Rog, I forgot to tell you what I found out about Samantha in the personnel files. There's someone who could be our potential way in to the mainframe computer of SI, Terence Cummings." I took a breath and continued. "Sam's been working at Spartacus Industries for fourteen years. And get this, according to the CIA employee document, she has been at the agency for only thirteen years." Roger just looked at me and shook his head.

Everything we found out about Sam was contradictory. We couldn't catch a break, and we needed one fast.

"This can't be possible!" Roger gasped.

"What is it?" When I minimized the file and saw the look on his face, I knew it was bad.

He glanced over and whispered the file path. I searched through a couple of files until I had it open in my sight.

He waited a moment while I skimmed through the information.

"Lauren, this can't be happening." Panic invaded his expression.

I pushed my hand toward him making him stop talking and I read it to myself a second time.

*While the "prototype" or nano technology could be quite useful in everyday circumstances, the objective in shifting its purpose outweighs the value for the 'average' citizen. The financial outcome of domestic and foreign governments' demands will be unprecedented in SI's history.* I kept reading when I came to a paragraph that caused chills down my spine. *The 'prototype' is the future of all securities and warfare worldwide. The factor of total control and swift complete action is unarguably superior and unprecedented. Governments will have unparalleled authority over their military. This will give levied power to the country that procures the technology first. With the development of future programs, and unforeseen potential in biological applications, governments could use said technology to facilitate population management. Giving said proprietor the ability to effortlessly and anonymously control the spread of infectious diseases, political unrest, civil disobedience and terrorist activity without significant risk to general populous.*

I stopped reading and looked at Roger. My feelings mimicked his as his eyes grew glossy and every ounce of color was gone from his face.

"Do you know what this means, Roger? There will be nothing to stop governments from wiping out hundreds of thousands, if not millions of people. All they have to do is create code for lethal viruses and upload it into people's heads. They can easily make it look like a pandemic outbreak. Nothing can stop them from targeting and controlling specific groups. They won't ever have to deal with germ warfare again … all they'll have to do is mandate the installation of your technology in every person's head and within seconds they'll have the ability to track people, collect data, manipulate and control them, and when they can't get anything else from that person, they will simply wipe them out."

"I had no idea they were going to use my technology for that. Lauren I give you my word, I didn't consider the capability of virtual germ warfare."

"What did you think would happen, Roger? You can't create a technology like this and expect people to embrace the humanity it unwittingly destroys."

"Lauren, I swear."

I just stared at him, unable to give him the expression he desperately needed from me. I couldn't make him feel okay with this. And he knew it.

A voice suffused the speakers in the plane, uttering something about starting our descent into

San Francisco. Great, we didn't know who killed Doctor Finway, no idea who Sam was loyal to and no concrete plan of action for California. A five-hour flight and we were still at square one. The only thing I knew for sure, I had to stop Roger's technology from being sold. I had to find a way to destroy it before it destroyed any more people's lives.

# nine

We landed in San Francisco at one o'clock, and by one thirty we were off the plane and heading toward the baggage claim. Roger needed to pee, so he hustled over to the first bathroom he saw.

In all of the hoopla of finding out Roger was alive and Sam was a backstabber, I forgot to call my mom to pick me up. I spotted some phones by the ladies room. Experience told me that most likely Marshall had my cell phone tapped, so I called her from a landline. On a good day she was about thirty minutes away from the airport, so I kept the conversation short. When I hung up and glanced across the airport, I saw Marshall and Sam walking from gate forty-eight. Both carried large black briefcases that hung from their shoulders. I watched them as they scanned the terminal and leisurely walked in the direction of the baggage claim. Suddenly, Marshall broke away from Sam and walked toward the men's restroom. The same restroom Roger was in. We had a problem ... nobody knew Roger was alive.

I had to think fast. "Call Roger" flew across my lips. The receiver icon lit green and appeared in the corner of my vision. Luckily for him, he answered on the second ring.

"Marshall's heading your way!" My voice was harsh and cursory. Then we were disconnected. I could only hope that he had enough time to ditch into a stall or find a place to take cover. Keeping my eyes on Sam, I got lost in the landscape of people. She was scanning the area, looking for anything out of the ordinary. I worked my way into the middle of the group, keeping my eyes on Sam the entire time. I wasn't about to look away. I was relieved when she didn't notice me; instead she entered the women's restroom. It was time Roger and I got out of the airport.

A tiny fuse of panic surfaced when I tried to contact Roger and he didn't answer. My panic quickly diminished when I remembered that had Roger been dead, it would have flashed across my vision when I tried to contact him. I slipped past the security exit and peered back to see if Roger was there. That's when I noticed both Sam and Marshall had met back up and were working their way through to the front of the airport.

Fortunately all I had was a carryon; I walked out of the terminal and found a taxi right away. I scanned the sidewalk and sky-cap areas for Marshall or Sam as I tossed my bag into the cab and hopped in.

"Hi, where can I take you?" the cabbie inquired.

"Ahh, do you think you could circle around a couple times, I am waiting for a friend," I answered.

"No prob."

I contacted Roger again and this time he answered.

"*Hey, Lauren.*" He sounded winded.

"You ok?" I asked.

"*Yeah, I barely made it into a stall when Marshall came in.*"

"Where're you now?" I asked, not waiting for him to finish his explanation.

"*I'm just goin' through the security exit,*" he replied. "*Where are you?*"

"I'm in a yellow taxi driving around the terminal, listen—I saw them not too long ago going through security. You need to forget your bags if you had any checked and meet me outside Boarding Area C. Be careful; make sure you're not seen and remember you're dead." We instantly disconnected.

"Do you mind pulling over here at this Boarding Area C?" I asked as he swerved sharp to catch a place next to the curb.

"Thanks," I answered.

I sat in the taxi, waiting for Roger. Relief enveloped me when I saw the enormous glass doors open and Roger came bounding toward the taxi. He looked hurried but not stressed.

"Are you ok?" he asked as he plopped down into the cab.

"Did you see them?" He shook his head.

"Excuse me, do you mind circling around and pulling over just past Terminal One?" Roger asked. The driver nodded and pulled from the curb.

"Why are we here?" I asked.

"I want to see if Marshall and Samantha are together. If they aren't together then we'll need to find out why," he responded.

We peered out the back window of the cab and watched every time the glass doors slid open, scanning the mobs of people that hurried out to waiting loved ones. Several swarms of people had exited when I caught an abrupt movement out of the corner of my eye. I instantly recognized my mom's gold Lexus as she pulled to the curb; my heart fell to my stomach. At the same time another cluster of people spilled from the automatic doors. That's when Roger noticed Marshall was deliberately centered in the group walking toward the curb. We watched as he searched the waiting taxis.

"Roger, that's my mom in the gold Lexus," I cried, hoping he saw what was about to happen. My heart raced as I worked out what I needed to do.

I watched as my mother reached across the inside of her car to the passenger's seat and struggled to pull out a huge white poster board. Suddenly, everything around me moved in slow motion. Marshall was creeping closer to her car, and knowing my mother, she probably had a sign with a clever slogan on it using my name. I couldn't allow her to hold that sign up. I turned to Roger for help when I saw the cab door was left open and he was gone. I was frozen, as I watched Roger work his way to my mother and her gold Lexus. I connected with him and was able to communicate Marshall's every move. Everything Roger did was deliberate and focused as he worked to get to my mother. Unexpectedly, someone pushed into my cab and slammed the door shut.

The figure held up a fist of money to the cabby and told him to drive.

"Did you honestly think I wouldn't find you, Lauren?" a raspy voice asked, taking off a small-rimmed hat. Her fire red hair spilled past her shoulders revealing that it was Samantha. "Come on, Lauren, you had to figure out that I wasn't going to let this trade go down without me."

"Trade? What are you doing in—" She backhanded me across my face. Stinging pain ripped across my cheek.

I lunged at her, wrapping my hands around her neck. I tightened my grip as pure rage surged throughout my body. Her thoughtless actions unleashed something deep in my core and I was ready to kill her.

"Like I was about to ask before you decided to make such a big fucking mistake. What are you doing in California?" I demanded, growling as the blood from my cut dribbled down and landed onto her colorless face.

I watched her as she gasped for air, knowing in a matter of seconds she would be unconscious and lifeless.

"*Lauren! Stop! Don't do it! You need to let go,*" I heard Roger bellow. He was still in my head.

"I can't, Rog, not until she answers me," I slurred, seething with every word.

*"Lauren, you have to listen to me, we need her."* He paused and then continued; I could hear desperation in his voice. *"Lauren — Marshall. Marshall's got your mother."* It was those words that pulled me back just in time to discover Sam was unconscious.

*"And it looks like you're heading on East Grand toward the waterfront."* Roger's voice boomed in my head.

"Just don't lose sight of my mom," I barked.

I remembered the only things down at the waterfront were warehouses and industrial businesses. Visions of different scenarios crept into my head. If the taxi driver was working for Marshall, I would be taken to an abandoned warehouse and roughed up just enough to keep me in line. If the taxi driver was working for Alejandro, my body will be found in about a week floating face down in the bay or in pieces in a garbage heap at the South San Francisco Dump.

Samantha moaned, her naturally raspy voice was reduced to a harsh croak as she spoke. "You know Marshall will find out about this and you'll be sorry," she threatened. "I know people, people that are not as forgiving as I am," she snarled as she struggled.

"I know the same people, Sam." I looked through her and watched as her eyes narrowed.

"What are you saying, Lauren?" She stopped struggling.

"I know who you work for." *All* of the people you work for. I'll let you go once you remember where you told the driver to take us." I was done with her and this situation.

A burning pressure in my rib cage interrupted my thoughts. Suddenly, I couldn't breathe and my body was being hammered against the taxi door. Samantha was pinning me against the side and kicking me with the sharp pointy ends of her stilettos. She was twisted in such a way that I couldn't get to her to stop. Every time I tried to catch her by one of her ankles the other stiletto would come in and stab my body. All I could do was holler with every strike. Dark red blood began to seep from my side. The gashes on my hands stung with acidic pain.

"I didn't tell him to take us anywhere … I just told him to drive," she yelled, kicking me. I had to stop her; I caught her legs, pinning her between me and the back seat. Excruciating pain shot through my ribs.

"Sam, I'll kill you before I'll let you out of this taxi. I need answers. You give me the right ones, you live. Do you understand?" I demanded. She nodded.

"I want to see what other files you have in your head."

"I can't let you do that, Lauren."

"You're going to let me; you have no choice … understand?"

"No, you don't understand the power Marshall has over me."

"Yes, I do, but that can't matter now."

"No, Lauren—Listen, Marshall has installed an app on my prototype that records every keystroke, every file accessed and every download from my head. He told me he'd kill me if he found out that anyone accessed any information in my head."

I ripped off her stilettos and threw them on the other side of the cab. That's when I felt the taxi jolt to a stop. I looked out the window and noticed we were at a warehouse close to the waterfront.

"Listen to me. I'm going to slide off of you. Don't fucking move. If you do, I will tie up your legs. You got me?" Sam nodded in agreement.

I gently pushed up and off her body while excruciating pain radiated up my left side. I bit my lip trying to keep from screaming in agony. I looked down pulled the side of my shirt, dragging my fingers over the shallow puncture holes that dotted my side. Small drops of blood were hidden in the design on my shirt.

"*Hey, ya there?*" Roger's voice startled me. "*I got it! It wasn't Marshall that paid off your driver.*"

I felt my breath escape my lungs before suddenly I could hear my heart beat echo loud in my chest.

"*You ready for this shit? It was able to access Marshall's prototype and it wasn't him.*"

"*Ok, well Sam won't let me get into her head, so what do you suggest I do to get the information?*" I thought to Roger.

"*Well, that's the least of your worries; Marshall just found you.*"

The hostility I had pushed down welled in my body again. Samantha looked back and saw Marshall in my mom's car; fear captured her face. I recognized how they looked at each other and that's when I knew our driver was working for Alejandro.

There was a copious pause before the door of the taxi swung open.

**ten**

A sinfully gorgeous man slipped in next to me. Arrested by the seamless mixture of his bronze complexion and his five o'clock shadow, I knew he must have been Alejandro. My body paralyzed by his presence, my lungs static as I tried to take a breath. I could only feel my heart rate as it hurriedly thrashed against the thin bones of my chest, leaving me with nothing more than the ability to blink. I was supposed to be afraid of him, my intuition and his energy played right into that shallow emotion. I broke from my thoughts and regained my ability to evaluate the situation in seconds. Be it a blessing or curse, in my line of work, moments like that were rare. Never caught speechless or tangled by the mere appearance of someone, this man had caught me off guard. My god, he looked like he had been plucked from the pages of a GQ magazine.

The taxi door closed behind him; unmoved and unaffected by the space we were sitting in, he stretched his strong lengthy hand out to me.

"My name is Alejandro Fernandez. You must be Mrs. Matthews." His Spanish accent and sensuous tone betrayed my instincts. Hypnotized by his frothy green eyes that danced when he spoke my name;

thoughtlessly words instantly stumbled across my lips.

"It's Miss. I'm not married."

Confused by the feeling he evoked in me, everything within me screamed that he was dangerous. My head shuffled around techniques to protect myself while my heart bounced weightless in my chest.

"Oh, my mistake, I just assumed — you are such a beautiful woman." I leaned toward him in a trance; my hand still delicately placed in the warmth of his grasp. I pulled myself together, unhinged from his trance and didn't let him pull me into his game.

Pressure swelled in the gash under my right eye as blood rushed to my cheeks. I realized that I hadn't looked at myself since the fight with Sam; I wondered if I had a black eye or if dry blood colored my face.

"Samantha, I hope your flight was — comfortable." Alejandro addressed her as he continued to gaze at me; his sultry eyes shuffled between mine.

"Everything was fine, Alejandro, thanks," she countered him, pushing toward the other side of the cab. My heart skipped as he dropped his eyes from mine. He tilted his head toward her, his eyes peering across the taxi as his voice was filled with poignant and precise demands.

"Samantha, leave Miss Matthews with me. There's a car waiting for you and Marshall."

For a brief moment it crossed my mind that she was going to stay, but our eyes met and I could see that she was relieved. I pulled her forward and unbuckled my belt from around her wrists. Without a word, she stretched to get her stilettos and was out the door. I watched her through the back window, making her way past my mother's car into a waiting limousine. *Did I just let the one person go that could have saved me from something worse than death?*

People say that your life flashes before your eyes when you're about to die. For me it was thoughts of *how* I was going to die that ran through my mind. Images of my body in the bay, or a bullet in my head kept filling the gaps of silence that crowded the back seat. I could feel Alejandro staring at me, waiting to make eye contact again.

"May I call you Lauren?" he asked while he raised two fingers and motioned for the taxi driver to return to the car. His eyes clung to mine, unhinging and twisting everything I was trained to do; I could feel the effect he had on me. He had a chemistry I was trained to snuff out and wipe away so my body wouldn't react and my mind wouldn't bend to his cleverness.

I've seen his type before and have dealt with them so often that I almost could tell what he was going to say next. First he'll attempt to win my loyalty with his charm and etiquette and then he will try and seduce me with his sensual words. It's not going to happen.

"Sure, Lauren is fine," I answered in a controlled and uninterested tone. One thing was for sure ... I couldn't let him win me over.

"Lauren, who did this to you?" he asked as his hand tenderly pushed into my hair and his thumb brushed back and forth under the gash in my cheekbone.

I didn't answer, I shook my head as uncertainty flooded my body ... I was losing.

"Shame on whoever hurt you. Beauty like this should be cherished, taken care of, pleased," he answered, shaking his head before looking at the cabbie. "Head toward North Beach," he told the driver and I felt the taxi pull forward.

My heart lodged in the back of my throat; we were heading straight to the area I grew up.

Memories spun like a torrent through my mind and how my life was back then when my concentration splintered by Alejandro.

"Marshall, take Sam to your hotel. Tell Lauren's mother that her daughter is ... with me. We just have some business we must handle. I will make sure she is returned to her hotel." He switched the phone to his other ear as he stared at my pale face. I hung on every word he spoke. His expression became hard and he pressed his lips until they drained to a pale line. After a moment of wondering what was being said, his demeanor changed and he spoke with an innocence I could only compare to a young boy's need for acceptance.

"Hello, Mrs. Matthews. My name is Alejandro Fernandez—oh—I see—my deepest apologies—remarried—oh, I see—Mrs. Wilson. *Yes I am* with your daughter." He stopped speaking and his face became soft as his eyes widened. "Yes ma'am—I understand—I will make sure."

*What was she saying?* All at once my neck grew fiery hot. Flashes of my childhood crowded the space between the words that wrapped my stomach in knots and the moment he pulled the phone from his ear and handed it to me.

"Your mother is demanding that she speak to you." His sexy tone kept me blushing. I wasn't prepared for him to use my mom to get to me. It was brilliant on his part and completely unfair.

I grabbed the phone knowing I had to sound like I was okay. Last thing I needed was for her to become totally unglued with me.

"Hi, Mom, I'm sorry I forgot to call you back."

"You should be. I was worried; you should have called me. I haven't seen you in over a year and you pull this?" Her voice rang loud in my ear.

"Mom—stop—please—I'm okay." I spoke between clutched teeth.

"I thought I was picking you up? You called me, remember?"

"Yeah, I know, I'm really sorry." I tried to calm the storm I knew she was about to create.

"It's a good thing you have friends like Marshall. He told me about your meeting with Alejandro." I could hear the anticipation in her voice.

"Yeah, he's a good friend." Fear grappled with my heart and clawed its way to my throat. *A friend that better not harm my mom.*

"It's about time you started dating again. It's been so long since— I love you and miss you *so* much." I could hear her voice crack; she was starting to cry. *How did Marshall know that dating would be the only excuse my mom would accept?*

"I miss you too! Don't cry, Mom. I'll call you before I head over to your place," I told her quickly before I said more than I should.

"You better," she answered.

"I've gotta go. I love you." I hurried my speech. I could have gone all week without hearing about the lack of dating in my life.

"Love you too, honey! Bye."

"Bye," I ended.

I couldn't keep the insecurities I felt as a teenage girl from rising in my chest when I handed him the phone.

"Sorry." The word tumbled from my mouth without thinking.

"Please don't apologize. I respect her concerns. She's a smart woman." He was amused by the exchange that we shared with the one person I had always kept in the dark about my life.

"Lauren, we have a lot to discuss; but first, why did you refuse my car? It's more comfortable than this and we could have a lot more privacy." He was charming with a hint of irritation brewing just under the surface.

Chastised by a man I just met for refusing his limo was ludicrous. Even if a lump formed in the back of my throat when he spoke, I was a highly trained field agent for the CIA; I should have known how to handle the situation. I swallowed, took a deep breath and pulled myself together.

"My mother wanted to pick me up. I haven't seen her in a while. She insisted." I had no problem spitting out the truth, even if it was a half-truth.

"Oh, that's it? I see. Well, I am sorry that didn't go as you hoped," he said as he looked away and focused his attention to the driver.

"Pull over here," he demanded. His body moved in a sweeping motion toward the door. My chest tightened as stress radiated up through my shoulders and perched in my jaw.

"My car is just up here," he insisted as the taxi parked at the curb and a man in a tuxedo pulled open his door.

*What was I going to do? I knew the percentage of women that lived through a situation like this wasn't a high number.* Alejandro collected my carryon, handing it to his driver, and slid his perfectly groomed body out the door.

Alejandro, debonair in his manners, turned and offered his hand to me. I hesitantly grasped it and carefully exited. The sharp searing pain from Samantha kicking me flared across my side. A small part of me was grateful to be out the taxi; however, I was defensive because I still didn't know what he wanted. My head told me he had ulterior motives, while my heart battled fiercely and won.

He walked behind me as we made our way to an eye-piercing white stretched limousine with pitch black windows. Desperate to know if he had other plans for me, I slowed my stride to be even with him. He brought his hand to my back, urging me to keep my steps slightly ahead. The driver opened the door and stood there waiting for me to get in. I turned to Alejandro and at that point, I knew my choice was made for me. I got in and he followed closely behind. The soft black leather seat gave way as my hands manipulated my way in. The partition between us and the driver was made of black smoked glass with the metallic, masculine shaped letters S I centered perfectly in the middle. I slid my body next to the door on the other side, taking advantage of the space available.

He snatched a bottle of champagne from the ice bucket and filled two glasses that were intentionally set out on the dark mahogany table.

"Please have some. I know we are not celebrating anything." He paused and whispered, "Yet." I took the glass he held toward me and drank. I hoped the pain in my ribcage that came at me in waves would subside with the champagne.

"Home," Alejandro told the driver. His attention shifted to me.

"I think we will be more comfortable there; I hope you don't mind," he said, his body crowding the space next to me.

"Do I have a choice?" I asked.

"Absolutely," he pressed.

I knew someone with his reputation wouldn't really give me a choice, but was smooth enough to make it look like he did.

"Where do you live?" I asked solid. A question I knew the answer to, but figured I would keep my head focused on details and information.

"Twenty-nine oh one Vallejo Street," he stated. Flashes of my new driver's license appeared in my head. It was the address on the license that Marshall had given me.

I wanted to get my hands on it, but I was going to have to wait. My carryon was in the trunk of the limo. I prayed he couldn't read my expression as he studied the contours of my face. I pushed the vision away and kept questioning him.

"Nice area, Pacific Heights. How long have you been there?" The conversation had to stay generic, because every time I looked at him, a craving would well in my body and I would lose my train of thought.

"You are very inquisitive for someone who is in a compromising position."

"Compromising position?" I asked.

"Well, you are an extremely beautiful woman, who has something I am very interested in and you are here ... alone with me in the back of my car."

"I have people who know where I am and will track my every move."

"Well, then, I'd better be the gentleman I was raised to be. I've lived in Pacific Heights for several years." His earthy green eyes raked leisurely up my body. There was a slight lull before he continued. "Lauren, I have to confess to you." I watched his eyebrows furrow as he paused.

My heart fell with a strong thump. I eyed him anxiously waiting for the confession. What would this powerful, heart-stopping man want to confess to me? "Confess?"

"Yes, dare I say, I'm already confessing. After the way Marshall spoke about you last week, my curiosity got the best of me," he declared as he moved toward me.

Normally my reaction would be to honor his personal space and back away; however, this wasn't normal and I couldn't find the space where he began and I ended. I desperately searched for the right words to push him away ... any excuse to look in another direction ... I needed an out and every justification I had abandoned me in my search. I drew in a breath to ask him about his curiosity just as his aroma captured me.

"What did Marshall say that left you so, curious?" The question rolled uncontested across my tongue.

"Now, Lauren, that wouldn't be very gentlemanly like."

"Really? And why not?" I said baiting him.

"Because certain conversations are better kept right where I decide they should stay." His eyelids lowered as he teasingly smiled and tapped his hand across his chest.

*Stop! This was crazy! What in the hell am I doing? Why am I being so ridiculous? This can only lead to trouble.*

"You're right, it's better left unsaid." I tore my eyes from his and sat back into the plush black leather seat. I needed to end this before it led to something more serious.

"Have I done something?" he asked sincerely as he grabbed the champagne from the ice and filled my empty glass. Commanding in his words, but delicate in his actions, he suddenly became anxious.

"No," I answered, fidgeting.

"Have I offended you?" He worked to catch my sight.

"No, you've been very ... accommodating." I brought my eyes to meet his.

"Accommodating ... hmmm, a word beautiful women use after they've been disappointed." His eyes cased my face, his lips, full of a moment I'd like to experience. I could feel his desperation trying to figure me out. God, he was good. I was beginning to become uncomfortably warm below my belly.

"Tell me, Lauren, what is it?" He put his drink down. I could feel the air shift between us as he brought his hand toward my face. I had to talk before he touched me.

"What are you doing?" I asked feeling the pressure of the question leap off of my chest. Silence fell between us before he spoke.

"Well, it seems I am answering an awful lot of questions you feel necessary to ask me," he answered perplexed.

"No, not that ... what are your plans for me ... what are you going to do with me?" The words tumbled from my mouth.

"You've just flown across the country to meet with me. I figured you would be tired and hungry, so I would like to make you dinner at *my* home where I thought you would be more comfortable. Unless, you prefer to go out?" he asked.

I know how to read individuals. My job requires it. As a matter of fact, I am very good at figuring out motivation and what drives people. How is it that he had me questioning my reading more into his hospitality than there was? I was tired, done from the flight and fighting Sam. Maybe he was just trying to make me feel comfortable.

The snow-colored limo came to a stop and I could feel the need to eat stir in my belly. Before anything, I still needed to contact Roger and tell him I was okay.

"I'm sorry, you are very kind, but I think I should go to my hotel," I mumbled.

"Let me make you dinner." His body language was asking as much as his words were. He leaned toward me to anticipate my answer. I just kept the thoughts of the mission in my mind. I had a job to do; my mark just so happened to be a god from Spain. I inhaled on the thought of his offer and closed my eyes as I tried to brush away the endorphins that surged in my body.

"We're already here. Come in, have dinner with me. That's it, and then I will take you to your hotel." He looked at me, his eyes begging and his lips pouting. Every womanly part of my body was pleading with me to say *yes*, while my mind diplomatically tried to quiet the riot.

"I don't think that's a good—"

"Just dinner … I promise," he interrupted.

"… idea," I finished. "Why?" he questioned seriously.

"Well, for one, your interest in … the prototype and Marshall."

"What does that have to do with me having dinner with a beautiful woman I want to get to know?"

"See there you go, making me uncomfortable."

"Well, then maybe I shouldn't compliment you?"

His eyes burned through my skin, taking me in with every breath he drew. Silence poured between us as he watched me squirm under his watch. His eyes begged me to stay, his pout rose to a smirk.

"Maybe you shouldn't," I rebutted.

"Fine, it's settled; you will eat what I cook, and I won't say another nice thing about you," he insisted.

"Is that a promise?" I exhaled.

"Are you agreeing to dinner with me?" His grin lit up his eyes. *Oh, holy hell, what am I doing?*

"Fine, I'll stay for dinner," I grumbled.

"Then I promise to keep my compliments to myself," he retorted, smiling.

"Perfect." *At least until I lock myself in your bathroom and freshen up from the Samantha fiasco.*

His house matched the expectation and Alejandro refined my mental picture. It was nice to be in a house that radiated wealth, but exhibited a reserved extravagance. Moderation seemed to be the theme that united each room. He was still tied to his humbled beginnings and frustratingly enough, I found it highly sexy.

Right now sexy didn't own me. I couldn't help but feel self-conscious about my face and how bad it probably looked. My body betrayed me as a shiver thrust itself down my spine and Alejandro noticed.

"Are you okay?"

"I'm fine; I'd just like to freshen up a bit. It's been a pretty trying day. Which way to the bathroom?" I asked, pointing toward the hall and the kitchen.

"Absolutely, you can use the one off of the kitchen. Through that doorway and to the left."

After I closed the bathroom door, I immediately peered at my face in the mirror. I noticed the gash across my face was already starting to heal. Shocked by how fast my face was healing, I pulled my shirt up and inspected my side. The wounds across my hip and ribcage appeared to be healing quickly too. I finished cleaning up and returned to the kitchen.

Alejandro watched me as I sauntered back from the bathroom and I found myself liking it. Cleaned up and feeling much better, it was the way his eyes dipped across my body and his teeth collected his bottom lip that created a frenzy in my belly.

"After dinner, I will show you the rest of the house." He plucked a wine glass from the cabinet and filled it half way with red wine before he pushed it across the marble island that separated us. His hand slid back off and into his pleasing jet-black hair, pulling my body with it. It must have been his way of telling me to sit.

It was a pleasant surprise to see he really was going to make me dinner. I watched him move effortlessly around the kitchen; he was fluid and at home as he pulled rare ingredients from cabinets and the refrigerator. Thirty minutes passed in an instant. I didn't think watching a man cook could be so sensual, until now. *God, I like a man that can cook.*

He slid a plate of Spanish tapas with mussels in front of me. Incredible colors burst from an artist's palette. Saffron yellow and charcoal roasted red with sprigs of dark forest green were delicately swallowed by midnight black shells resting on beds of purple leaves belonging to the sea. The aroma made me realize how ravenously hungry I was. He grabbed his plate and joined me. We ate almost in silence. Strangely enough I didn't feel the need to talk. It must have been the mussels that I couldn't stop shoveling into my mouth. He was the first to break the quiet when he pulled in a breath.

"So, how do you like it?" He let his eyes meet mine, looking for the answer. I swallowed the mouthful of food that I wanted to continue to taste and replied almost choking.

"It's edible," I teased.

"Edible?" he asked.

"It's good." I played flippant. I knew full well our banter was stirring the same desires that he ignited within me.

"Just good?" he played back.

"It's exceptionally good. Better?" I held his attention and then dropped my eyes and stabbed at another mussel.

"Yes, and I'm glad you like it. It's my favorite dish to make." I watched him pick up a shell from his plate and tilt it deliciously into his mouth. His chin pushed at the space above while his glossy black hair stumbled back exposing his strong jaw. I wanted to be that shell, more so, the mussel that entered his mouth. I wanted to taste his lips, his flavor. I wanted to be consumed by him. His voice broke my private thoughts.

"Tell me about yourself, Lauren." He pulled another shell to his lips and swallowed.

"What do you want to know?" I put my fork down on my plate; my head was swimming.

"Tell me about your family."

I took a breath and began to say something when Roger popped into my vision; he was trying to contact me. It was perfect timing, even if for a brief moment I forgot I had the prototype in my head.

"I'm sorry, I really need to use the bathroom. Excuse me."

I didn't want to make eye contact so I focused on my hands. He pointed the way; I glanced back at him, knowing he was watching me walk away and I could feel his eyes boring into my back. I wondered if he was as aroused as I was.

I closed the bathroom door, turned on the water from the sink and I drenched my hands pressing them to my cheeks. I couldn't stop the deep tingling urge to walk back out there and get lost in his universe. I needed to bring myself back down to Earth. This wasn't what I was supposed to do. I took a couple of deep core groused breaths. I had to be ready to talk to Roger.

I left the water running; I wasn't about to take the chance that Alejandro was going to hear any part of my conversation with Roger. He was dead to everyone but me. I wanted to keep it that way. I was relieved to hear his voice. The last time I heard him was by the warehouses in south city. I cleared my throat.

"Hi, Rog. Are you ok? Where are you?" I couldn't find anything comfortable to do with my hands, so I forced them under the running water.

"I'm fine. I followed your mother, she's home now. I'm heading to Marshall and Sam's hotel. Are you ok?" he asked; his concern was present in his voice. I also didn't forget that he could track me with the GPS on his computer. It was a shame that my computer didn't reciprocate.

"I'm fine. It's taking a little longer than expected to get Alejandro to talk. I will contact you the minute I find anything out. Stay on Marshall and Sam. And for our sake, don't get caught." I shivered, turned the water off and dried my hands.

"*Lauren, don't spend too much time there. You don't know what he's capable of.*" He spoke like a protective older brother.

"I'm trying my best to get him to talk."

"*Just be very careful. He can be very dangerous. Stay alert.*"

"Okay, Rog." Our connection was gone. It is a good thing he couldn't pick up on my emotions. *How could he say that?* Surprisingly, I was irritated at Roger. I was being protective of a man I barely knew. And I knew without a doubt, Roger had to be wrong … Alejandro wasn't dangerous, he was misunderstood, and he was nothing less than a gentleman.

I found my way back to Alejandro's marble island. I smiled at what he had done while I was in the bathroom with Roger in my head. He had cleared our dinner plates, refilled our wine glasses and had a small plate with a slice of cheesecake waiting with one fork.

"I thought you might like dessert?" he asked.

"Thank you." My body moved into the stool next to him. Before I could take in what he was doing, he grabbed the fork, pushed it through the cake and held it in front of my mouth.

"I want to know what you think." His words knotted my stomach and stopped my heart.

"About what?" I played back.

"The cheesecake I made." He met my eyes, they were craving my answer.

I pulled my lips apart giving him a chance to ask again. He gently answered by sliding the fork to my mouth. I closed my eyes and allowed the flavor wash over me. He pulled the fork delicately from between my lips. I swallowed; it was delicious. My eyes rebound opened almost expecting the fork to be there again but instead his hand was moving toward my face.

This was starting to get dangerous. He was dangerous. I couldn't tell if it was want or fear that kept swelling in my chest. He was touching me, and the problem was I really liked it. I turned my head and reached for my wine glass, his hand dropped to his lap. His eyes defeated.

"I'm sorry, I am being too forward."

"No. I think—thanks for dinner—dessert, but I think it's time I go to my hotel." I started to get off of the stool and move from his island. My legs weak and my groin moaning, I needed to get out before I betrayed all that I had worked so hard to obtain.

"Lauren, stay and finish your drink. I will behave, I promise—please." He held his hand over his heart and looked deep into my eyes.

I tried to look away.

"Ok, it will take time to call my car for you." His hand cradled my elbow and forearm. "And besides I owe you a tour of my home." He interjected guiding my face with his free hand to recapture my eyes. I was trying to settle the feelings raging in my body. He was touching me again. I was weak; I had to decide.

"Please, call your driver." I forced the words.

"Sure." He forced a smile and I melted. He slid his hand down from my chin and brushed my hair back from my shoulder. With that he reached for his phone and made the arrangements.

"He will be here to pick you up in twenty minutes." My heart sunk and twisted wickedly. *A lot could happen in twenty minutes.*

I slid my wine glass back onto the black and rusty gold veined marble island before Alejandro subtly brushed his fingertips down the inside of my wrist and pulled me up from my chair.

"Come, follow me. I want you to see my favorite room." His voice pulled and my body followed. His aroma filled my lungs, clean and just savory enough to create an ache deep within my belly.

We passed his modest living room where Spanish tile ruled under our feet and a hand carved armoire filled the warm space. Alejandro never once let go of my hand as he strolled me down the unassuming adobe-colored hall where oil paintings methodically hung on both sides of the walls.

"Here we are," he said pushing open the only solid wood dark brown door. I stood there breathless, unable to move. He slipped his arm behind me and pressed his hand on the small of my back. I stumbled forward and was in the room.

Dimly lit sconces were situated every so often against pure black walls. Comfortable dark maroon loveseats formed a half circle and a gold travertine tile floor peeked out from underneath plush black area rugs. A massive white screen spread square on the wall. There was a picture framed in gold across the room. It was a black and white photo of a family in front of a movie theatre. The mother and father stood behind two boys, one much taller than the other. I moved closer and noticed the father had the same eyes as Alejandro. I scanned down to the boys; both with silly faces.

"Is that you?" I asked, breaking the silence between us. He came up behind me and pushed his finger toward the picture as he spoke.

"Yeah, those are my parents and that small one there, is me. It was taken in front of the Cine Doré in Madrid." He smiled; his face froze as the time capsule in his mind unraveled. His eyes became distant as he pointed his finger to the other boy in the picture.

"That is my older brother Vicente. He was killed before we came to America." I felt him exhale as the weight of his memories forced the air from his lungs.

A moment hung entrenched between us and I didn't know what to do. He was lost in memories sparked by the photo in front of me. I didn't turn around to him; I just let him speak when he was ready. I heard him tug a shallow breath in.

"I am sorry. I didn't expect this picture to affect me like this."

I listened with every ounce of who I was. My entire body was ready to react to his words. Truthful or not, he pulled me in when he took that shallow breath. Nothing mattered to me, all I craved was to be invited in, and all it took was a string of words he exhaled in one of the most private moments of his life. I listened as he let me in. "I remember we had packed all that day. My mother had asked Vicente to go pick up some cleaning supplies down at the market. She would never consider leaving our house dirty for the next tenants. I remember my mother was so excited to be coming to America. She was glowing that day. Her black hair was pulled up off her face. She smelt like lavender flowers."

I turned to him. The agony was alive in his eyes as he relived a taste of his childhood.

"I was on the phone talking to my father when our neighbor busted through the door. I can still see his face; no color, no life, just nothing. He grabbed my mother as she collapsed to the floor. The next thing I remember—my father was standing in the doorway. I had heard much later that Vicente was trying to stop a fight between a woman and her husband—he couldn't stand by and watch this happen. When he had tried to stop the man from hurting her—the man stabbed him—left him for dead."

He shook his head like he was trying to force the thoughts away. I needed to say something. It was for my sake as much as his. Remorse welled in my chest as I watched him begin to crumble.

"I'm so sorry. That must've been the worst day of your life," I said, consoling him. He looked at my hands dangling down by my waist.

"That was bad, but the day we left him buried in Spain and came to America—that was the worst."

His eyes closed and I watched the few tears that clung to his eyelashes spiral off into the space between us.

"I don't know what makes me so comfortable with you," he whispered, "like nobody I have met before." His words pierced my soul and I found his eyes. I couldn't contain the urge to reach up and capture the remaining tears that fell from his eyelashes.

"You're dangerous for me," I whispered under my breath as I brushed my damp fingers across his sullen lips. I started to pull my hand away from his face when he captured my arm. Delicately he brought my wrist to his sharp nose before he inhaled. Taken by his actions, every spark that collided within my body, collected down low in my stomach. He pressed his soft, warm lips against the taut tendons of my wrist as he spoke one convincing word ..."stay." My body reacted to his sated word, nailing me to the very cross I had pinned my burdens on for years.

Danger didn't own any part of my consciousness at that point. I didn't see the power-ravaged demonic man that Marshall saw. I didn't feel the same fear that Sam felt earlier in the taxi. I saw an accomplished man emotionally broken and strangely enough, I felt the need to protect him. Make him whole again. What I didn't want to admit was that I didn't really know him at all. The warm spot where his lips rested ran cold as he pulled away. His unhurried eyes opened and met my gaze. I knew what I wanted, but it would have to wait.

"The driver must be here by now," I forced out in a whisper as I pulled my arm from his hand.

I knew he wanted to continue kissing up my flesh until his lips were emphatically ruling mine. I knew it because, I, just a badly wanted to kiss him back. I wasn't stupid, light-headed maybe from the wine, but not stupid; I had to draw the line, even when I knew my body had already crossed it.

"I will see you tomorrow morning?" Alejandro's voice was rasp, captive by the visceral chemistry percolating between us.

"Yes," I whispered, desperately trying to keep in control.

"Very good, then I will have my driver pick you up," he answered, more collected than before.

I nodded, hoping a wordless answer was enough. He gave me a slight smile before he slipped his hand against the small of my back and led me to the foyer. Without anymore words, our eyes pinned against the curves and bends of each other's bodies, we silently made our way out onto the front porch. He ardently walked me down the steps, leading me across the driveway, before he pulled open the limo door and made sure I was safely tucked inside. My eyes narrowed and casted upon his. He must have read my expression as questioning, because he gave me a slight shrug before he spoke.

"Lauren, I promised your mother I'd get you back safe." He slowly smiled as he fashioned a wink that quite possible could have stripped me of my virtue if he hadn't shut the limo door.

It didn't take long to realize I was sitting in the same limo that brought me to his house, but this time it wasn't as comfortable. I didn't have someone to preoccupy my mind and the wine I drank earlier started to wear thin in my blood. My cheek didn't let me forget the damage Sam inflicted earlier and my left side was throbbing. Either way, I was an exhausted mess. My heart wouldn't let go of my regret for not staying while my mind fought to think about tomorrow. Problem was I needed to contact Roger tonight.

I focused on the cursor in the lower right corner of my eye that became part of the scenery in my vision. I pulled up Roger's contact information. It didn't take long before Roger's voice permeated my head.

*"Hey Lauren — did you' find out anything?"* he whispered, getting right to the point. The fresh memories of Alejandro pasted themselves across my mind; the sparks that rushed my skin when he kissed my wrist; the pull of his voice when he wanted me to stay, and the tears that wet my open hand as I collected them. I tried to force the memories away. I didn't know the level of access Roger had to my mind with this prototype.

I cleared my throat, "No—nothing. But I'm working on it. What about you? Where are you?" My throat went dry and my voice sounded strange. I hoped Roger didn't pick up on it.

"*Sam and Marshall are staying at the Radisson Fisherman's Warf. Been watching Marshall down in the bar. He keeps checking his watch like he's waiting for someone — whoa, wait — what's this?*"

"What? Roger—what?" I asked.

His tone made the hair on my neck stand up. Roger started talking to himself; I had no choice but to listen.

"*It looks like there's someone here to meet him. Who's that? — Ok, Marshall, this is interesting. What are you planning now?*" he mumbled. Frustrated, I broke his dialogue.

"Who is it—what's going on?"

"*Lauren, gotta disconnect. I'll contact you back—trust me.*"

He hastily minimized me in his eye. Unaware I was still in his head, I was able to hear him talking under his breath, only too low to make out every word he was saying,—"*black—huge—agent—database.*" I needed to find out who was there with Marshall.

The limo came to a gradual stop and I jumped out, not taking any time to look back. I could only hear Roger breathing as I rushed to the entry of the hotel. The minute I was through the front doors, I spotted the bar.

I pushed past a group of people working to pull a few of the tables and chairs together and searched for Roger. Sweat marched down my temple, tickling above my ear. I began to think Roger had already left. The bar clatter was too loud to listen for him in my head. I forced my fingers into my ears hoping to void the outside noise.

*"What are yo- do- -ere?"* I heard him but his voice was breaking up.

"What?"

*"La-r-n, -at are you d-ng here?"* His voice was still breaking up.

"I can't hear you." I was almost screaming.

*"Look up."* Finally I heard him. I raised my head to meet his fierce eyes behind his black rimmed glasses. Seconds later I was across the room with him. I was shocked by his strength as he clutched my arm pulling me over to him. His nostrils flared and his face glowed red.

"What are you thinking? I told you I would contact you later."

"Rog, you can't do that to me. We are partners, remember? You're the only person I can trust. Don't forget that." My words flew at him, betrayed and left out.

"I know we're partners, but you can't go running around right now, especially here. Who knows what would have happened if he'd seen you?" I watched his eyes shift from me to a spot in the room and back at me.

"Who's he with?" I asked.

"I don't know. Never seen him before," he said as he pointed to a spot in the middle of the room.

I looked over and immediately recognized Terence Cummings. He was a magnificently built African American man with flawless dreadlocks reaching past his gigantic shoulders. "I know him. Oh my God! I know him—" The words tumbled over each other as they came out of my mouth. *I only knew him in my head, but I knew him.*

"He's the guy in the file. You know, the file Sam uploaded. He's in it. Oh my God, that is him." The wave of familiarity brushed over my skin. The hair on my arms stood.

"Are you sure that's him?" Roger was skeptical.

"I would bet my life on it. I remember his picture and file. He was the one assigned to modify your prototype, he works for Spartacus Industries. He was the one that recommended Sam work with him on the project—but what's he doing with Marshall? I need to get in closer." I stood up. Roger pulled me down.

"Don't worry, I'm recording it," he said and pointed to his eyes.

"Well, aren't you too far away to record their voices?" I asked.

"I'm recording it through Marshall's eyes." Roger looked at me like he expected me to know this capability already existed.

"I didn't know we could do that," I stammered.

"*We* can't, only I can," he boasted.

"So you can take over my head?" Shock radiated down to my core. Roger nodded his head. I was capsizing, drowning in the idea that he had the ability to access my deepest personal moments.

"Have you done that to me?" I asked, not really wanting to hear his answer.

"No, and I don't plan on it. I wanted to secure my prototype, in case things went sour. I didn't do it to invade anyone's privacy." He tried to convince me, but his words anchored one of my worst fears.

I felt a flux of regret surge in my throat. Now more than ever, since I had this *thing* put in my head, I truly wanted it out. I didn't like the idea that he had that type of access.

Terence shook Marshall's hand as he stood up from the table. Panic like a jagged lightning bolt radiated down my spine as I watched him leave the bar.

"I'm going to follow him," I choked.

"No wait, don't—not yet." Roger grabbed my arm; he was looking at Marshall.

"He's contacting Sam using his prototype." Roger's mind was taken by Marshall's actions. He mumbled as his eyes quickly bounced to different spots in the bar. I could tell he was navigating through files in his eyes and not seeing anything beyond that.

Roger started to recite what he was hearing. "He's telling her that she's going to fly back to D.C.

in a couple of days. He told her that she isn't meeting Alejandro tomorrow. She's really upset and asking why. He's really mad at her for letting you go with Alejandro in his limo. She told him that she thinks you're at his house." Roger stopped reciting, his face flushed with doubt.

"What is it, Roger? What is he saying now?" I asked pressing on his shoulder.

"Marshall's leaving. He told her to stay where she was, he'll be back. He's going to Alejandro's house." Roger's eyes filled with resentment.

"We need to stop him. He's going to blow the whole thing. We've come too far to have—" Roger stopped me. He kept his hand up and turned from me. He became surly and I could feel his energy twist and turn in anger. What had he heard?

"Roger, what did Sam say?" I asked while my heart pounded loud in my ears. He wouldn't look at me.

"Sam told Marshall that you were with Alejandro." His voice broke down.

"I was with Alejandro today," I answered. I didn't catch what he was alluding to. "We had dinner," I continued.

"No Lauren, Sam told Marshall that you had sex with him ... What the hell were you thinking? I never thought of you to be someone who would jump in a man's bed so quickly," he chided. "I mean, really it's none of my business what you do on your time, Lauren, but if you screw up my opportunity, I swear—"

"Who's opportunity? Aren't we in this together, Roger ... Don't make this about you and your precious piece of shit in my head! How dare you assume what anyone says about me is the truth! You want to know about what I am doing ... ask me, talk to me!" I hollered. I was pissed that he believed Sam and Marshall over me. He knew me better than that.

I stood up to leave. I wasn't going to stay and deal with his jealousy, his self-centered bullshit attitude about this technology. This wasn't just about him or this shit in my head. He was calling me out on something I didn't do.

I wouldn't call myself a prude or a wallflower. I would say that I am inexperienced. Maybe it was the fact that I was so wrapped up in being the perfect daughter, perfect student, perfect agent that I didn't learn how to be the perfect one-night stand.

Roger caught my arm from across the table.

"I'm sorry, Lauren. I believe you," he said through a deep breath that allowed his color to return to his cheeks.

"It's fine." In a deep hidden corner of my heart, I was guilty of wanting his jealousy to be justified.

We left the bar and headed back to the hotel. I decided against checking in. It was late and figured it would be safer if I just roomed with Roger in his suite with two queen beds. He claims that the hotel made a mistake and that he wasn't supposed to have such a huge room. I think he wasn't being all together truthful and planned it that way.

When we got into the room, he was quick to slide out a chair and motioned for me to sit. He filled the chair opposite me. His eyes staring off, vacant of present time, he was working on his prototype.

"What are you doing?"

"I want you to see the recording between Marshall and Terence, without uploading it to your head," he rambled. I was grateful. I didn't want him rummaging through my mind.

"I'm going to directly link you to my prototype." He was working and talking at the same time.

"My prototype acts as the master, while yours will be the slave—Okay, there, I've uploaded the file," he informed me. "All you do now is find where it says new network connections, and open it. See that?"

"Alright, I'm connected. There it is," I said, dumbstruck. My eyes focused on the file and my mind went blank.

When my vision came back, Terence was sitting right in front of me. I was in Marshall's head. I was looking at life through his eyes. I felt his voice reverberate in my body, anxious like I had information I needed to share with Terence. I felt angry and disappointed. *What was happening to me?*

"Roger! What is going on? I'm feeling pretty strange," I tried to ask out loud.

Suddenly I could taste beer. It washed over my taste buds as fast as I began to smell it. The pungent aroma of strong ale made me want to vomit.

"Why do I taste beer?—Roger!" I was irritated.

"That is the side effect of being in someone else's head. Not only will you see what they see, you will taste, hear, smell and feel what they do. The only problem is your traits mix with theirs. That's why you feel sick at the taste of the beer. He likes it; you don't," he told me comfortably. It gives a whole new meaning to, 'getting into someone's head.'

I kept tasting the beer and feeling anxious. Being in someone's experience wasn't very comfortable, at least to me. Marshall was blunt and to the point when he addressed Terence.

"Terence. Thank you for meeting me—please sit." Marshall swung his hand to a chair pushed out far enough for Terence to sit down. "I don't know how much time we have. So I wanted to get right to the point. I hope you don't mind."

Terence swung the chair around backward in one motion. His giant legs straddled it as his dark shining arms folded, resting on the back, swallowing it up as he sat. His shirt pulled from the collar across his chest and around his biceps. I could feel the insecurity in Marshall's body.

"I need you to help me out with Sam. I know you've worked with her at Spartacus Industries." Marshall kept his words convoluted trying to find a weak spot to push his agenda.

"Yeah, well just cuz I worked wit' her at SI don't mean I'm interested in helpin' you out," Terence said. Whether he meant to be or not, he was really intimidating. I think my fears mixed well with

Marshall's in this instance. Both of our hearts were pounding.

"Hey, no disrespect intended. I just thought if you could help me with something, then maybe I could help you back," he pushed. "I figured we could do each other a favor. You help me with Sam and, well, I help you with your brother." I felt sweat beads form on my, Marshall's forehead. He was pulling out all the stops in hopes of manipulating Terence.

"Wha-chu think you know 'bout my life or my brother's?" His eyes filled with angst, narrowed and pinned. He cocked his head to the side and flicked his hand toward Marshall as he spoke. "You know nothin'." Terence stared him down. "You know nothin'."

Marshall responded in a calm voice. The same voice that used to give me chills.

"I know that your brother has a third strike against him— possession of a concealed weapon. Isn't that life in prison? Well, it would be a shame if you knew of a way to save him and you chose to ignore it." Marshall leaned back in his chair and I felt it press into my back. It was creepy, I couldn't get used to it.

Terence looked straight through Marshall's soul. Of course I was looking into his. I could tell his back was against the wall. His eyes widened and his arm muscles twitched.

"Wha-cha goin' to do for my brother? You tell me that! Then we'll talk business." Terence was trying to play hardball. What he didn't know was that Marshall was the master of ultimatums.

"Well, Terence. First he is going to need a great lawyer; I have the best money can buy. Then he will need to get lucky with which judge hears his case. That's really important. I hear that Judge Blankenship is the one he'll want to get. Judge Blankenship owes me a favor. Do you get the idea?" Marshall roused him.

"I get the idea. Wha-chu *want* me to do?" I saw the injustice of his situation own his body. His head swung, broad shoulders curled in, and his face winced as Marshall's words hurt like the sting of a whip against his back. I could tell he was an honest, hardworking man that had the unfortunate luck of having a criminal for a brother.

Marshall leaned in toward the middle of the table, closer to Terence. Terence didn't move. He just looked at him, waiting for the demands that would be thrust upon him to save his sorry excuse for a brother, one more time. He knew getting his brother off on a third strike would be near impossible so the trade was going to be something huge involving Samantha.

"I need you to pick up Samantha from the hotel tomorrow morning, six thirty sharp. You need to take her to the airport. Make sure she gets on the next flight out to D.C." Marshall wasn't real clear on what he wanted him to do. Terence wasn't convinced that that was the end of it. The mistrust swirled in his earth brown eyes. His shoulders bearing the burden of what he thought was the only way to save his brother's life. Knowing there was more to the request from Marshall, he pressed. "Once she's on the plane, what then?"

"Well, then you come back to me and we discuss options for your brother," Marshall answered Terence. My throat burnt as Marshall took a huge swig of the nauseating beer again.

"I wanna know wha-chu' playin' me for? I don't trust you. I know you're holdin' back. Give me respect enough to come out with it." He pushed up from the chair. I was staring Terence in the eye through Marshall. That's when I felt the words bounce out of his mouth.

"I need you to extricate Samantha's prototype." I felt the pressure leave my chest as he said it.

I could see the wheels in Terence's head start to spin. He was really contemplating Marshall's request before he answered.

"Why can't you just do it? You're smart enough," Terence stated.

"I need someone who knows how to leave no trace of it. I figure you're a software programmer and she wouldn't think anything about it. She trusts you. I can tell she doesn't trust me anymore," he rambled.

"Do you blame her?" Terence asked as he lowered his body on the chair that was swallowed by his enormity. "If I do this, you'll call your judge and make the charges against my brother disappear, right?" he questioned in a firm tone. Marshall nodded. I felt like a puppet. I didn't have to wait long for the pull of the strings attached to my arm to reach over and shake Terence's hand that impatiently waited for Marshall. They shook hands and Terence was gone.

The recording stopped and I was back in Roger's hotel room. I took a deep cleansing breath. I was physically exhausted and mentally beat, let down by my expectations surrounding Terence. I really wanted him to fight harder for his moral being. I didn't want him to give in so casually to Marshall, except I had more to think about than just that. Sam has been nothing but a thorn in my side since I've learned of her existence, and even though I should hate her for what she has done, she was in trouble. No matter what, we had a strange bond, a connection if you will. We were the only two women in existence to have the prototype installed. At least I had one ace in the hole — Roger. Nobody knew he was alive.

twelve

Sleep had found me fast, fortunately, and so did my desires for Alejandro. *He pushed his lips to mine and it felt like a sunny day filled with an afternoon breeze tickling across my skin. Goosebumps scattered across my flesh, telling the world I wanted more. His fervent green eyes and the sprinkle of his five o'clock shadow caroused to every part of my body that needed him. His tongue tangled with mine and his thick, strong fingers twisted into the tresses of my hair, causing every piece of lonely I ever owned to become nothing more than the dust under my past experiences. He was perfect, and I wanted to live in his perfection. He pulled back from our kiss, written on his face was every desire I had that ached for him to fulfill. His mouth brushed across my neck and up to the sacred space behind my ear. Sparks rushed through my body and pooled between my legs; God, I craved for him to find each and every one of them. His tongue leisurely swirled around my earlobe before he let out a moan mirrored by his hips swaying against me. I was going to explode …*

The alarm clock belched at five thirty in the morning and I was awake at once. Heartless enough to rip me from my fantasy of Alejandro, I hated my alarm clock. I didn't remember falling asleep. All I had was the memory of Terence trading his morality for the freedom of his brother. What choice did I have to change that experience? I had two options: either I was going to Spartacus Industries today to meet with Alejandro and show him the prototype; or I was going to get the file off the mainframe and destroy it. No matter how Alejandro made me feel, it was at that point I had to make the choice to be the agent I knew I could be. I needed to stop Terence from getting to Sam before he sent her off on an airplane.

I pulled the blankets off and embarrassingly I had spent another night in my clothes. I was grateful for the fact that Roger ordered something to eat.

"Good morning, I hope you don't mind I ordered you room service."

"Good morning," I replied in a rough voice. I tried to make eye contact but he was too busy readying his scrambled eggs and potatoes.

"Well, Lauren today is the big day," he said in a way that had made my skin clammy. I had conceded to the fact that it was the day that I was going to find out what I was made of. I knew Roger was thinking about the options of the day while I was thinking how I was going to control the desires that surged through my body when I was in the presence of Alejandro.

"Yeah, what are we going to do about Sam?" I asked, pulling the thoughts of what I lived through last night over my preoccupied mind belonging to Alejandro.

"I need to stop Terence from getting to Sam," Roger breathed. "We both need to stop Terence from getting to Sam," I told him. I wasn't about to let Roger handle this without backup. We didn't know Terence and seeing what I saw last night, I wasn't about to let Roger take any chances alone with him.

"Lauren, Alejandro is expecting you to be ready by seven this mornin'. I'll be fine," he reassured me, making our eyes meet and shaking his head. I didn't like the idea that he would be dealing with Terence without some type of backup.

Roger wasn't a field agent. He was a weapons engineer in a highly restricted department of the CIA. There weren't too many people at the agency able to do what he did. I had to let go, trust and believe he could handle this type of work.

"Fine, but once you have her safe I'm going to need you at SI. I can't do this without your help," I said.

"I'll make sure I'm with you. I'll keep connected to you the entire time," he stated with a firm voice, making me understand that he really did have the ability to live in my head if he wanted to.

I immediately backpedaled my demands. "I don't think you'll need to do that the entire time. I'll connect with you once I am in the server room at SI." I scrunched my hair back onto a messy ponytail.

"What if something happens between the time you leave here and reach SI? I don't think that's such a great idea." His voice sounded just like my father when I would ask if I could stay out an hour past curfew on a Saturday night.

"Nothing's going to happen. Even if Marshall shows up, I'll make sure I'm safe. Besides, you're going to need to focus on Terence." I was trying to facilitate a conversation that I should've been able to control.

"I'm not comfortable with that. You need to — "

"No, Roger, stay out of my head until I say," I demanded as I interrupted him. His head swung toward the floor and a dark cloud consumed him.

"Fine — but I'm not happy about it," he complained.

"I can't focus on the job if my mind is clouded with thoughts of you invading me. Promise to stay out of my head," I told him. I had to make sure he wouldn't get into my head until I wanted him to be there.

"Promise," he agreed. We finished eating in silence. "Well, I need to get moving, so you know how to contact me." He paused then finished. "Your gun and a couple of knives were the only weapons they forwarded. Just be careful. If I don't hear from you by nine — well you know what I can do."

He snatched up his CIA-issued pistol, forcing it into his shoulder holster and walked out the door. I hated when Roger would do that. Not giving me the last word really pissed me off, but today the fact that he had a gun just flat out concerned me.

I didn't realize that six thirty could creep up on me so quickly. I had to be down in the lobby in thirty minutes. I prided myself on the fact that I could get ready to go within a half hour. Today, I was stuck in a rut of trying to find a shirt that had the right amount of cling that would accentuate my curves to hold Alejandro's eyes. I knew what I was doing and as much as I knew it was totally crazy, I couldn't seem to stop myself.

I ended up choosing a thin white v-neck knitted cotton shirt that pulled just enough in all the right places. I found a big mirror behind the bathroom door and put on a minimal amount of makeup. I gave myself a couple of turns to check my clothes and how they fit. I left my hair in the messy ponytail but adjusted it out of habit. I grabbed my gun, made sure it was loaded and shoved it into my ankle holster under my flared jeans. I put my knife where I would be able to get to it quickly. I usually had two knives pushed up under the band of my bra, but I had to opt for a single one under my left side. I double-checked it in the mirror to make sure it wasn't obvious and then left the hotel room.

The elevator took its painfully sweet time making its way down from the fifteenth floor to the lobby. I became preoccupied with thoughts of what Roger might be doing. Without warning, his file popped up into my eyes. I noticed an unlocked file labeled *useful tools* with six applications including the remote access and the tracking software Roger showed me before. I downloaded them immediately without requiring any password or security warnings. By the time the elevator reached the lobby, I had the two new applications on my prototype.

The elevator slowly rolled open. Anxiety pulled as I sucked in a deep cleansing breath and looked for Alejandro's driver.

After a claustrophobic quarter-spin in the rotating door, I came out onto the busy sidewalk that invited people to begin their lives in the city by the bay. I wondered what life I was going to embrace. That's when I saw him and my heart dropped. His tall muscular structure leaned against a midnight black Ford GT that matched the color of his hair. His eyes captured mine and I couldn't pull them away. My mind was thrust back to yesterday, his sharp nose and warm lips against my wrist as the magnetic urge to have him kiss me all came flooding back. He pushed himself up from the side of the car and came toward me. I couldn't help but take him in as he walked with a confident swagger. From his head to his toes and back again, he was a vision that I drank up entirely, causing me to forget who I was and where I was standing.

"Good morning, Lauren, I hope you don't mind that I came to get you this morning?" His accent was even sexier today. "I assigned my driver to Marshall today. Mmmm, so I guess you're stuck with me." Alejandro cocked his head, brandishing a smirk that sparked a swirling energy low in my belly. His long soft fingers found my hand and pulled it to his mouth. Every sacred place in my body reacted when his warm breath poured over my skin as he pushed his satiated lips to the back of my hand and his forest green eyes closed. He shrewdly lowered my arm as his eyes met my stare.

I wanted to have my mind clear today. I had to get my prototype to record Roger and I was relying on the time I would've had in the limo to do that. Now that will be impossible.

"Um. Well thank you—I don't mind." I fumbled for words to say.

He turned toward his car, taking an intimate moment to run his hand around the back of my waist. His fingertips almost wrapped around my side. I shivered with the pressure he used to guide me to his car. The image of my pistol flashed in my mind, I was glad I didn't carry it in the waistband of my pants. He pulled the door open and wouldn't let go of me until I was in. I watched as he hurried around the front of the car, getting in like he had done it for a lifetime. He fit effortlessly behind the wheel. His scent filled the car and I automatically began breathing through my nose, allowing his smell to rush my taste buds in the back of my tongue. Lost in him, I knew I was in for a crushing tough day.

The car roared to life, electricity surged in my body. I never considered myself someone affected by the sound of a powerful engine, but then again, I never sat in a car so close to someone that captivated me so quickly and completely. As he pulled from the curb, my body became heavy and pressure rushed across my chest as the strength of the car matched its sound. It was exhilarating, scary and sexy all at the same time; words that became the metaphors of my feelings for Alejandro. I couldn't tear my eyes off of him, he had me mesmerized. Even when he met my gaze, I couldn't pull away.

"Are you hungry?" he asked, indicating there were restaurants we passed in the universe that existed outside of the atmosphere in his car.

"No, thank you, I already ate." I regretted saying it as the words spilt from my mouth.

"Well, how about a café?" He perked his brow.

I was glad he came up with some other reason to stop. I figured some coffee would be innocent enough.

"Sure." I tried to sound casual.

He pulled into a small hole-in-the-wall coffee shop. He looked at me curtly as he turned off the engine and waited. I smiled and nodded letting him know I was okay with his choice. His hand found the comfortable spot on my lower back as he led me to the coffee shop and opened the door. It felt good to be treated like a lady; something that just didn't happen too often and I was innately aware it was my career which contributed to the lack of chivalry in my life.

After we ordered, we sat in a corner away from the frothing gurgle of milk being heated and the sounds of people's dynamic conversations that just didn't matter to us. It was the perfect location for a private conversation that we both knew we needed to have.

"Thank you for the coffee." I held the paper cup toward him.

"You're welcome. It was my pleasure." He looked down at his coffee, twisted the lid around and continued a little unsure. "What have you learned about me? Marshall must have told you something about me," he breathed, meeting my eyes as he finished his sentence

"Marshall didn't tell me anything about you. I don't really know much, other than what you told me last night," I answered sheepishly, trying to avoid the messages my mind was sending my body.

I was drowning; I wanted to tell him what I thought. I didn't want to be so torn between what was right and wrong, black and white, good and bad. For the last twelve hours I had been living in between everything that seemed real; up was down, right had to be wrong and good doesn't ever conquer evil. My life was gray, and for the first time in a long time, I was being forced to embrace it.

I wasn't going to tell him about the file I read and the warnings Sam and Roger gave me. His face loosened and a slight smile that caught up to his eyes. I didn't look away. I didn't want him to know that I knew more than I let on.

"What? Is there something you need to tell me?" I asked with a false confidence. I didn't break my gaze; I wasn't about to let him off that easy. He shifted before his expression became dismissive.

"What do you *think* I need to tell you?"

Alejandro was playing a game of cat and mouse with me. I knew he was testing what I might know about him and I'll be damned if I didn't play into it perfectly.

"I want to know why you're after Roger's prototype. What are you going to use it for?"

There it was. I called him out. His expression dropped blank before bewilderment usurped his face. I wanted to see him work his way out of the corner I pinned him in. I needed to see why he had the reputation of being someone I was supposed to fear.

"Well, I'm a business man and I want to do business with successful business people." His words were abundantly charged with his Spanish accent.

"That's not answering my question," I pointed out. So I asked again.

"What are your plans for Roger Clarke's prototype?" He twisted his coffee around and took an exaggeratedly long pull before he paused and set his cup down on the table. A moment grew as he searched for the right words buried deep in the back of his mind. Words he must have believed I wanted to hear.

"I want to use the prototype for healing and helping people."

He paused. In the gap of silence, I wanted to believe him; I wanted him to be as honorable as I needed him to be.

I waited.

He continued. "What if I told you that doctors could use this nanobiotechnology in surgery? Mechanics when fixing elaborate cars. Lawyers could pull up files while defending their clients. Don't you see it, Lauren? The potential for this technology is virtually endless and I see that. I see what it is capable of doing." His eyes grew, fueling his energy and excitement as his hands pushed and pulled between us and his words streamed across the table at me. He was completely taken by the technology that Roger brought to him. Did he know it had the viable ability to wipe out nations, the world?

"Okay, but what about opposing governments, political parties, or military extremists and terrorists? What about the people who want it for all the wrong reasons? What about those people?" I asked, hoping the level of my insistence bore some weight to the validity of my concerns. Maybe I was trying to catch him in a lie; part of me wanted to know if he really was about 'the people' like he said. Damn it, I wanted to know, was he really a humanitarian or was it about pure profits, and bottom lines like it was for so many others? Silence was filled with an undeniable presence, which remained until he answered my question honestly.

He dragged his hand across his brow, collecting the few strands of hair misbehaving before he inhaled an extended breath. Up until that point, I believed he was perfect, that the words of so many were just simply wrong ... but it was his words, words that would have been best left by the side of the road, buried in a ditch; words which poured out of his mouth tainting my illusion of his perfect image.

"You want the truth? Here's the true, Lauren. I am all about helping the people. I'm about giving what was never given to me and if there is a chance to help people, and I can make money while doing it? Lauren, I am all for philanthropy, but I am still a business man." He grabbed my hand from across the table pulling it into his palm as he spoke. "I see the potential of his invention. It will be very profitable for everyone involved. I want to be a part of that. It would be foolish not to be."

His hand was warm from holding his drink. I didn't try to pull away; I just lingered in his grasp and drowned in his gaze.

He never did answer my question.

"Alejandro, have you thought about the real possible threat of the wrong people doing whatever it would take to get their hands on this technology?"

"Lauren—I don't think you want to hear what I would be forced to do." He broke the gaze and let go of my hand. He grabbed his coffee and stood up. "I think it's best if we get to SI. You still have something very important to show to me." He pressed his long fingers to the side of my head before tucking a few straggling tresses behind my ear. "I have no doubt it's going to be the most spectacular thing I've ever seen." His words caressed my flesh as he dropped his hand and ambled to the door. He wasn't ready to give me the answers I wanted to hear.

The drive to Spartacus Industries was quiet. Alejandro seemed to be thinking about the questions I raised and, well, the fact I decided to wait patiently for his explanation might have helped break the silence that filled the car.

"Did I upset you in the coffee shop?" Alejandro asked.

"No," I replied.

"I feel like you are upset by my answers."

"How can I be upset by your answers if what you said wasn't even an answer?" It felt weird talking to him like this. He wasn't my boyfriend and yet I felt myself play the emotional card like he was.

"Well, I don't want you to be upset when we meet with Marshall," he said, trying to change the subject.

Immediately, after he mentioned Marshall, I couldn't stop my thoughts from swirling around Samantha. If it was a normal situation, I wouldn't think twice about walking away from helping her, but this situation was anything but normal. Marshall wanted her taken care of, and not in a good way … why? What would switch his feelings off so fast for her? He's killing off all of the people with the prototype in their head ... My heart unexpectedly raced, fueling an immense pressure in my chest. It was as if an elephant decided to perch across my ribs, causing me to struggle for each breath. The space around me began to dissolve the unwelcomed humidity that licked my flesh. I recognized it immediately; I was having a panic attack. This attack was different, it was deeper, core rattling; it affected my entire body. I really didn't want Alejandro to know what was going on. I couldn't get the window down fast enough in the car. With every turn and acceleration, I felt the chunks of anxiety crawl up into the back of my throat.

"Pull over," I demanded, holding myself together as much as I could. His eyes widened, I guess the shade of green I turned convinced him to pull over. The car hit loose gravel skidding to a stop, my head kept traveling and my face hit the dash.

"Oh shit! Are you okay?" Alejandro yelled as he jumped out of the car and ran to my side.

"I'm fine," I squeaked. I pushed the palm of my hand to my left cheek, trying to get the burning pain to cool. At least the panic attack was gone.

Alejandro flung my door open; his hands covered mine that clung to my cheek. He pulled my hands away and pushed my forehead up so he could see the damage to my face.

"Oh, okay, not bad," he said as he opened the glove box and pulled out some napkins, pressing them to my cheek.

"Look at your car! Oh, I'm sorry about that." I was mortified that my blood was on his dash.

"Please Lauren, it's just a car. I should be apologizing to you." He kept dabbing my cheek and folding the napkins. I looked past him and spotted a GP station across the road. A restroom with water, soap and fresh towels would be a much better solution.

"Gas station—I just want to clean it up." I pointed across the street.

"I think I should get this to stop bleeding first."

I tried to wiggle out of his car and stand up. "Oh, no, I'm going to drive you over there ... get in," he said as he pushed my legs back into his car. I didn't argue.

The engine roared alive and he had me across the street before I could focus on the Goldstein Petrol sign lit in the corner of the property. He helped me out of the car and into the restroom.

"I'll be right out," I said, letting him know I wanted to clean up alone.

He slid his hand down the outside of the door as it closed shut. I could hear the gravel crunch under his feet as he walked away and I pressed the lock.

I turned on the water and pulled several paper hand towels from the box on the wall and thrust the paper towels under the ice cold water and started to clean up my cheek that was taking a beating the last couple of days.

Stowed away in a locked restroom, I had a perfect opportunity to contact Roger, and like a habit that was second nature, I said his name ... out loud.

"Roger Clarke." I spoke clearly.

His information appeared and I noticed now he had an icon that was a compass and another that had two computers with a link between them.

I told him that I didn't want to connect with him until I was at SI but figured taking this opportunity to see what he was doing with Terence and Samantha would be one way to keep him from contacting me later. I focused on the icon with two computers linked and instantly a little white bubble started to bounce between them. I clicked around and with only a couple of minor set up details and I was in. I could see his files, apps, and data ... everything he could see. I could even access his recorder. I shuffled around his head for a short moment before I activated his recorder. My mind went blank as my vision slowly faded out to black. I prayed I wasn't too late to find out the details on Sam and Terence.

I should have known that Roger could tell when someone accessed his mind. I was stupid to think I could enter his thoughts and prototype without him noticing.

*"Lauren, what the hell are you doing? You don't belong in my head!"* His voice boomed in my head.

"Well, Rog, I'm sorry but I am stuck in a filthy restroom in a stinking gas station and we haven't even been to SI yet," I answered in a meek and broken tone.

*"What happened? Did Alejandro hurt you? Are you okay? Do you need me?"* His questions fired rapidly across my aching mind.

"No, I'm okay."

*"Are you sure?"* Roger asked.

"Yeah, I'm sure," I responded.

Suddenly, my body felt strange, like I was running, breaking a sweat. I blinked and suddenly, Sam and Terence were in front of me. They were walking fast with their arms intertwined. She didn't appear to be struggling. As a matter of fact, she seemed to be willing, at least from my vantage point.

Roger broke into a sprint and ran around to a group of people walking in front of Terence and Sam. Hidden behind the cluster of people, Roger saw that Samantha was smiling and Terence was totally relaxed.

"Roger, I need you to drink something," I croaked, my throat had gone terribly dry and it felt as if blocks of wood were being drug across rough sandpaper.

"Hang on. I need to catch Sam."

"Rog, I really feel like I am going to pass out!"

"Ok, give me a minute. There we go." He hustled over to an unused drinking fountain bulging from the wall. Pressing the button, he lowered his head down to the stream of cold water. He drank so much I almost couldn't breathe. He pulled up and ran his hand across his lips wiping the excess water dribbling from his mouth and for a moment I felt comfortable in his masculine world. Unfortunately, my comfort didn't last long when he saw that Samantha was through security and was now walking toward the gate with Terence, hand and hand.

His heart thundered in his chest as his hands crashed against my aching head. I saw his thoughts race while different ideas popped up from the dark murky corners of his mind. His frustration grew quickly into anger. Replaying the scene in his head, the drink we took, the water dripping, the moment he realized that he couldn't get to them once they had past security.

"*Get out!*" he screamed out loud.

"I'm sorry, Roger. I am so sorry," I begged him.

"*Get out of my head,*" he demanded again banging his fists to his temples. I watched from his eyes as people stared at him like he was crazy. I had to stop him.

"Roger. Please."

"*Get out. Get out now. Get the hell out of my head.*"

"Okay, please stop. I'm gone." I disconnected and found myself back in the filthy gas station restroom staring at the mirror, dried blood dribbles crusted on my cheek. I really screwed up his opportunity to save Samantha. I felt so ugly and disgusted.

"Are you ok, Lauren?" Alejandro asked, knocking lightly on the door.

I didn't answer.

Shifting his intentions, Alejandro's soft knuckled raps turned into tight fisted thunderous strikes against the door.

"Lauren, answer me! Are you okay? Lauren?"

"I'll be out in a minute," I sighed.

"I'm right here. I'll wait right by the door."

"Thanks," I whispered so low he couldn't hear me.

I pulled the hair band out of my messy ponytail and recollected the loose strands of hair that escaped. I took another handful of paper towels, wetting them and removing the dried blood off my face before pressing them to my puffy my eyes red. The cool water gave me a reprieve I desired. When I pulled the restroom door open, sure enough Alejandro was right there. I didn't mean to be dramatic but when I saw him my knees buckled and I fell into his grasp. My heart pounded a thousand apologies for what I had done. My skin wept tears of sweat as the image of Roger freaking out and rejecting me filled my mind. I couldn't pull myself together. I heard Alejandro call my name while images of Roger popped off in my head; everything I saw around me fizzled into black as I passed out.

I woke up to a freezing ice pack across my face and a rolled up blanket tucked under my knees. I pulled the ice from my eyes and struggled to focus on the person who sat attentively across from me.

Instantly, Alejandro rushed over, slipping his big warm hands behind my back to help me sit up. I didn't recognize where I was. A black lacquered desk sat across the room with a brass lamp radiating a shallow yellow glow.

Alejandro brushed my cheek with a warm damp cloth.

"Hi, beautiful, there you are. You made me concerned," he whispered.

"Where am I? What happened?"

"You passed out after you came out of the gas station lavatory and I brought you to my office." He pushed the ice pack to my cheek and held it there.

"We're at your office? I passed out?" I looked around frantically. Everything in my head was wishy-washy and swimming, like my eyes was left behind while my head continued on.

"Where's Marshall? We're supposed to meet him."

"Don't worry about Marshall. Don't worry about anything right now," he said as he pulled the ice pack from my cheek, inspecting my face before he dragged his thumb soothingly under my gash.

I ached deep in my body and the most awful part about it was that it wasn't physical. Beat me, tear me apart, rip my body to a thousand pieces, all would be easier than what I had faced with the disappointment I caused Roger. He didn't save Sam and it was entirely my fault; regret ripped through my spirit.

"Where did you go?" Alejandro's voice pierced my deep remorse; his other hand pushed my loose strands of hair away from my face. His eyes filled with trepidation as they belonged to me.

"Nowhere," I lied.

"Yes, you did. You were far away, somewhere deeply painful ... I recognized it in your eyes."

"I'm just grateful you were there to catch me when I passed out," I told him, hoping to change the subject.

"Me too. Someday I will figure out what makes you tick, until then, you ready to go?" He held his hands out to me.

"Go, go where? I thought we were meeting Marshall."

"No, I took care of it."

"I don't understand," I piped up.

"See, you bumped your head harder than we thought." He pushed his fingertips to the space below my gash causing me to flinch.

"I don't understand, what about Marshall?"

"There is nothing to understand, *mi dama*. You obviously hit your head pretty hard. I canceled our meeting with him until tomorrow ... Now, I am going to take care of you." He leaned down to slip my feet down off the sofa.

"No!" I groused. "You shouldn't have canceled the meeting. I could have handled it." I cautiously slipped my feet off the sofa.

A smug smirk grew on his face as he held up his hand. He was done hearing anymore arguments from me.

"Lauren, it's already done. I am taking you to my house." He lowered his body, swallowing me in his fresh aroma. Dizzied by his attention, he slipped his arms around my back and as if he had been planning it, he inhaled against my exposed flesh as he pulled me up into his body.

"Just take a moment to collect your balance; I'm here," he whispered against my ear. Shaky, I took my time to steady myself. He helped me back into his car, remarkably the blood that splattered from my face was gone from the dash.

It wasn't hard to notice he was driving much slower this time. Every time I closed my eyes, Roger's anger would creep into my thoughts, my body would jerk and I would let out a muffled whimper. I turned away from Alejandro, my hand fisted against my thigh; I just wanted the visions to stop invading me so violently. His fingertips brush across my knuckles as he slipped his hand over mine. Affected by his touch, a growing craving burned low in my stomach; I let his fingers slowly tangle with mine. A comfort flooded my body as he caressed his thumb across my thigh. I was able to close my eyes for the last couple of turns to his house. Maybe humanity did exist in my world.

# fourteen

It was only eleven forty-five in the morning when Alejandro pulled me from the car. The sun stung my tear-soaked eyes as I looked up at him. The choice of the white clinging t-shirt was for not. Blood-soaked stains dotted the collar and down the front of it. I didn't want to own any part of this nightmare anymore. The only solace I clung to rested in the eyes of the man that was holding me as we entered his house.

"Lauren, I'm calling my physician. I want him to tell me you are okay."

"You don't have to do that, I'm fine," I insisted.

"I'll call him; he can be here quick."

"No, please I'm fine," I pushed and started getting upset. I wasn't going to let just anyone exam my body now. Who knew what doctors would see or find out with me having this thing in my head? Besides, Alejandro was convinced that my collapse was due to hitting my head. He didn't know about the blowup between Roger and me.

Alejandro gave me the once over as his unconvinced expression broke to frustration. "Okay, fine, I will let you win … this time. However, I insist you rest and let me take care of you," he said as he

169

closed the front door and slipped his hand comfortably across the small of my back and led me up a massive staircase.

"Where are you taking me?"

"My bedroom, so you can rest. I want to get you a clean shirt."

He swung the door open to his bedroom. It was modest, masculine, sexy, and called my name as I shuffled my heavy feet through the threshold. Brown suede-textured walls hugged me as he pulled me in. Piles of different shaped pillows innocently invited me to his massive king-sized bed, draped with a burgundy comforter.

"Go on ... I'll let you rest in my bed."

I turned around and gave him a long gaze. He nodded to me before he held his hand out.

"Nothing more than me offering you a place to recover before I take you back to your hotel room."

I sat on the edge of his bed, restlessly bouncing my knee while he made his way to his walk-in-closet and came back with a button-up white long sleeve shirt and held it to his chest.

"Is this ok?"

"That's one of your dress shirts; don't you have a tee-shirt or something?"

"No, this is what you'll wear."

I gave him a startled glance. His words rubbed at that place inside me that piqued my defenses.

"What if I refuse?" I quipped.

He looked at me questioningly, like he didn't understand my response.

"Lauren, why do you keep refusing me when my only concern is you? I didn't think you'd want to pull a tee-shirt over your head. That's all."

He tossed the shirt to the bed; it bellowed a slow dance before it landed. A moment of time dangled clumsily between us. "Good. I will be downstairs if you need me." He made sure our eyes met and then closed the door behind him.

I pulled my t-shirt off over my head and felt the cling of the shirt push on my cheek. Pain shot across my face.

I walked to the full length mirror and didn't recognize the shirtless body that stared back at me. She had bruises and cuts on her face and down her rib cage, evidence of Samantha's rage. She looked pale and meek. Her hair was messy, clumped and dark. It took me a second to pull myself into the body that stared back in the mirror. I noticed a door open behind me, it was the master bathroom. My body craved to feel clean again. I pushed open the bathroom and was instantly consumed by a whirlwind of peace.

Enormous slabs of dark brown marble, tangled with rusty red and gold lines, embraced me as I curved my way to the center of the huge shower. It was spacious enough for four people with room left over. Deliberate pocket shelves were concaved into the wall to hold soap and shampoo while a solid black granite bench protruded from the back wall. The brass shower heads were deliberately mounted every three feet, one for every section of my body. I tugged off my remaining clothes, found a drawer to put my weapons in and pushed the faucet handles to hot. I began to relax into the water that poured over my head, pressed down my back and pulsated on my thighs. Steam pushed its way up and out the top of the shower as I kept turning my body. All the different shower heads were heating every inch of my body; it was relaxing and stimulating, confusing my senses.

I fantasized how the water that ran down my spine were his hands finding the curve of my waist. I turned toward the rush of the spray that was his breath as it warmed the space below my breasts. The stream of water that trickled down my face was his wet lips pressed hot against mine as they found their way to my neck and down to my chest. I turned, letting the hot water press on the back of my spine as I pulled my hair away. I felt warm pressure push on the inside of my arms and down to my thighs like he was memorizing my body.

I dragged my hand across my stomach, fielding the desire to satisfy the ache that raged between my legs when I heard the bathroom door slide open. My heart dropped when I heard it shut with a click.

"Lauren, I brought you fresh towels," Alejandro called to me. His Spanish accent mingled with the water as it slammed against my skin.

"Thanks. I hope you don't mind that I jumped into your shower," I replied, as I peeked out from around the corner.

"Please take your time," he answered, looking at me. I felt the temperature in the room rise and I was suddenly aware of the water that found its way to the inside of my thighs. I pushed my face back into the shower and waited for the door to close.

Even though my body didn't want to leave the sensual haven created by Alejandro's shower, I hurried to finish. I grabbed at the towels he set out for me, and wrapped up my body and hair before I regretfully stepped out of my fantasy.

When I noticed the pile of clothes I left in the middle of the bathroom floor were gone, I went in search for them; that's when I noticed a pair of silk boxers on the bed, folded and neatly placed next to the shirt he had picked out for me to wear. Every warning light and siren went off in my head and I had played right into his hand. I had allowed his actions to effortlessly pull me into his world. Every ounce of my intuition was screaming for me to question his motives and yet my carnal desire to touch him, taste him, and feel him was ruling my body.

I un-wrapped the towel from my body and pulled my legs through the warm soft boxers. I rolled the band down a couple of times to make them tight around my waist. I snatched the see-through white button-up shirt and swung it around my body. The scent pushed toward me, thrusting at my soul. His shirt caressed my skin as I slid so comfortably into it. I tugged at the edges, pulling it to wrap tight around my chest before I dragged my fingers across the edges and buttoned it. I rolled the sleeves as I went back into the bathroom.

I looked in the mirror, seeing what I had become, damaged by the events that made up the last couple of days. Even though my face was clean, it was not free from the wounds beginning to heal. A wave of disappointment pushed its way into my mind about Roger. The anger in his voice at my innocent mistake with Samantha sent jolts of guilt and pain through my body. He didn't even let me apologize for my mistake, he just pushed me away. My arms became heavy and the space that hurt so deep within my soul began to churn. I didn't deserve to be treated that way. I thought about Roger and how angry he was this morning. All the insecure feelings of inadequacy and loss began to fill my body. I could feel the lonely, lost woman I was so many years ago, pushing to be healed. I was desperate to be held and made whole again. I dropped my hands to the vanity and I fought to take a deep breath.

"Lauren?" Alejandro's voice mused through the bedroom door as he knocked lightly.

"Yeah?" I answered startled. I froze waiting to hear if he was going to answer.

"Are you decent? May I come in?" his voice permeated the door.

"Yes, come in," I answered quickly.

His hands were full with a tray overflowing with fresh fruit and a bottle of mineral water. He walked over and placed it on the foot of the bed.

"I thought you might be a little hungry," he said with his back to me. I stared at him, blinking to keep from having tears converge in my eyes.

"Thank you."

He turned toward me and froze. His eyes slowly caressed their way from my feet up to my face; soaking in every curve and bend, overflowing my body with warmth. I felt his desire fill the room and rake my body, as the most private places in me ached to be touched and filled by him. He didn't say anything as he gradually sauntered his way toward me. The space between us became non-existent. He let out a low visceral breath as he reached for the collar of my shirt. I noticed his jaw flex and roll as he tilted his head to one side and pulled the back of my collar free. I felt his shirt drag across my hardened nipples. I was vibrating inside; I ached to feel him touch me, placate that lonely girl that resided somewhere between desperate and durable. I wanted him.

"Your collar is tucked under. Now we can't have that, can we?" he said through a whisper. His hands, warm against my neck, induced a shiver down my spine, collecting between my legs. He was the perfect diversion I needed to fill a vacancy I didn't want.

My mouth watering, I parted my lips enough to take in his aroma. I felt a bone shattering chill as the tip of his nose brushed across my ear. He pushed his lips against the pulse in my neck before making his way to the edge of my jaw. Every nerve fired sparks that flooded the space deep in my stomach. His hands clung below my shoulder blades. He plucked his lips from my flesh.

"I want you," he whispered as his eyes caught mine.

Speechless in his wake, there was nothing I was willing to question about his plan to use me.

"I can't," I breathed. God knows I wanted to taste him and I ached to have him quench the desire burning inside of me; but, I had to be smart; I had to stop what was happening between us before we went too far.

"Lauren, let me take care of you." His eyes danced with mine as he flashed his smoldering smile, tearing me open to his charm. His fingers pushed at my cheek before he stroked his thumb delicately across my bottom lip. "I want to taste you from here down," he breathed and I melted.

My knees weakened and my head swam with images of him taking me to places I hadn't been in years. My breath quickened as he pressed his lips against mine. I kissed him back as my body was answering his plea.

Alejandro pulled his mouth slightly from mine and I felt his breath tickle my lips as he asked me again. "Do you want me, Lauren?"

I swallowed resting my forehead against his, our lips barely touching as I nodded.

"I want to hear you say it. Say it, Lauren, tell me you want me to taste you from here down to there," he murmured as his hand traced from my lips, across my body, down below my navel until his fingertips brushed across the silky boxers I was wearing. My hips automatically swayed against his fingers as they lingered down between my legs.

He had me. I wanted him. Every moment of lonely I had lived surged through every sensual part of my body ... I needed him to take me.

"Yes," I huffed as I pushed my mouth against his.

His large strong hand anchored to the back of my neck as he urged me to open my mouth with his tongue. Kissing me vigorously as my hands tangled in his hair and he pulled me closer as his erection hardened against my stomach. He tasted so sweet, better than I had imagined. He kissed down the front of my neck across to the hollow of my collarbone. I arched my shoulders and leaned my head back inviting him to continue. I closed my eyes, my breath caught as I ached for him to take me where ever he was willing to go.

Alejandro picked me up and carried me to the bed. His eyes fixed on mine; god, I wanted him. I wanted him more than I ever thought I'd want someone ever again. I shivered, longing to feel him against me; feel him press so hard that I'd lose my breath and get lost in his touch.

"You cold?" he breathed.

"No," I whispered.

He gently laid me on the bed, his mouth finding its way back to my lips. I tugged at his buttons trying to take off his shirt. I needed to feel his chest, his pulse, and kiss his scorching flesh. He dragged his lips from mine with a low hum and backed off me just enough to make me ache.

My eyes sprang open as he stared at me. My hands empty, frozen in the air, begging to be captured by his strong grip. My heart throbbed loudly, waiting for him to touch my skin. His arms on either side of me, pressing into the bed, flexing, I could see he was going to say something.

Desperate, to have his mouth against my flesh, hoping beyond all hope that I'll be able to go through with this, I reached up to the pearl white buttons that held my shirt together and started to unbutton them. Little by little the fabric fell apart, opening him to my heart; when I reached the third button, just below my breast, his hand slid under my shirt and pushed it back. I gasped for a charged breath. His soft hot fingertips caressed my firm pebbled nipples, creating an uncontrollable craving that pounded between my legs.

His eyes never broke from mine as I reached up and unbuttoned his shirt. His lips found mine again while his hands attentively learned the topography of my body. Kissing me between my breasts, he dragged the tip of his tongue across my skin before his teeth nipped at my hardened nipples.

It's been too long since I've had someone touch me like this; years of burdens, dropped at the altar of this moment. He was teasing me while everything I was begged him to touch me. His hands methodically explored my body running down my sides across my stomach and ready to pull on the waist band of my boxers when he stopped and noticed the damage to my one side.

"What happened?" he asked.

"Nothing," I answered as I pushed him off me and rolled onto my side.

"Lauren, who did this to you?" he asked, as he pulled me onto my back. His eyes were fixed to my side as he waited for me to answer.

"Nobody," I answered. Suddenly I was self-conscious about my body.

"*Mi dama,* that won't do. I must insist, who damaged you?"

"These are just the scars. The wounds I bury everyday lay deeper than this. Don't ask me to tell you who damaged me, there are too many to count."

Delicately he caressed his fingertips over my cuts and punctures, before he pressed his lips to each one. I could hear him trying to heal me as his lips lifted. "Someday, Lauren, someday you will tell me."

"Someday is a moment which will have its own time, and for whatever reason, be it right or wrong, I am here with you willing to give you a part of me that hasn't been offered to anyone else in a very, very long time."

His eyes flickered with a sinful possession, narrowing as he dragged his lips across my abdomen hovering just below my navel. His fingers caught the waistband of my boxers and pulled them down past my thighs. A wicked urge rushed between my legs as my hands tangled into his thick, tousled black hair. I wanted to feel him drag his tongue along the crest of my desire, and taste for the first time what I have kept sacred for so long.

He pulled his mouth from my flesh, smiling at the raging storm he was creating in my body. His eyes soaked in my exposed flesh; he stood up off the bed and unsnapped his jeans. Unhurriedly he lowered the zipper, and dragged them down off his body. His erection pushed diligently at his silk boxers. A soft fabric bound his rock hard intentions; they were the last thing separating us from complete and utter discovery. I looked up at him and his eyes caught mine before I wrapped my fingers around the waistband of his boxers and tugged, making them fall into a crumpled pile at his feet. He pushed his leg between my knees and lowered me onto the bed.

He slinked on top of me, meticulously possessing every inch of my skin with his mouth. He caught my wrists and pinned my arms up over my head. A rush of apprehension tanked in my stomach before desire saturated my most intimate spaces. My body was his road map to unabashed pleasure. His mouth pressed and drove against my skin, first the bend of my neck, then the curve of my breasts, next the stretch of my stomach, and finally, the span of my thighs before he spread my legs apart. Cool air charged my edges, dampening and throbbing for him. His eyes caught my smile as I waited for his tongue to tap and dance against me. Bursts of heat flowed against the crest between my legs, his breath evoking the sway of my hips as he smiled and lowered his lips to the inside of my thigh.

"Lauren, I'm going to make you beg," he said as the cool air of the room replaced the heat of his lips. "I'm not going to stop tasting you until I feel you explode against my tongue."

Anxiety reared its cruel intention and I was vexed.

"I don't beg," I breathed.

An unabashed smile crept across his face. Giving Alejandro complete control over me wasn't something that was going to come easy, especially when I am the most vulnerable. His eyes were wickedly sexy while the muscles across his jaw pulled taut. My body surged with a desire that had been unfulfilled for too long, my hips automatically rolled and swayed waiting in anticipation of him tasting how ready I was. My hands knotted into his shiny black hair and I pushed him to where I needed him to please me. Deep lingering groans rose from my throat as his tongue lapped at my desire. Swirling and sucking, pulling and pressure, dampened with the heat of his mouth and the cool chill of his release. Everything I had missed, everything I had pushed away for so long filled my soul. Strong waves vibrated through my body, tingling with jolts of electricity that shot through my core. Was this the freedom I had been missing for so long? I couldn't remember if I'd ever felt that way before. Maybe Alejandro was a master of making women beg, or maybe not; but when his fingers breached the loneliest place on my body, I lost my breath, and wordlessly begged him to take me.

I pulled up my legs hoping the crashing thrust of my hips would drive his fingers deeper, his mouth still tasting the swollen space he now owned, as his other hand toiled and pressed my breasts. I rolled up, clawing at him, trying to force his fingers faster and deeper into my body.

"That's right, *mi dame*, beg me. Beg me with your body." He pushed his mouth against me, catching his breath with a low rumbling moan and that was it. My body craved his weight, ached to feel him push and pull deeper and harder inside of me.

"I need you ... inside of me. Please Alejandro, I can't take this anymore," I huffed between thrusts of my hips against his fingers and tongue.

His hands left my body and his mouth withdrew from between my legs and suddenly I was floating in a sea of incomplete. Alejandro leaned across his bed and pulled a condom from his nightstand. Never have I had such an unalterable craving that owned me entirely. For over ten years I had been denying physical passion and my carnal needs, but today I easily became a slave to its pleasure. As much as I hated to relinquish control to someone else, in that moment, no matter how anxious I was ... I couldn't stop it ... my body wouldn't let me; and, quite frankly, neither did my heart.

"You okay?" he asked as he dusted my face with kisses. I nodded, wordlessly still begging him to fill me. His body hovered over me as he pushed his lips hard against mine. Our bodies, molding perfectly as he rolled his hips between my legs and my body welcomed his length. Slowly he pressed, deeper; quickly he pulled back, and then slowly again he'd push until he felt my body accept his size. My hips bucking under his thrust; he answered with a sway of his pelvis. Deeper he'd press, faster I would respond.

"You like that ... don't you," he growled.

"Yes, faster," I huffed. My body easily remembered what my heart had forgotten. I wanted to explode against him as the walls of my desire clenched and accepted their fate. I wanted to be revered, adored, and loved. Alejandro thrust faster and deeper as our bodies worked in rhythm. I dragged my hands down his muscular backside urging him to thrust harder. His grunts and moans with each push and pull were salacious. The velocity of our bodies quickened balancing on the sharp edge of oblivion as he kissed me, sweeping his tongue across mine. Our bodies pumped and thundered solid against one another as we grabbed with such force that the line between pain and ecstasy melded. We shivered and jerked simultaneously for what seemed forever. Our breaths panting in unison; he didn't stop thrusting inside me as his fingers found my spot and rubbed causing me to explode around him again. Bolts of white electricity exploded behind my closed eyes, ripping through out my entire body. Deep-seated moans escaped in rapid succession as I cried out my satisfaction. He owned my pleasure, twice. As I began to come back from where he took me and reality tickled at my being, my whole body relaxed into the aftermath of his talent. He rolled over to his side and pulled me in into his arms, pressing his lips to my temple as his words melted into my flesh.

"Promise me you'll make that noise every time I make you come."

I answered an inaudible yes as we finally lay there tucked in each other's arms, tired, sweaty and satisfied.

He stretched over the other side of the bed where the tray of food rested precariously on the edge and plucked a couple of grapes from their stems. He popped one in his mouth before he teased and dangled one above me. I reached for it and he pulled it away. Control, that's what he desired, so I opened my mouth and let him, feed me. As soon as I closed my mouth, his lips connected and pressed against mine, not as forceful as he did earlier, but gently like he was reminding me that he was honorable. His tongue languidly tangled with mine, the flavor of sweet grapes mingled with his zest.

"You really are beautiful, I couldn't help myself," he said as he pulled away from our kiss. His hand swept the hair back from my eyes.

"You sure it wasn't the see-through white button-up?" I joked with him. He smiled and an animalistic desire mounted in my body again.

"Well, that helped. Are you hungry?" he asked as he pulled the huge tray of food to his side. I watched as his muscles flexed from his shoulders all the way down across his backside to his ankles. His shiny black hair fell and tumbled, almost daring my hands to get tangled up in its waves. I felt like a lioness that wanted to catch him, bring him to my den and ravage his body.

"Yeah, I'm starving," I told him as I pushed against his back spooning him to reach the tray of food. He was so warm and we fit so comfortably together.

"Well, I better feed you so you're prepared for round two," he said, smiling with a handful of juicy red strawberries and plump green grapes. I gave him a ravenous look before I laid back on the bed and let him feed me.

# fifteen

The second shower of the day felt just as good as the first. Alejandro's fingers pressed down my spine, catching every last ounce of passion he sparked in the haven between my legs.

Like bees to honey, his lips traced the same paths they discovered hours before. We wanted more than the limited discovery in the confines of soft sheets. The shower pummeled our bodies, its water protected us with its heat and steam, and its chills rolled in waves over our flesh.

I asked for more by hitching my legs around Alejandro's hips, he answered by pinning me against the heated granite. Our kiss feverish; he was carnal and demanding when he pushed inside of me. I lost my breath in the first couple of thrusts that my body accepted him. He was spreading me more than the physical with the roll of his hips; the huffs of his breath took me farther than any urge I've experienced before. It was lascivious, more than any will to survive; with every push, he pulled me deeper into his possession.

When Alejandro stepped out his skin glistened with the remnants of water beading across his olive skin and as I watched his muscles move under his dampened skin I wanted to believe he was mine. The visions of our bodies entwined and twisted played over and over in my mind, his hands capturing me, pushing and pulling my body beyond the confines I had created for myself. My heart sped, my stomach swirled as I relived everything Alejandro did to me. Suddenly, my vision dissolved into solitary flashing cursor blinking spastically in the bottom corner of my eye before Roger's name glowed solid. Frustration flooded my body as the sheer dread of talking to him drizzled across my skin, what was I going to say to him? I wasn't ready to talk as his voice flooded my head.

*"Lauren? Hey Lauren – I'm sorry. I really shouldn't have reacted the way I did,"* his voice quivered.

"Roger can't talk right now," I answered, aloof.

*"Lauren, please don't. I'm so sorry."*

"Fine, I know you're sorry, but I can't talk right now," I answered deliberately. Severing my connection to Roger, I was back in the shower alone. My pure oasis was trampled by the angst that Roger left in his wake.

At least Alejandro had left my clothes from earlier today folded, clean and smelling like him. After getting dressed, I grabbed a brush and ran it a couple of times through my hair, before pulling it into a wet ponytail. As much as I didn't want to, I knew I needed to contact Roger. Tension throbbed up through my back settling in my jaw. Roger had hurt me and at this point I wasn't ready to forgive him.

I poked my head out of the bathroom and noticed the bedroom door was closed. Mirroring the bedroom door, I shut the bathroom door and locked it. I needed to get a hold of Roger. Easy enough, I was beginning to understand how to use the prototype. Roger's file appeared before my eyes. The phone icon glowed bright green and the graphic equalizer came to life as the ringing climbed in my head.

Roger answered by the third ring.

*"Lauren, hi, I wanted to tell you sorry for my reaction."* Roger spoke in a hushed whisper.

"No problem," I answered indifferently.

*"I shouldn't have reacted the way I did."*

I accepted his apology, while making some of my own. Long explanations were not what I needed right now. I was relieved and glad to have that out of the way but deep down I wasn't ready to forgive him completely.

*"Did you get anything out of Alejandro? How was the meeting this morning with Marshall?"*

I didn't want him to know what I did with Alejandro today. Even though I was still holding a small grudge, I knew it would devastate him and I didn't want to do that.

"I actually didn't meet with Marshall. I — ah — hit my head." There, just enough information but not too much.

*"Are you ok?"* he asked.

"I just needed a rest. That's all. I feel a lot better now. Besides, Alejandro rescheduled our meeting for tomorrow," I said, still trying to keep my day private.

"*Well, Lauren, I needed to tell you. I'm ... well ...*" He paused for a long moment. "*I, oh man, I'm on a flight to D.C.*"

A long silence rested between us. I tried to suck in a deep breath, but my diaphragm went rigid, like someone punched me in my gut. I wasn't expecting him to be heading home. Without Roger here, I was the perfect target. An uncomfortable silence clung to the empty space between us.

"*Lauren, listen, I had to go; Sam's in trouble. She has my prototype in her head and I had to trust my gut feeling that you'd be okay.*"

"What the hell do you think is in my head, Roger?"

"*I knew you'd be upset, but I have to go. If I had a choice I would stay with you. It's just — I have to find out if Sam is playing the middle against the ends.*"

"Don't worry about it. Take care of the situation. I understand. I can handle things on this end." Relief poured over my body, at least he wouldn't find out about Alejandro, yet. But that meant I was going to be alone. No back up, nothing. If Marshall decided to take me out — I was on my own.

"*Are you sure? I'm hoping to handle this in a couple of days then be back to get you home.*"

"I'm sure. Take care of Sam." I disconnected first this time. I closed my eyes and visualized a sunset where shades of red drew strength from the mountains pushing on the lake filled sky. It was my favorite place to go when I needed to feel peace.

I searched the house for Alejandro. I was about to give up when I found him in the kitchen.

"There you are," I murmured. A strange awkwardness built between us, disappointment filled his eyes. I dropped my hands to my sides, wondering what had happened in the short period of time that he had left me in the bathroom. I didn't say a word, waiting for him to break the silence or stare whichever came first.

"Who would want to hurt her?" He looked away and mumbled as he walked to the other side of the kitchen.

"Hurt who?" I innocently asked, breaking the trance he was under. He grabbed my shoulders squaring his body to mine. He looked deep into my eyes trying to find answers.

"Lauren, tell me, do you know what happened to Samantha?" His grip grew tighter. I was nervous. I didn't want to be put into this position. This wasn't what I wanted to spend the rest of the day discussing.

"What do you mean?" I played dumb.

"Do you know where she could be?" he asked with desperation in his voice.

"Did you try her cell phone?" I asked, encouraging my innocence.

"Yes, there was no answer." He looked at me, his eyes filled with hope.

"You can contact her right—with your prototype? Call her?" His words ran from his mouth so fast, almost tripping over one another, anticipation radiated through his entire body.

"Oh, well, yeah—should be able to. What do you want me to say?" I was suffocated by jealousy. The image of Sam kissing Marshall passionately at my house just days earlier shoved its way into my mind. Resentment smoldered deep in my abdomen. I didn't want to feel jealous, but it just oozed over me like an erupting volcano. I wasn't a heartless bitch, I was concerned for Sam because I knew where she was and what her future was going to be if Roger didn't catch her soon, but seeing Alejandro's reaction to her threatened me.

"Tell her—I know what she was planning to do to SI."

"What was she going to do?" I asked, knowing full well her intentions; I had the proof in my prototype.

"Nothing that would concern you, *mi dama*; she needs to call me. I will work it out with her, but she needs to get in touch with me. Understand." He wrung his hands. I watched him pace back and forth.

I didn't like this obsession he seemed to have for her and I wanted to ask him what he was planning to do with her. Instead, I did what he asked me to do. He watched me speak and stare out into a vacant blank space in front of me.

"Contact Samantha Wilkins," I said in a clear firm voice, but nothing happened. The file lay wide open but the phone icon didn't turn green. I cleared my voice and repeated her name ... nothing.

"Something is different. I don't get it. Usually, I can just pull up a file and contact people. I can try one more way," I said out loud. She had an application Marshall installed to record any access she's had to her head and what files they might have opened.

"I won't be able to talk to her, but I can get an idea who's been in her head," I informed Alejandro.

"Will it tell you where she is?"

"No," I answered quickly. I looked at him trying not to indicate that the prototype could track her.

I knew what I needed to do. I had to contact Roger and explain what happened with Sam.

*Roger Clarke.* I thought to myself. I watched as the same phone icon light up as it rang in my head.

*"Lauren. What's goin' on?"* Roger asked, his voice cracking against the question.

I pulled together my mental strength and projected my thoughts to him.

*"Hey, Rog, I'm okay, just needed to connect with Samantha and couldn't."*

*"What, Lauren? Why? What's goin' on?"* I could tell he was disturbed by my attempts.

*"I wanted to know if you've heard from Sam. I need to talk to her; is there a different way to contact her?"*

*"I noticed yesterday that she and Marshall fell off our network. That's what stopped me from catching her as she went through the metal detectors down to the gate. I couldn't use the apps I downloaded in her prototype,"* he

said clear as day; yet I felt like I didn't understand him.

"*Roger, we need to fix this now,*" I commanded.

"*I don't think her prototype was hacked or anything. Marshall did something to disconnect them,*" he volunteered.

"*What are you going to do?*" I asked him silently.

"*There's nothing I can do.*"

"Is there something wrong? Were you not able to get information on Sam?" Alejandro interrupted my secret conversation with Roger while looking at me, seeing I was anywhere but in the room with him.

"No, nothing's wrong. Well, I'm not able to connect with Sam," I answered Alejandro, confusing Roger.

"*What? Whose there with you? Is that Alejandro?*" Roger's voice roared.

"Why can't you contact her?" Alejandro asked me.

"It looks like she has been disconnected from the network," I told him. Finally it registered for him that I wasn't going to be talking to Sam anytime soon. As long as she was disconnected, I wouldn't be able to track or talk to her. All of this added up to more reasons why I had to stop the prototype and find a way to destroy every last one.

"*Roger, I think it's time to show Alejandro what Marshall ordered Terence to do.*" My mind was worn out and I really wasn't interested in his answer to my solution. I disconnected and told Alejandro there was something he had to know … and it was about Sam.

# sixteen

When we arrived at my hotel, the chauffeur quickly pulled open the limousine door and Alejandro insisted I exit first. His old world chivalry wasn't lost on me. Once outside, he slipped his arms around me from behind and pulled me back against the contours of his body, his warmth enveloped me.

"I know we are at your hotel to take care of business ... but you, standing there like that ... I couldn't help myself," he whispered against my ear.

I spun around and he tightened his arms around my back and pressed me into a deep thankful kiss.

"Lauren, today wasn't casual for me," he said low and only for me.

I nodded, because trying to speak would be a failure at making sense.

"I never make it a habit to bring just any woman into my bed." His words tangled my insides.

"Me either," I whispered back.

"I'm glad to know you don't make it a habit to bring just any woman into your bed." He teased as he nudged his lips to the side of my head before nuzzling his face down into my neck.

"Ha ha, very funny." I pushed him back. "You know what I meant."

"Of course I do. Just knowing you haven't come that hard before me … makes me want to take you again right here in the elevator," he said in a whisper.

"I never admitted that I hadn't come that hard before," I countered.

"You didn't have to, *mi dama*; your body told me."

I felt the most intimate place between my legs tingle as I thought about him making love to me. I brought Alejandro up to my hotel room, knowing it could lead to something much different than we came here to do. When I pushed the door open, I was relieved to see the room had been cleaned and the beds made. I shuffled around the room, grabbing my laptop and setting it in front of him on the small table.

"Sit there and turn that on," I told him.

"Sure," he answered as he opened it and pressed it on.

"I am going to network it as a slave. No comments." I stole a glance at Alejandro's face, his eyes glinted with surprise. He pulled open the laptop and powered it on. Even in a stressful situation like this, the comfort and ease we felt around each other was undeniable.

After several moments, I was able to get the laptop to recognize and link with my prototype. "Master and slave," I mumbled. I was surprised at how easy it was to get these technologies to merge. I knew the only way Alejandro was going to be able to see the plans Marshall had for Sam was to connect with Roger and download the recording to my prototype. I took a deep breath and began to speak.

"Roger Clarke." I watched the confusion flood over Alejandro.

"What?"

"I am connecting with Roger."

"Wait, he's dead. Isn't he?"

"No, Alejandro he's not." I watched carefully as he tried to deduce the answer I gave him.

"What? How? Marshall told me that he was murdered!"

I didn't answer him. I focused on the phone icon in the file and instantly I was connected to Roger's prototype.

"Lauren. I'm almost to D.C. What's going on?" he responded as I saw it in my head and now heard him through the speakers of my laptop.

"Roger. Listen I have to tell you something," I said out loud. My eyes focused on Alejandro, I held my finger up in front of my mouth, silently pleading to Alejandro to stay quiet.

"What Lauren? What is it?" Roger asked, picking up on the tension in my voice.

"I need the file with the recording of Marshall and Terence — where they talk about Sam."

"Lauren, you think that's a good idea?"

"Yeah, Roger. Unfortunately, it's about all we have now."

"I don't know how Alejandro is going to react to the conversation."

"It's okay Roger, I do."

"Fine — I'm sending the recording. My plane is landing and I need to find where Terence is taking her. I'll do whatever it takes to save her. You work on Marshall, I trust you — and Lauren — be careful." He disconnected.

I didn't break my eye contact with Alejandro as I had the conversation with Roger. I was desperate to know that I hadn't lost the one man I had let possess my heart. Alejandro shook his head and dropped his eyes from mine. He was lost to me. I wanted him to see I was still the same woman he was with earlier, that this didn't change anything.

"Lauren, what do you mean you have Terence on a recording with Marshall?" Alejandro asked in a hollow voice.

"I don't, Roger has it. We didn't — I didn't mean to hide this from you. Everything moved so quickly today and when we saw the recording last night — "

"You saw this last night?" he roared. Suddenly, my thoughts led me to think; all he saw in me was a despicable woman who chose pleasure over someone else's life. I was left completely alone with Alejandro. I had no way of explaining that I was honorable and no one else to help me explain what we saw in our heads last night. There was only one thing I could do. Show him the recording.

I accessed the file Roger sent to me and held my breath as I focused on the play button that lit green. I minimized the file in my eyes. I had already lived through that recording I didn't want to do it two days in a row. Besides, I didn't want to take my eyes off of Alejandro as he watched it play on my laptop and not in his head.

Rage filled his eyes as he watched Marshall blackmail Terence. Alejandro cursed under his breath as his beautiful forest eyes became dark and clouded. He pushed himself from the table and stood up. I was frightened by his quick action. His hands balled to rock hard fists. I didn't know what to say, so I stood facing him in silence.

"Why didn't you tell me?" Pain curtained his expression.

"I didn't know you cared. Roger was handling it, I was told to go with you to SI. Marshall and you were my responsibility. Roger was going to handle Sam and Terence." My answer seemed twisted and convoluted as it came out of my mouth. Not at all how I wanted it to sound.

"What do you mean that I was your responsibility?" he questioned.

"I just meant—I was going to go with Roger to help with Sam," I answered.

"Sam and Terence are my employees, Lauren. If anything happens to them, so help me—" His eyes pierced mine.

Frustration drowned any sense I was making. Suddenly, everything I said wasn't justifiable. "When I realized that you were going to be expecting me; I thought that we would have a chance to talk in the coffee shop and I would get the opportunity to tell you, when we were alone. When I hit the dash everything started to tail spin from there. You canceled the meeting with Marshall. You took me to your house and —"

"We got carried away with each other," he said.

I looked up and paused. He just stared at me. My head swam as each pounding thrust of my heart carried his poisonous words throughout my body.

"Is that what you think? That we got carried away?" I whispered.

"I don't know what to think. Who can I trust? Marshall is trying to hurt Sam, Terence can be blackmailed into anything and you—you kept it *all* from me. How did you think I was going to react?" He met my eyes. His shoulders heavy, his expression wrecked; he turned away from me and headed to the door.

"Wait. Don't do this. Don't spew your anger with me and then walk away." My chest rose with each breath I was fighting to catch. "I can ask the same thing. Who can I trust, Alejandro? Who do I believe? Marshall tells me to stay away from you, Roger tells me you're dangerous and Samantha is so terrified that she shakes at the mention of your name. You're asking me about trust. Have you been completely honest?" My words grasped at anything that would protect me from pain.

I looked at him. His body swayed with each breath I took as he walked back to me. I didn't want to be the owner of this busted harmony between us. I didn't want this to be the scene where we broke up a relationship that didn't altogether even exist. "Okay, Alejandro, so I screwed up, but don't give up on saving Sam. Roger needs your help." I grabbed at his arm and pulled him toward me. I kept forgetting how strong I was with the prototype evolving in my body. We looked into each other's eyes. We were mirrors shattered by each other's words.

"I'll help Sam, without Roger," he said before he turned and walked out the door.

I fell to my knees; broken beyond anything I had been before, I held my heart out for the sacrifice. I gave myself to him so completely and all I could do was watch him dissolve my heart to nothing more than dust in my hands as he walked out the door. I had nothing left in my chest; I slammed my fists against my head and contacted Roger.

"Roger Clarke," I cried. Within seconds he answered.

"*Lauren, what's wrong? Are you ok?*"

"No, Rog, I'm not ok. I need to get out of California now!"

"*Why? What happened? What the hell is going on?*"

"Damn it, Roger, I just do. Stop talking and listen. Get me out of here!" I screamed at him.

"*Fine, fine, okay, look in my suitcase; you'll see a black zip-up leather case the size of a checkbook. In there you will find some money. Take it, get a ticket and get back to D.C.*

"Thanks, Roger."

"*Just get back to me in one piece, Lauren.*"

"Okay."

I couldn't stop my body from shaking. It started in my core and radiated out to my arms and legs as I searched Roger's suitcase for the leather pack of money. I found it, a huge amount of money all perfectly stacked, tens, twenties and hundreds all in the right order. It was more than enough to get me out of here. I rubbed the tips of my fingers across my eyes and typed American Airlines on my laptop. If there was a flight available, I was going to find it. I found a redeye flight out of SFO at eleven fifty five. I tried to pack everything we brought but kept dropping things I'd pick up. They just slipped from my grip. It felt like all control I had over my body ceased. My head was swimming with all the shit I had to pack before I flew back home. An hour and a half later I had mine and Roger's bags packed and ready to go. I wasn't going to worry about getting my weapons from Alejandro's house. I would just have to cut my losses.

Cut losses, losses bigger than weapons in a drawer warped my thoughts and the reasons why I never opened myself up to the crippling pain of relationships. I was content with making my career my lover; I didn't need anything else. The pain of my life ten years ago flooded my soul. I couldn't breathe. I couldn't keep my lungs from shriveling up abandoning their post, while the strangling pressure returned from a fucking elephant sitting on my chest. Left abandoned like so many times before, everything short-circuited and faded to nothing.

Maybe the pinprick date of my dying in three days was wrong ... maybe it was this moment, right here where my life would just slowly slip away.

Time passed into a gaping hole of null and void. I don't know how much or what occurred but my eyes popped open to the rapping on the door.

"Room service, Mrs. Clarke," A male's voice spoke against the door. I was surprised at the name he called me then remembered the room was registered to Roger.

"Thanks," I whispered.

"Would you like me to leave it out here?" he asked.

"Yes, please," I answered as I pressed my body against the inside of the door. The pain in my stomach wasn't from being hungry. I was aching for Alejandro.

**seventeen**

I was wrapped inside the memory of that night I had dinner with Alejandro. I remembered the pressure of the fork as he pulled it from my mouth, the sweet taste of cheese cake when I swallowed. The warmth of his hand as it brushed across my cheek and the deep pounding of my pulse. I longed to go back to that night where I still wondered what he felt like. What his lips tasted like. Instead I was interrupted by Roger in my head.

*"Lauren? Hey Lauren, how are you? Did you get a ticket home?"*

I shivered at his voice. Home, what was that? My thoughts switched to D.C. Was that really my home? It's been my home since I turned my back on California. I didn't anticipate a long day in the city would make me feel like I belonged here and sadly, at the same time left me feeling so alienated.

*"Lauren, answer me. Did you get a ticket home?"* I could hear the alarm in his voice.

"Yeah, it leaves tonight. Eleven fifty-five. Thanks," I answered absent as I pushed the memory of Alejandro from my mind and the slice of shitty room service cheese cake from the edge of the table.

"What time is it there? Two in the morning?"

*"About that time. I wanted to make sure you found the money and was able to get a ticket. What time do you land in D.C.?"* He paused, but not long enough. *"What happened? Did Marshall do something to you?"* He waited for me to answer.

I really didn't feel like talking about it. I wanted to avoid my life right now. "No, Marshall had nothing to do with it." I didn't give him anymore details. I busied myself by collecting my clothes.

*"Is this your way of telling me it's none of my business?"*

I let out a deep low sigh. "Something like that. What's going on with Sam?" I was a bit hesitant to ask and stood still waiting for an answer.

*"She's home. I didn't see Terence at the airport, so I don't think he got on the plane with her. He must still be in San Francisco. Her plane landed before mine and by luck I found her at baggage claim. I've been following her, waiting to contact her. Keep your fingers crossed she doesn't freak out."* He seemed like the old Roger I knew.

"Terence wasn't with her?

*"No,"* he answered.

The wheels in my head started to spin and I began to think about the meeting with Terence and how Alejandro found out about Terence's deal with Marshall.

The gap of time caused Roger to speak up.

*"What are you thinkin'?"* He could tell I was working something out in my head.

"Alejandro must've called Marshall about Sam. Marshall didn't give him what he wanted so he came to me and found out about Terence and Marshall's deal. If Terence wasn't on the plane and Alejandro was pissed. What's to stop Alejandro from finding Marshall and—"

*"Lauren, Your flight is leaving in a couple of hours. You should already be at the airport."* Panic swelled in his voice.

"I will be. I just want to—"

*"No, Lauren, no want to's. You get your ass in a taxi and get yourself to SFO. Get on that plane!"* Roger demanded.

I appeased him with a short answer and we disconnected from each other. I grabbed the phone and called down to the front desk. They were very courteous and made sure I would have a ride to the airport.

A gentle rap at the door pulled me from packing up the toiletries I left in the bathroom. I was so close to being ready. I wish the driver wasn't here for just another half an hour. Still, then again I just needed to get out of the city and California. I pushed the rest of my items into my bag and zipped it up. I was in a whirl wind getting ready to go so when I swung the door open I wasn't prepared for who was on the other side.

My body didn't move. I was paralyzed by shock. He stood there silent and unmoved waiting for my reaction.

"Lauren Matthews?" he asked as I watched his dreadlocks sweep at his shoulders and his enormous coffee-painted hand reached out to me. He continued. "I'm Terence Cummings. I work for Alejandro Fernandez at Spartacus Industries." He waited for me to grab his hand pushing it closer to me. I watched my hand disappear, swallowed completely by his grasp. I was stunned.

"May I come in?" he asked.

I stared up at him as I tried to figure out how he knew who I was. *It had to be Alejandro, he must have told him about me. That's it. He told Terence about me — But why? Why would he come to see me? Marshall? It could've been him too. Sam?* My head spun as I tried to figure out how he knew me. He automatically ducked his head and turned his colossal body sideways to enter my hotel room. I pressed up against the wall as he walked by me and lumbered to the plain reading chair in the corner of the room. I let the door close and with the snap of the latch I knew I wasn't going to make my flight.

"Sorry to barge in on you, but this couldn't wait," he said standing, waiting to sit in the chair that I thought was huge until he stood there.

"How did you find me? Who told you I was here?" I asked as I pushed my hands up and down my jeans trying to get the blood to flow through them again.

"Alejandro told me where to find you, after I convinced him not to kill me," he said as his body consumed the good-sized chair. My body ripped with a fever burning a hole through my heart when he said his name.

"Kill you?" I grabbed the back of a chair keeping some distance and the table between us.

"He won't kill me if I convince you about the truth." He looked at me curiously. "Do I frighten you? Don't be afraid of me," he stated in a calm tone.

"Afraid of you? No. What do you want from me? Why did he send you?" I shuffled my body around and sat down. I figured that I would look more confident if I was sitting.

"Alejandro told me 'bout Marshall's plan to take the file from SI and destroy its mainframe, making it *look* like an accident. Then sell the prototype and its technology the country that's willing to pay the millions he's asking for." His earth brown eyes narrowed struggling with what he said. He shifted his body giving the chair a moment of relief.

"I knew about selling it to the highest bidder and I thought I was brought here to convince him to buy it. What's on the file?" I felt pressure squeeze at the back of my neck.

"Marshall and Alejandro entered a business contract several years ago that gave Alejandro exclusive rights to any product that came from Grayson Technologies. Didn't you ever wonder where Marshall got his money?" He looked at me and smiled.

"The file's proof that Marshall is Alejandro's bitch." The words rolled off my tongue. He seemed more comfortable with me. Or maybe I let go of the preconceived ideas of a huge black man with me alone in my room and the fear it invoked in me. My back loosened and the tightness in my neck released to a flush of chills down my shoulders.

"I didn't know about the contract. How long have they had it in place?" Time tables rumbled through my mind. "Six months? One year? What are we talking about here?" I hammered him with questions.

"The contract was signed three years ago and it's expiring at the end of this week." He had pulled out his phone and checked his messages as he spoke. When he looked up at me, my mind flashed back to the conversation he had with Marshall. The same one I experienced in my head. Why was he warning me now or telling me this information? What was I going to be able to do with this?

"I'm a little thrown by what you're saying. Why did Marshall ask you to take Sam and disconnect her prototype then?" His eyes became huge and his body swelled. The muscles in his shoulders and arms became rigid.

"Who told you that?" He clutched the arms of the unadorned chair thrusting his chest forward. His knotty knuckles bleached a slight muddy brown.

Every cell in my body shrunk and shivered in fear. This was exactly what I was afraid of. I didn't want this, not now. I pulled the core of my body tight and brought my head straight so I could look him in the eyes. I was scared, but I wasn't going to give in.

"Nobody told me, I saw—experienced your conversation with Marshall in my prototype. Roger recorded your meeting. I was in Marshall's head. What he tasted, I tasted, touched, I touched, heard, I heard." I scratched my eyebrow, rubbed my forehead and pushed my loose hair away from my eyes. Nerves took over my hands as I talked to him.

"Wait, that thing in your head can do all that? You can be in someone's head and experience what they are doing? Naw, what else can it do?" His eyes twinkled. I could see that he had some ideas of his own for this *thing* in my head.

"I don't know. Roger didn't get a chance to show me." I lied the best I could. I felt the swell of disenchantment fill my body. Whatever else this could do I didn't care, it was already sitting too long in my head. I changed the subject just as quick.

"Terence? Why did you let Marshall bully you?"

"He didn't bully me; nobody bullies me." He pulled the stereotypical masculine persona from his arsenal.

"Do you think your brother is really going to be taken care of? Really?" I stood up looking at him and walked into the kitchenette, he followed. I continued my questioning as I grabbed a bottle of water. "Sam was someone you really trusted and liked."

"What was I suppose to do? My brother needed me—had to help him."

"I watched you sacrifice your integrity to do it." I tossed him a bottle of water. His gigantic hand moved quick to catch it. His voice became loud and I watched his stance shift to defensive.

"You know nothin' about my family. He's my little brother; don't tell me you wouldn't have done the same thing."

"I wouldn't. I'm an only child." I took a huge swig of the water and went to sit at the table again. I didn't want to make him mad, but I wanted him to see that he didn't need to sacrifice his morals for anyone.

"I didn't disconnect the prototype like he told me to. I just took her to the airport and put her on the plane. What she does in D.C. is her business." He was smug as he looked for approval in my eyes. I wondered if he thought he was being noble volunteering the information.

"Why didn't you go to Alejandro for help? You're his employee after all." I grabbed at my knees under the table and started to bounce my right leg unconsciously.

"I couldn't. It isn't like that."

"What is it like?" "I don't know, but not like that. He's got enough to think about. He doesn't need me coming up and buggin' him about my family problems. Besides, Marshall knows the judge and he owes him a favor." He cracked the lid of the water and took a swig that drained half the bottle.

"Was Roger aware of the contract between SI and Marshall?" Every bone in my body was hoping that Roger wasn't involved with these negotiations.

"I don't know. You should ask him. I gotta go. Thanks for the water." He seemed nervous as he abruptly ended our conversation handing me the empty bottle telling me to recycle it and headed to the door.

He looked back, tossed his hand in the air above his head and waved as he shut the door. Abandonment flooded my soul as pictures of Alejandro, and now Terence, walking out the door owned my mind. I looked at the clock on the dresser and saw that I had one hour to get to the airport. I wasn't going to make it. I sat back down at the table, grabbed the fork that was perfectly set next to the cheese cake, pushed it through the pointed end and brought it to my mouth.

# eighteen

I was staring at an empty plate littered with a slight layer of graham cracker crumbs and the pitch-forked weapon that obliterated it fit comfortably in my hand. I couldn't believe I ate the whole piece of cheesecake. I wasn't hungry, but when you need something to do while your mind is elsewhere that will suffice.

A gradual knock at the door turning into an impatient bang startled me out of my sugar-induced daze. I heard deep fast breathing when I pressed my ear to the door. Whoever was out there was trying real hard to catch their breath. A low deep growl filled the hall before I felt the last attempt vibrate across the door and heard the rub of damp skin skid across the outside. I pressed my eye to the peep hole trying to see as my toes held my weight the best they could. I felt my knees decision to give up, my ankles weary as my eye sent my body the message of what it saw. He had given up at hammering and retired to walking away when my mind registered who it was.

I pulled open the door that seemed heavier than before. He didn't hear the door open, he just kept walking. I rummaged through my mind trying to find the perfect word that would turn him around and bring him back. I was afraid he was going to reach the elevators and I would lose my chance to catch him forever. This was not the way I wanted to end it.

"Hey!" I blurted out.

He stopped and slowly turned to face me his dark green eyes constrict with sin. The lines in my face grew tight, my heart pounded harder and my eyes betrayed me as tears crammed the small ledges of my eyelids. I pushed the tears away enough to see Alejandro standing there. His black hair twisted and disheveled, his nose flaring with every breath, his lips ripe agony. He was mouthwateringly gorgeous.

I grabbed the door jamb trying to hold on for life. My legs trembled as the door began to weigh even heavier against my choice. All I wanted to do was run to him. Feel him around me again. Hear him say my name, touch my face, exist in his smile.

He took a strong decisive breath and came toward me. His breathing slowed, his mouth relaxed, his eyes softened with concern and I felt warmth wash over me. He came at me with determination reaching for me as he got closer. His hands brushed at my shoulders, pushing the door open and releasing the pressure that lay against me, I stumble, pulling him with me. I felt his weight shift as he tucked me against his chest, trying to protect me as we fell. He landed on his elbows trying to protect my head from crashing into the floor. His body pressed heavy against mine; I could feel his breath hot against my face and his legs bestriding mine. We laid there on the floor as I heard the door slam shut by our feet.

"Are you okay?" he asked as my head lay cradled in the palms of his hands.

"I think so," I answered still stunned by the fall.

We stared at each other, not saying anything else. Studying what we might have missed the last time we were together. He lowered his face closer to mine and brushed the edge of his nose against mine. His moist lips tickled below my cheek as he cleared away the evidence of my pain. My mouth pined to taste him and feel his lips persuasively devour all the doubt I had let consume me. I dragged my hands around his back and slid them up past his shoulders before I anchored them in his thick black hair. He caught my lower lip between his teeth and tugged, causing a carnal need to mount low in my core. I opened my mouth, inviting him to extinguish any doubt between us. He thrust his tongue deep into my mouth and our kiss tangled into the invitation we both desperately needed.

Alejandro's body pressed so heavy against mine, I couldn't breathe. His mouth devoured mine before he lifted his lips, pulling away. Hungrily, I followed trying to capture what little moment of heaven he created. I craved the burn he sparked low in my belly.

He dragged his body from mine and lay next to me for a moment before he rolled up off the floor and offered me his hand. Undoubtedly, he was collecting his wits and testing his self control. I took a shallow breath and let him pull me to my feet. He continued to hold my hand as he led me to the ordinary table near the foot of my bed.

He sat me down and then I watched as he slowly sat in the chair across the table from me. At that single moment, nothing else mattered to me. I wanted him, like nothing I've wanted before. His gaze stoic, I sensed that he needed to tell me something. He pushed his hands across the table, holding my hands delicately into his. Electricity bolted from my fingertips to the back of my neck as he caught his lower lip between his teeth and rolled it loose to talk.

"You need to know, I tried to keep you safe." He tightened his grasp on my hands.

I narrowed my eyes as I looked at him, hoping my expression would get him to explain. I was lost. What did I need to be safe from?

"You were mad—you left!" I exclaimed before dragging my hands from his hold.

"I *was* mad and extremely ... disappointed." His eyes bore into me.

I was uncomfortable ... the way he looked at me made me feel uneasy. I got up and went to the sink area next to the bathroom. I couldn't look at him knowing that he felt that way about me.

"Are you still?" I asked as I picked up the towel on the sink and busied my hands.

"Mad? Yes—but I understand why you did what you did." He rose from his chair and walked toward me.

"What do you understand? That I was jealous of Sam? Or that I didn't tell you about Roger because I didn't want to lose you. I had a job to do, I didn't expect—" My voice cracked as I continued, "you hurt me, too." I turned away from him. I couldn't look at him; his eyes were my kryptonite. They were my weakness that consumed all the strength it took me to walk away.

His body pressed against my back and his breath warmed the edge of my ear.

"I don't want to hurt you—ever." His arms tightened around me as he pressed his lips against the space behind my ear. I pulled my head to the side, needing him to continue to explore the back of my neck.

"Why'd you come back?" I whispered.

"I came back to warn you." His words registered breathy across my flesh.

"About what?" I turned toward him, still wrapped in his embrace.

"Marshall."

He dragged his fingertips lazily across my body as his focus stalled on my eyes.

"Lauren, Marshall's going to try and disconnect every active prototype. I came back to protect you," he said solemnly before he dragged his lips across the bridge of my nose and planted them on my forehead.

Immeasurable chills twisted and thrashed at my insides. It was a matter of time before the evil that lay just below Marshall's skin would surface. In a moment of his blatant greed and unhinged power, all of our humanity ceases to exist.

Marshall wasn't into this deal for lifting and enlightening the human race, he worked this deal so he could keep this technology for himself and ruin anyone who got in the way. This prototype of Roger's wasn't worth dying for ... not even the advancement of the human race would justify handing my life over to him.

"Alejandro, how do you plan on protecting me?"

"I don't know yet, but until I figure it out ..."

I looked over at the clock on the nightstand, eleven fifty-nine. I wouldn't be making my flight to D.C. I'd be spending another night in San Francisco. I wondered if I was going to be sleeping alone or with him. He drew me closer. I let my chin fall as my head rest in the curve of his chest and shoulder. I knew he wasn't telling me everything, but I didn't care. Not tonight.

Alejandro began to pull away and desperation flooded my body. I ached to feel him kiss me, touch me, love me the way he did before. I wrapped my arms up around his neck pulling him down against my lips, kissing him until he knew I wasn't ready for him to leave. His sweet clean aroma rushed my senses, creating sparks that bust free across my skin. I needed him to possess me. He pulled me to the bed and thrust me down like his prey. His carnal desire radiated from his skin; his deep-seated need to consume my body flared wickedly in his eyes. Trepidation drifted through my head only long enough to be thieved by my body's reaction to his strength. I didn't care; I wanted him, and I was willing to let him have me ... whatever way he saw fit.

He snatched the edge of my shirt and wrapped his fists in the fabric. I heard the seams stress and break under the pressure of his strength as he yanked it up and over my head. He balled it up between his hands and buried his nose, inhaling my scent before he tossed it across the room. His attention refocused on my body, his eyes ravaging every inch of my exposed flesh. I forced my hands down to the waistband of my pants, trying desperately to unsnap them before he changed his mind. I thrust my hips in the air, struggling to remove my pants as he grabbed my wrist and flipped me onto my stomach. There was nothing delicate or lenient in his actions. He let out a deep breathy sigh against my skin before his scorching lips pressed firm in the small of my back. His hands skimmed down the sides of my pants, gripping where they could as he feverishly ripped them from my body. His hands unsnapped the clasps on my bra, while his mouth skated across the curve of my waist.

"I need to see you," I huffed trying to turn over onto my back.

"No," he answered pressing down against my body.

"Why not?" I whispered.

I needed to turn over I craved to watch him, but his determination was overpowering.

"Because. I need to discover every inch of what I must protect. I have to know that you'll trust me."

He raked his fingertips down my spine. I felt my panties pull from my rear and drag down the front of my thighs. I wanted to trust him. My gut argued with my head, hoping to convince the fear pulsing through my veins that Alejandro wouldn't hurt me. Fear clutched my heart, thundering in rhythm with the pull between my legs.

He pressed his mouth against the curve of my bottom, his hands squeezing my flesh as his teeth caught part of my skin. I let out an unexpected whimper. His hands massaged down my thighs, catching the chill his touch created. Still lying on my stomach, I thrust my hands forward and clutched onto the headboard.

"I want to trust you," I breathed.

He pulled back, my flesh tortured by his vanishing touch. *What was he doing to me?* I rose up onto my knees, ready to use my strength to flip over and tug him down onto my body. Instead, Alejandro snatched my ankles, yanked and spread my legs wide open. My stomach pressed into the bed, the tops of my toes dug into the comforter, and the swollen folds between my legs begged for his touch. I knew what he wanted and it invoked a twisted fear in my soul. All of my life I was the one who made the calls. I was always the one in control; I was the one that chose career over lust, responsibility over recklessness … it was my way of making sure I wasn't going to end up with a broken heart. Now, Alejandro sparked a dark force in my belly that I didn't expect to feel. His demanding touch shattered every burden I clung to, owning my loneliness. Suddenly, I ached to glide on the thin edge between autonomy and compulsion.

His hands slid up between my body and the bed. My breath hitched as he pressed his lips to my calf, dragging the tip of his tongue up the back of my leg before cresting the top of my inner thigh. With the swipe of his tongue, he made my body hungry. His hand clutched my soft bottom, his other circling my sensitive flesh, as he piqued my curiosity. *What if he spanks me? I've never been spanked before.* The thought excited me and yet pulled at my nerves. Fear surged in my gut, mingling with the restlessness of my newly found desires.

"Tell me that you trust me."

"With my heart?" I asked breathlessly.

"With your life," he answered as his hand collided with the edge of my skin. I felt the fear of punishment and euphoria swirl between my legs.

"I don't know," I whimpered as I pulled my knees under my body.

His fingers circled my hot stinging flesh, relieving the burn.

"That's not the answer I expected."

His touch disappeared from my backside before slamming against my rear again.

I've never let a man touch me like this before. I never gave so much control over to one person. The pleasure of his demands frightened the shit out of me and confused me. I craved to have him devour my body and yet the rational side of me knew this would only lead to trouble. I pushed my head into the bed letting the anticipation fill me to almost combustion.

"Come on, Lauren ... Say you trust me," he said as his fingertips stroked at my needy parts before pushing inside of me.

My muscles clutched; my hips swayed.

"I trust you," I moaned. "God, I trust you."

"Well, maybe you shouldn't," he growled.

In a single motion, smooth as the rush of water over rocks, he turned and slid his face under my pelvis. His nimble fingers spread me as he pushed up between my legs. I thrust my hips down hard against his pulsating tongue lapping at my wetness. The rhythm of my pleasure and the deep moan he released against my flesh goaded me into wanting to please him at the same time. I wanted to make him feel the surge of pleasure he was giving me. I swung my leg around bringing my body opposite of his as I unbuttoned his pants. He continued to taste the sweet space between my legs while I yanked his zipper down. His erection was strong and significant as I stroked its length; dragging my tongue from the base all the way to his tip. His voracious appetite deliberate and his deep bellowing moans he clustered against me drove me insane with pleasure. His fingers trapped my firm nipples, pulling and caressing them, causing me to gasp. He pulled away; disappointment flooded my body as the cool air replaced his mouth.

"Get on your knees," he demanded. His eyes wicked with sexual desire, his crave fed my body. My stomach clenched as apprehension and pleasure twisted and vibrated throughout my body.

"What do you want me to do?"

He didn't answer. Instead he yanked me across the bed. My knees on the edge of the mattress, my feet dangling, he pushed my head down against the comforter, his mouth near my face, his breath rolling across the bend of neck.

"I want to watch you trust me," he whispered at the same he dragged his fingers down my spine.

I felt him push against me, my body ravenous for him. I pressed back as his willingness thrust deep and unyielding inside me. He rolled his hips. I gasped before he pulled back and thrust again. The slap of our skin, his low heady huffs as he drove himself deeper inside me, ecstasy wasn't a good enough word for what I was feeling. His hands clung to my waist as he drove himself into me even faster, harder and rougher. Our sex was different this time, less forgiving and more demanding. Nothing mirrored his delicate discovery of my body the first time we were together. Escalating to quicken my body's reaction, my insides clutched and quivered at the friction he created. I gasped and howled as he plunged into me unrelentingly.

Desperation gripped my motivation as every breath I fought to catch and every nerve in my body rushed my skin. If someone asked me where I was, I couldn't tell them, I couldn't give them the reasons I let Alejandro take me so tirelessly. It was exponential discovery, freedom in its purest of form. I was noisy, uncontrolled and animalistic as he unhinged the loneliness that kept me prisoner for years. My legs and arms shook uncontrollably for a long couple of seconds as my core ignited in the most intense orgasm I'd ever had.

"Eres perfecta, mi amor!" Alejandro hollered as he threw his head back and his body convulsed under me just seconds after I came. His arms still tightly wrapped around my shoulders as he continued to pump inside of me. All the amassed insecurities and sexual inexperience that resided in my body were washed away when I felt him explode. I was satisfied.

We lay there, our bodies limply tangled. His arms bound me tight against his moist skin, and my head locked under his chin as he whispered warm words he strung together as he caught his breath. In seconds I realized the string of breathless words were in Spanish.

"Gracias a Dios, que confia en mi."

I let him pull me down onto his chest as I fell fast asleep, still wrapped in his arms.

**nineteen**

My eyes sprung open so quickly that my mind didn't have time to register where I was. Pillows piled and sheets twisted in front of me. I slowly stretched my hand toward the space expecting to feel his warm skin. I visualized my morning yearning fulfilled. My lips stretched stern across my teeth into a smirk while my leg searched below. My expectations were thwarted by the cold empty sheet my hand explored. My eyes confirmed what my hand and leg reported to me. He was gone and desolation swirled stronger than ever before.

What's happening to me? My emotions were so raw, much more than ever before. My body was becoming stronger, my senses heightened and I was experiencing feelings I didn't think I was capable of. Ever since Roger installed that thing in my head my body hadn't been my own. I sat up, my thoughts reeling because of the prototype. I needed to get it out of my head. I didn't want to help Marshall or be invaded by Roger. I didn't want any of it anymore. I wanted my thoughts back and my mind left alone. With Alejandro gone, alone is exactly what I had. It just wasn't what I wanted.

My cell phone rang, kicking me from my self-induced nightmare as it vibrated on the night stand next to my bed.

"Hello." My voice was raspy and my throat dry. Goose bumps rose on my skin proof of how cold I was in the huge bed alone.

"Hi."

"Alejandro?"

"Forgive me, I didn't want to wake you; you looked so peaceful." My body warmed and the goose bumps stayed.

"Wish you would've. Where are you?"

"My office. I wanted to take care of some business and clear my schedule today. I'm sending a car for you."

"When?"

"An hour."

I didn't say anything. I could hear him shift the phone to his other ear.

"Lauren, you there?"

"I'm here. I was supposed to fly out last night."

"Glad you didn't," he teased. I could visualize the smile across his face.

"Me, too." I shivered; the images of last night packed my head.

"You're not leaving today, right?" His voice dropped to a whisper.

"That depends on Roger."

There was no sound on the other end of the phone. I struck an uncomfortable chord and I was immediately sorry. A flurry of regret blasted my thoughts as I searched to find a way to bring him back in the conversation with me. Silent seconds passed awkwardly before he cleared his throat.

"When is he contacting you?" His voice was low and hollow.

"Looks like I'm contacting him," I answered cautiously as I took a shallow breath and continued. "I was supposed to be in D.C. already. He's probably wondering where I am."

He exhaled a low jealous sigh. "Better call him."

"Yeah, I better. I'll call you back." I didn't hear him say goodbye before the line went dead.

I worked hard not to take it personal. He was preoccupied with his concerns for Sam and I knew that. Besides I was the only connection he had to Roger and we both knew that Roger was the one person that could save her now. I focused on the blinking cursor in the lower corner of my right eye that has become a constant in my vision and spoke out Roger's full name. Once his file appeared in my eyes I scanned automatically and focused on the phone icon that lit green. The ringing in my ears only repeated once before Roger's voice crammed my head. He answered out of breath.

"*He got to her! He got to her!*" His voice was brimming with hysterics.

"Roger. Talk to me. Who?" I was deliberate in my tone, hoping he'd settle down.

"*Marshall! He got to Sam. I couldn't stop him!*" His words were frenzied as he still struggled to catch his breath.

"Where did he take her?"

*"I failed. I screwed up and now she's gone!"* I had never heard Roger so distraught.

"What are you saying? Gotta give me something — anything," I responded, as a surge of adrenaline began to rush through my body.

*"The fucking monster took her from right under my nose,"* His voice was weighty with desperation as it trailed off.

"You were there? You saw him take her?" I asked pointedly.

*"Yes, I couldn't stop him. I couldn't fucking stop him."*

My mind spun, racing with different scenarios and Samantha. I needed to get to D.C.; I should've been there hours ago. Guilt pulsed through my body knowing that I was with Alejandro when I should have been on a plane back to D.C. I wish I could have seen what happened. Instantly, the ability to record from the prototype flashed across my mind.

"Roger ... your recorder, connect me to it."

*"I don't think — "*

"Roger, connect me now."

*"Lauren, it's gnarly. Are you sure?"* His voice echoed the unsettledness in his heart.

"Yes, I am," I pressed.

We were losing valuable time and if I was going to help, I needed to know what I was up against. I scanned his file, found the link icon and focused on it until the little white bubble bounced between the two computer images.

"I'm connected. Where's the file?" I held my palms tight against the table; trying to steady myself.

*"It's in my personal video files under Sam. It should be the last one."* His voice grew louder as it pitched up an octave.

I scrolled down through the stack of dates and titles until I saw it, the last entry. Focusing on the file, it opened and instantly I was thrown into Roger's video ... as him.

*The Washington D.C. breeze had tousled my short hair causing it to thrash and tickle my ears as I had brushed away sporadic rain drops that showered my face and the back of my neck. Roger's glasses had filled with raindrops and steam from the heat of his cheeks. I rubbed away the rain drops that ran down his cheeks. It was strange; I shivered as the cold air caressed my neck Roger's hands felt so much softer than mine and much bigger. I was standing in front of an enormous red brick building. When Roger's vision pushed and instantly I was heading into the building.*

*Soft classical music played in the lobby as I walked toward a long wooden counter. A gorgeous young woman reading a poly-sci textbook, her curly black hair tumbled back from around her dark brown complexion as she looked up at me. Her eyes filled with so much life, something I must have had when I was her age.*

*I felt Roger's entire body react to her beauty, reminding me where I was. His thoughts and urges swirled from my mind to between my legs.*

"*Good morning, how may I help you?*" *she asked with a sweet twang in her words.*

His pushed his hands against the cold smooth counter, rubbing them back and forth against the sharp edge. "*Why, yes you can. I'm here to see Samantha Wilkins.*" I could feel his nerves. His eyes registered the voluptuous curves of her lips and I noticed a surge of energy rushed between his legs.

"*May I tell her who's here?*" She picked up the phone receiver and waited for me to speak.

"*Actually, what I would really like to do is surprise her. She hasn't seen me in a couple of months; it's like I've been dead to her.*" I felt his cute charming smile as he never broke eye contact.

"*We're really supposed to call first.*"

"*The last time I saw her, I was being shipped off to Afghanistan. She really doesn't know if I am alive or dead. I just thought –*" Roger broke off, rolling his shoulders forward.

"*I could get in trouble for this ... but you seem nice enough. And who am I to keep you from surprising your friend?*"

"*Thank you. I can't wait to see the look on her face when she sees me. What number was she again?*" I felt his head tilt as he pulled his hand back to the edge of the counter.

"*Three-thirteen – third floor. Take the elevator behind me and when you get off turn right.*" She stood up, turned around and pointed as she gave directions.

He took a long glance at her backside before he inhaled a deep breath and shook his head. I never thought I would *ever see the day when I was in a guy's head as he flirted to get what he wanted.*

*He pressed the elevator button so hard I could feel my fingertip begin to go numb. His shoulders dropped and I could feel his lungs burn with cold air as he inhaled a massive breath once the elevator doors closed. In no time, the doors slid open to the third floor and he hurried to Sam's apartment. The door was ajar and looked like someone busted it open. My stomach dropped, twisting into knots. Roger slowly pushed the door open and looked into Sam's apartment.* "Sit down and shut the hell up." *The words were gruff.*

"Who sent you? What do you want from me?" *Sam asked before I heard shuffling followed by a cry.*

"Told you to shut the fuck up," *he repeated as he slapped her.*

*Samantha let out a howl before a loud thump filled the room.*

"Get up!" *He sounded wicked and evil. Suddenly, I heard scuffling and footsteps before Samantha whimpered at being dragged across the floor.*

"Why?" *Samantha gasped.*

"Bitch, I told you to shut the fuck up!" *The raspy voice interrupted before I heard a hollow thud and Samantha cried.*

*Roger's arms tightened, clutching his hands into fists, as he listened to Samantha being beat. I needed to help her, but I was watching a recording and there was no way of stopping it. I was a prisoner to what had already been done.*

*Roger peered around and saw Sam with her assailant. A sick familiarity rolled through Roger's body as he recognized the man. Visions of his encounter snapped into my mind. This was the same scumbag sent to kill Roger just a couple of days ago. Roger's eyes seated with anger and his heart thundered with adrenaline.*

*Sam was hunched in a wooden kitchen chair; blood was dribbling from her nose and seeping from the cuts on her cheeks. Huge dark purple bruises stained her face, arms and upper chest and her eyes were swollen almost shut. Her once white shirt was checkered with her blood; she looked almost close to death.*

*I saw the man ball his fist, pull his arm back and clock her full force upside the head. Her body flew off the wooden chair, through the air and land on the other side of the hall. I heard the sickening thud as she landed, and an echoing crack as her skull hit the floor. I heard her body slide across the floor before it came to an abrupt stop. Her blood-curdling scream filled the room and my mind.*

*I was a prisoner in Roger's head. Why wasn't he doing anything to stop this? The assailant stepped over her, deliberately kicking her in the back and stomach as he towered over her. He bent down and grabbed at the collar of Sam's shirt he leaned in close, her arms dangling by her sides her body bouncing with every cry.*

*"I told Marshall I'd take care of you ... just like I took care of the other pieces of shit." He let go and let her body drop to the hardwood floor. Suddenly, he determinedly started to scour the room for something. His demeanor changed when he stammered over to Sam.*

*The man had snatched Sam's chin and pulled her face over to see what he had. The gurgle deep in her throat as she whimpered for help had been agonizing as I watched him pull out a long thin metal skewer and shook it in front of her. Torturing her as he brought it to her right ear, Marshall had hired him to finish the job Terence never did.*

*I felt Roger's body lunge forward as he caught Sam's assailant around the neck and yanked him down to the floor. Searing pain tore through my left side as Roger's hands ripped at the man's face. Hate had surged from the depths of my soul. Roger cocked his arm back and punched the man so hard that I heard the bones in his face and Roger's hand shatter. Every feeling Roger was experiencing, thundered through my body.*

*The assailant's wicked right hook had blasted powerfully across the side of Roger's skull. His head had swung across his body and suddenly the ceiling of the room had spun above me and my eyes had rolled up in the back of my head. Roger's body had hit a piece of furniture and slide to a stop as I had heard objects falling around me ... everything had gone black, Roger had passed out.*

I opened my eyes. I was back in the hotel room disconnected from Roger. Immediately, I hustled to the nearest mirror and checked to see if there was any evidence of what that fucking monster did to Roger reflected on my body. It was so real, so evil. I pulled my hair back behind my ears examining my face, nothing. I pulled my shirt up to see if the skewer that pierced Roger caused any damage, again-nothing. I was okay but I knew that Roger and Sam weren't.

I struggled to contact Roger. Too much time collected as I waited for Roger to answer.

"Roger!"

*"Lauren, did you see it?"* He sounded exhausted.

"Oh my God, Roger, are you okay?"

*"Yeah, I'm fine."*

"I'm on the next flight out." I paced the room as I spoke to him feeling immense guilt for not being there.

*"Where are you? I thought you would be here already."* His voice dropped to a whisper.

"I'm still in the city. I will be there later today. Just do what I say! And get to a hospital; someone should take a look at you." I paused to swallow and finished my rant. "Do you hear me, get to the hospital."

He made a short wounded noise.

*"Fine, but I need to find her before he — "*

"I know, I will do my best to get there as quick as I can."

I disconnected from him grabbed my cell phone and pressed the button for the last call I received. I felt my throat tighten as the ringing against my ear sped to an anxious pace.

"Hello," Alejandro answered quickly.

"It's Sam," I whispered in a trembling voice.

"I'm on my way. Stay there," he breathed as the phone went dead and three beeps confirmed he hung up. I collapsed into a chair, totally disbelief ravaging my thoughts. Suddenly, I realized just how alone I really was with this prototype in my head. Thoughts of my impending death swirled rapidly through my head. A textbox dictating my death by asphyxiation in two days and the only thing that keeps thundering through my head is finding ways to save Sam. Death by suffocation or at the hands of a monster, two days isn't enough time to contemplate the rest of my existence. Sam could quite possibly be the catalyst for my demise in the first place. Besides, I couldn't do anything right now but wait for Alejandro to show up. I laid my head across my arms knowing I should've already been in D.C.

## twenty

A warm pressure radiated in circles against my back causing me to open my eyes. I have no idea how long I was passed out before Alejandro arrived. I thrust my body up from the chair, wrapping my arms tight around his neck. I buried my face deep in his chest and started to cry. Something that happened more and more lately, it was the fear of losing him that weighed so heavy in my mind, even more than having to tell him that Sam could be dead. I inhaled until my lungs burned with pain, keeping my face crushed into his chest trying to find the ability to tell him what I knew.

"Roger didn't get to Sam in time." I pulled in another breath. "I'm so sorry, Alejandro," I cried. Desperate to move past this moment, the despicable words I was going to be forced to use. God, please help him understand.

He pushed the hair back away from my face and looked into my swollen drenched eyes.

"What do you mean, in time?"

He pulled at my chin making me look into his eyes.

"I should have been there! I belong in D.C. If I was there, I could have stopped this." My hands ached from holding him so tight. I was desperate, reeling from the fear of losing Alejandro. I couldn't lose him over this; fear surged through every thought that swallowed my words.

"Tell me, please, what happened to Sam?" Alejandro's desperation pulled at every string dangling from my heart.

"Roger went to her house. He ... went there ... He beat her badly."

Alejandro looked at me confused.

"Roger?" His eyes widened as his face lost all its warmth.

"No, the man, the man Marshall hired. Roger, he tried, I swear he tried to stop him, but he couldn't, Alejandro, the guy knocked him out. Sam ... she was gone once Roger came to." I was stammering; words wouldn't come out right, tears were swelling again as I had to relive that moment again. As bad as I wanted to look into Alejandro's eyes, I couldn't; I knew it was my words that were shredding his heart apart.

"Where's Sam now?" Desperation saturated his face, his body surging with the impatience. Caged with little information Alejandro frantically searched for answers I couldn't give him.

"I don't know." I looked away.

He turned away and pulled out his cell phone. His eyes burning with hatred, his cheeks flushed red matching the edges of his ears. Deep frustration pooled in his eyes and instantly I knew what this was. It was the nightmare ending to my perfect dream. It was time to see the awful person that everyone tried to warn me about. Here was the thorn of the rose I grew to admire.

His voice was low but I could tell he was speaking in Spanish. I heard one word that I could understand. One that made my skin crawl, a word that didn't need a translation ... *Marshall.* Then he tapped his phone, slipped it into his pocket. When he looked at me, determination deepened the lines in his face.

"Lauren, my jet will take you to D.C., be at the airport in one hour." The determination in his stride told me he had another agenda, one I wasn't privy to.

"Aren't you coming with me?" My hand drew forward to stop him. *This wasn't happening! There was no way in hell I am getting on a plane without him. Rip me open, tear out my heart ... no, this isn't going to happen. It.can.not.be.happening. Not when I just found perfection.* Every muscle in my body ached, struggling to keep me upright.

"I will meet you there. I have some garbage I have to take care of here, first." He opened his arms and invited me to him. He looked resolute, stern, like he knew this was going to happen.

I didn't move. I couldn't go into his arms; I didn't want to experience what I know won't be mine anymore. His comfort, his smell, the warmth of his breath as he presses his lips to the top of my head, if I get on that plane I'm afraid he won't be mine anymore and I'll lose him for good. I didn't want to accept this. I shouldn't have to accept this.

"I don't want to go without you. I can't, I can't go without you!" My hands hung heavy against my sides before all my insides start to crumble and I needed to double over.

"Lauren, look at me."

I couldn't look at him, I couldn't look at the man who took my heart, and resided in my soul.

"Please, look … at … me." He nudged closer and pulled up on my chin. I kept the space between us, my way of protecting the lonely girl from crashing into the pit of hell.

"I promise with everything I am, I will meet you when I can. But, Lauren, you must be careful. These people are dangerous. Promise me you will be safe. I don't know what I would do if I lost you." He pulled me into his arms and they were warm and secure, and yet at the same time I could tell he was anxious to leave.

I lengthened my neck kissing him so hard that he pulled away to lighten the pressure between us. Our lips moist with passion and fear, our arms pillared with the burdens of our unknown future together we embraced for a changeless flicker of time.

Time was not sensitive to us; I was the first to pull away. My arms became cold, lips dry and the spark he ignited in my core faded to a suspended ember.

"Keep your promise." My voice was barely over a whisper.

Our arms pulled to a bridge as our last connection before our hands broke apart and dropped to our sides.

"Promise," Alejandro mouthed as I watched him pull the door open and disappear into the west coast life I was abandoning.

Forty-five minutes passed from the time Alejandro left me, to the time the limo pulled next to the jet on the tarmac. I had fifteen minutes to spare before Alejandro's jet was scheduled to take off.

My life had changed dramatically in the last week. I've lost too many people and haven't felt so alone since I was a kid ... *Oh, shit, my parents! What in the hell am I going to tell them? I never called them or went to see them ... and now, I was at the airport leaving California.*

The limo driver opened my door and helped me out of the car. I looked back and saw two men loading the luggage into the belly of the plane. I climbed the steps and wished Alejandro was going to board his private jet with me. A familiar loneliness cascaded through my soul. I reached the top of the landing and greeted the pilot. "Welcome aboard, Miss Matthews, my name is Captain Gary Arrow. My co-pilot, Captain Robert Pulls, is performing our preflight check; once that's complete, and we get clearance for takeoff, we will have you in the air and on the way home."

"Thank you," I answered.

I step into the jet, and lost my breath. It was gorgeous, just like the ones you see on the television. The beige rounded walls parted with rich mahogany cabinetry pushed off the sides and over-sized root beer brown leather recliners. The temperature set to a perfect 75 degrees warmed the exposed parts of my body. I sat in the plush recliner, my backside warmed as I pushed back into a reclining position. A space fit for a tired queen.

When I opened my eyes I didn't expect to see a tall, thin man standing in front of me. He cleared his throat before introducing himself.

"Hello, Miss Matthews, I am Captain Robert Pulls, co-pilot for your flight today. We are about to be cleared for takeoff, we will need you to upright your seat and fasten your seatbelt, please."

I pushed the footrest down on the chair.

"And, Miss Matthews, Mr. Fernandez asked if I wouldn't give you this. He's requesting you don't open it until we are in the air."

"Thank you," I murmured.

I held Alejandro's letter in my fingers. It was so light it didn't feel like anything was in it. I flipped it over and noticed it was sealed. Maybe it was in my head, but I could swear it smelt like him. I held it to my nose and kept breathing in his scent. Every memory of us being together flocked to the deepest places he's been. Every tear I'd spilt, every kiss we'd had, every orgasm he'd given me swirled across mind. I was scared to open this letter. What was he going to say to me? What words was he willing to write on the paper? Was it the promise written in ink?

I felt the plane taxi to the runway and then suddenly the familiar pressure against my chest as my body pressed heavy in the chair. I felt my body adjust to the elevation changes as the pilot spoke from the Bose speakers above my head.

"We will be flying roughly two thousand four hundred and forty nine nautical miles today. Please make yourself comfortable and enjoy your flight Miss Matthews." I held the envelope still unopened waiting for a moment that my heart wasn't in my throat. Waiting for the tears that threatened my cheeks to dissolve. I pulled on the sticky part of the envelope and it pulled open so easily, easier than I expected. Part of me wanted it to fight with me, be stingy with its contents. I wanted to feel the need to rip it open but when I saw the white lined paper, I didn't care … I just needed to see what he wrote to me. It was folded so perfectly but, all I could think about was reading his words. I pulled on it and realized that I had never seen his handwriting before.

Dear Lauren,

By the time you get this letter you will probably be flying over Las Vegas.

A place I would like to take you some day. We haven't had much time together but what we have had has been incredible. I want you to know that I will forever be changed by you, mi dama. I didn't expect what Roger told me to be so absolutely true. Your loyalty is inimitable, your courage miraculous, your desires unstoppable and your beauty solid to your soul. Being able to experience it first-hand was a gift you gave me unconditionally. I thank you.

But now I must tell you news I know you will not like, but I need you to know all of me. Every part whether it's good or bad. I wish I could change my life to better suit you, but I can't. No matter how hard I try, I will be driven by the injustice and pain of my brother's murder. I can't change that part of my life, so I create solace in the justice where I can.

I wish so bad it didn't have to be this way, but there is nothing more I can do to make you understand. I won't be going to D.C. to meet you. Not today, not soon.

Just know that you are strong in my heart, every corner belongs to you. Every beat will call your name and with every rush of my blood, I will be regretful of this day. I am not wicked or immoral, please know that. When I am done with the demons that haunt me, I will come for you. Until then, please stay safe. I'm sorry I can't keep my promise to you, mi dama.

Yo no espero que me perdone, pero yo espero que.

Honorablemente Tuyo,

Alejandro

My head spun, my face ran cold and I couldn't stop my body from reacting. A hole as huge as a planet formed in the pit of my stomach. I felt the pain surging up my throat. The worst isolation crashed against the sides of my head as the vise of rejection clamped down. The chorus of his written words built the desperation my soul clung to. Suddenly I felt desperately angry.

*Why did I let him in? Twelve years I waited to invite someone in, someone who was worthy of me. Was*

*Alejandro worthy? Was this what a worthy person would do?*

My mind twisted, pulling away from my experience, it disconnected from my body and played a memory of my life I buried so deep inside that I almost didn't recognize it.

*Agony filled the halls of the hospital. The mustard-colored chairs bolted in a straight row uninviting to the desperation that weakened my legs. My mom grabbed me as I stood there. I couldn't cry anymore. I was physically out of tears. Her arms crushed against my ribs as she held me in a protective grip. I remember smelling carbon paper and mixed crayons. I didn't know if it was her or the slow loss of my mind taking place. I had just left the hospital room, without the man I allowed to live in my heart.*

*Peter and I were in love. We met in the summer between our junior and senior year at Stanford. We were going to move in together.*

*He was studying to become a pharmacist and had a couple more years left of school. I had graduated and was ready to start my life with him.*

*I was told it was a turf war between rival gangs, a drive by shooting. He was caught in the crossfire. The police found out later it was mistaken identity. The bullets grazed his heart and punctured his lung. The doctors tried everything. Within hours he had to be put on life support.*

You can't die, Peter. You have to fight hard, fight for life, choose me damn it! Chose to live for me!

*It wasn't my choice; I had no power. The doctors said Peter had no brain activity when his parents finally*

245

*arrived from Oregon. They never talked to me about it ...
never considered my feelings. Two days after Peter was
put on life support, his family signed the forms to take him
from my world. I watched as he took his last breath, his
chest stopped moving and the bouncing line on his heart
monitor fell flat. My Peter was gone. My life was gone. As
fast as my dreams came true, they had vanished in that
instant. I promised myself that day I wouldn't fall in love
again. I wanted to run. Run as far away as possible. Get
away from the pain that lay breathless in the hospital bed.*

*I went home that night, found the acceptance letter
from the CIA Training Academy, packed my bags for
Washington D.C. and never looked back at that agonizing
day – until now.*


Alejandro wasn't fair to me. He waited until I
was a prisoner, unable to stop the plane. The letter
crumpled in my hand, the words on the page blurred
by my falling tears I flattened it and read it again.
Maybe I missed something. I felt the same anguish I
did the first time I read it. I pulled my legs to my
chest, balling into a protective fetal position. I wished
I was numb to the world.

It wasn't going to be the case today. A woman I
had no idea was on the plane walked slow to me as
she called my name.

"Ms. Matthews, I have to ask you to buckle your
safety belt for our descent into Ronald Reagan
Airport. I think you dropped this." She held
Alejandro's letter out to me. My hand shook as I

collected it from her. The paper still damp with my tears; the creases still there from when I crumpled it.

"Thank you," I rasped.

I looked around the plane, nothing around represented who I was ... and yet, I was living in the pain of being here. I flattened his words against my heart ... Where did the five hours of my life go?

# twenty-one

I walked down the steps of the jet and watched the limo driver load my bags into the trunk of another limousine. The last thing Alejandro did for me in his attempt to keep me safe. My foot pressed firm into the dark tarmac removing me from the last reminisces of my trip to California. I couldn't look back. It was too painful to see where my life had dropped me off. I didn't want to meet up with the lonely girl that resided deep in my soul. I had lost the man that stole my heart and seared himself in my soul. Once again, I had to leave behind my life in California. I had to find my strength. The sooner I found Roger, the sooner he could take this thing out of my head. I was done with Marshall done with everything outside of the CIA.

I lowered my head and crouched into the back of the limo. The driver told me he had been instructed to take me home. I gave him a nod and closed my eyes. My mind filled with the one person I least expected to think about. Marshall Grayson. What a piece of work. How I ever found him appealing was beyond me. I let out a short breath of air through my

248

nose thinking about where he could be. Instantly, I was startled by Marshall's file filling my eyes. I noticed the GPS icon glowed bright. It was different than I expected, in seconds a map of the world appeared with each country being a different color. I noticed that the United States was the only one that had a bright yellow aura. I focused on it and it magnified across my vision. Four brightly lit red flashing bubbles bleeped on the screen. Three were in the Washington D.C. area and one that appeared to be slowly moving across Virginia. I focused on the moving one; a text box large enough to hold all the information I needed appeared next to it.

Marshall Grayson
Richmond, Virginia
Coordinates:37n33,77w28

My legs went numb and a crisp humming swamped my ears. The text box went blank, and an animated white circle spun like a record. Suddenly, the information appeared again but this time he was in Fredericksburg, Virginia heading straight to D.C. His bright red bubble was moving so steady, the only logical explanation—he was on a plane, that heartless coward. I repositioned my eyes on the three bubbles in the D.C. area and watched as information popped open for each one. My bubble was moving really slow, recalibrating as the limo drove toward my house on the outskirts of D.C. Roger's red bubble was undisturbed at George Washington Hospital. It was the third bubble that piqued my interest. It was Samantha's. I felt a wave of hope crash through me. Could this be the one time this thing in my head will be used for good! My heart clung to the back of my throat. The last time I saw Samantha she was severely beaten and had been abducted from her house. I noticed she was moving away from D.C. and heading north. My heart dropped into the pit of my stomach, where was she being taken?

The limo rolled to a stop, minimizing the GPS and saw that I was home. The door swung open and the driver helped me out before he led me to the back of the limo and pulled opened the trunk. The hair on my arms reached for the sky. I was wrong about Alejandro; he had one more thing to do for me. I shot the driver a questioning glance and then carefully reached my hand slowly down into the trunk and reclaimed my gun, its holster and my knife.

I pushed the keypad and opened my garage door. Finally, I was home and I was exhausted. I didn't want to check my messages or look at the mail that was piled on the floor inside my front door; I didn't even care to unpack my bags, all I wanted to do was to take a hot steaming bath. I wanted to soak away the pain of losing my heart today. Wash away the part of my life I wasted falling in love. I needed to find a place I could exist where I am just me again.

I pulled a towel from the hall closet, took advantage of the last little bit of mineral oil beads and headed to my modest bathroom, which in no way mirrored Alejandro's. My tub was just big enough to lay out flat to allow the water to reach my shoulders. No jets, no bubbles, my mineral oil beads were my only indulgence. I pulled the lever up so my bath would begin to fill and tossed the remaining beads in the water. They say lavender has a soothing aroma. I really hoped that was true. I caught myself in the mirror above my sink. Lovely, the dark circles under my eyes were more prominent than normal, the cuts and bruises looked better than a couple of days ago but still nowhere near gone and my hair looked like a fountain flying out of the middle of my head. I looked like hell. Well at least my appearance matched my feelings. Hit by a truck, if I was only that lucky. Maybe dying would have been easier. I pulled my phone from my pocket and looked at the date. Friday, two days from now I was supposed to die … asphyxiation … if I was only so lucky.

I tossed my phone on the vanity and pulled at my shirt stretching it around my forearms to fit it up and over my head when Marshall's full name appeared in my right eye. Nervous, I turned off the running water and sat on the toilet. I figured if I was as quiet as possible he wouldn't know I was home. The only drawback, he was trying to get into my head not my bathroom.

"Marshall," I answered. I knew where he was and what he was up to, I just hoped he didn't figure it out.

"Where are you? You're not in California, are you?" he asked. I could tell he knew the answer to his question.

"I couldn't contact you. Like you fell of the grid so I did what I was trained to do if I was compromised. I came back to D.C. Is everything okay?" I tried to come across genuine and hide the irritation soaking into every cell of my body. As far as he knew, I was totally unaware of him being in California. Our paths never crossed.

"No everything's not okay — Sam's gone missing. She went to California and hasn't come back," he lied.

"Do you have anyone looking for her?"

"Yeah, I have some people in California that owe me favors. So far nobody can seem to find her. I had to come back. I'll debrief you tomorrow. First thing in the morning — my house — eight o'clock sharp." He cleared his throat and waited for me to acknowledge what he said.

"Eight — your house — anyone looking for her out here in D.C.? Maybe she came back like I did?"

"No, I figured if they don't find anything in the next couple of days. Then we'll search this area. However, all evidence points to California." He sounded convincing — *scary*. We said our goodbyes and then I disconnected from him, sick to my stomach.

I knew he went to California, I knew he hired a monster to hurt Sam and disable her prototype. I knew she was in D.C. If he convinced me that she was still in California it gave him more time to hide her somewhere. This way he could remove any obstacles in his way including me. I was the last line of defense to stop Marshall from selling the prototype to other countries for massive profits and bottom lines. The longer this was in my head, the more I began to fear its absolute power.

I lost the desire to take a bath, even if it was full of soothing lavender oil. I pushed the lever and watched the water run out, mesmerized by the whirlpool it created. I didn't want to think anymore, I just wanted to sleep.

Normally I loved to sleep in my bed, but tonight my skin seemed to be overly sensitive. Every time I moved, I felt the hair on my arms tangle with the fibers of the sheets. My legs were affected by the razor sharp pin-pricks when I slid them apart. I couldn't get my feet warm no matter how much I rubbed them together, even with the down comforter. It wasn't only my sense of touch that was different. I could smell things, tasting them as the aroma filled the back of my throat. The lavender from the bathroom was strong, that was explainable, still on my hands; however, the gun powder from my pistol wasn't. Or the free sample of laundry soap that lay sealed in the pile of mail in my living room. My senses were on heightened alert.

I got out of bed and walked out to my living room in the dark, I could see as clear as day without reaching to turn on a light. I bent down to the mail and rummaged through it, each piece smelling of every person that handled it. The sender, sorters, the mail carrier, every person's scent until I found the advertisement for the new unscented organic laundry soap. I dropped it; shocked I pulled my hands to my face almost throwing up. The scent of all the envelopes I had touched was on my skin. I ran to the bathroom and tried to wash it away. *What the fuck was happening to me?* My only explanation, the prototype was malfunctioning. I looked for strange things happening in my vision. Strange dots, blinking flashes, blind spots where the prototype could be crashing. Maybe it would be my hearing next … maybe things would get so loud I would go insane trying to silence the white noise. What if it was my sense of taste next? Immediately I contacted Roger. It didn't cross my mind until he answered that I was in another bathroom with running water and talking to him, a habit that I had created, even subconsciously.

*"Hi Lauren, glad you're home safe."* He sounded a lot better than the last time we talked.

"Hi, Roger, how are you?"

*"Oh I'm a lot better. Just left the ER; they fixed my side and cleaned my cuts. The doc told me it would have been a lot worse if that skewer was even a fraction of an inch to the right. How are you?"*

I turned off the water and I could hear he was in his car driving, based on the sounds of the trees that passed him. He was going pretty fast.

"Are you on the highway?"

*"Yeah — why?"*

"Because I hear the trees whistling past your open window."

*"My window isn't open."*

I felt my stomach leap into my throat. I could hear trees whistling, his tires clinging to the asphalt and the hum of the engine. I could feel my skin crawl with an energy that vibrates at the level just between where my flesh meets the world. I needed to tell him what was going on.

"Roger, I think there's something wrong with the prototype."

*"What? What makes you say that?"* I could hear his doubt.

"I think it's malfunctioning or something, all my senses are really intensified. My sense of touch and smell are off the charts. Roger, it's freaking me out. I can't live with these feelings so intense. It's like my nerves scraping across my bones and my skin isn't doing anything to keep my soul from floating above me. I can't even find a place to exist where I can't smell people's essence."

He was silent for a moment then cleared his throat before he spoke.

*"Lauren, that's something you'll get use to. Like the blinking cursor,"* he said.

"Well, thank God I won't have to after tomorrow. I'm having this thing taken out of my head tomorrow after the debriefing."

*"What debriefing?"* Roger questioned.

"Marshall's house, tomorrow, eight in the morning." I knew Marshall was setting me up. The one defense I had, he didn't know Roger was still alive.

*"I want to go with you. I'll pick you up in the morning. Okay?"* I've known Roger for a long time and I could tell by the way his voice lowered he was apprehensive about me meeting with Marshall alone.

"It's a good thing Marshall doesn't know you're still alive."

*"Yeah – good thing."* He didn't sound convincing.

"Back to this thing in my head —"

*"The prototype,"* he interrupted.

"Back to this *prototype* in my head; is there any way you can adjust the sensitivity it creates?"

He was silent for a long moment and then started to bark instructions to me.

*"To dull the sensatory processor you need to enter settings. Next, scan down until you see the words sensatory processor. It should be about half way down on the right side. Run your eyes past it. It should say automatic. Highlight the word automatic and replace it with manual."*

He must've stopped driving; I couldn't hear the wind rushing past or his tires slapping against the road. I did everything he told me. Unemotional, to the point, that was who Roger was becoming to me. Maybe his prototype was already replacing his humanness.

"Okay, got it. That's it?" I was relieved.

*"No, we have to set the manual levels now."* His voice was steady. *"Close that window; it'll ask you if you want to save changes, say yes. Then it'll reboot, give it a minute."*

"Okay." I took advantage of the lapse in time to use the bathroom. I lost contact with Roger and my vision went black as the prototype reboot. He didn't tell me that was going to happen and I started to feel that familiar rock of apprehension cling to the space behind my heart as it climbed its way to settle the back of my throat. My vision returned and immediately my blinking cursor was transformed to Roger's full name as he attempted to connect to me. I swallowed hard.

"I wasn't ready for that." I washed my hands. The cold water felt refreshing on my skin.

*"Sorry, I should've told you about that."*

He explained how to keep adjusting settings and told me the more I do it, the easier it will become. I kept telling him it was a waste of time because tomorrow he was going to remove it from my head. He let out an intentional chuckle and unwillingly agreed with my gripe. Before we disconnected he reminded me that he was coming over to pick me up in the morning. Like I would forget at this point ... I just wanted one good night's sleep.

twenty-two

My eyes snapped open to ringing in my ears. I looked over at my clock; it was six in the morning. Groggy, I slowly reached for the phone next to my bed. When the dial tone mixed with the ringing in my ears I realized it was my prototype that rang and not my phone.

It was Marshall. *Why was he contacting me again?* Confused and still half asleep, I answered his impatient call.

"Marshall?" I could hear him breathing hard and his feet shuffling on the floor. *"Don't you understand, it's what I had to do?"* He was talking, but not to me.

"Marshall, what is it?" I asked confused.

*"You know me; don't let this affect our business."* He still seemed to be talking to someone else. It was like he called me on accident. He wasn't responding to what I was saying. I attempted a couple more times to get his attention, but failed. There was only one way to get him to listen and that was me accessing the recordable feature in his files. I clicked around and shuffled through to Marshall's recordable files. I focused on

the recorder icon and instantly his world appeared in my eyes. I felt his heart pound so heavy I thought he was going to pass out. His eyes were closed, almost like a long purposeful blink.

My eyes opened and I was in Marshall's head. I was him. He was in his library. I felt his throat dry and his eyes burn and his fingertips stroll up across the textured spines of the gilded hardback books. His fingers rose to into my eyesight and caught what he was looking at. I felt the excitement build in his chest and his hand move toward a black and silver 9mm semiautomatic pistol. His fingers tickled at the cold steel barrel and his palm warmed the black handle. He slowly pulled it from behind the book and slipped it into the front of his waistband. I heard a breath behind him, it was familiar but I couldn't place it.

*"I didn't want anything to affect my business with you. Doctor Finway was a mistake, okay. I didn't mean to kill him; all I wanted was to disable the prototype."*

When our eyes met and I saw who it was, my stomach wrapped into twisted knots. The muscles in my arms and legs constricted, instantly causing them to shake uncontrollably. I closed my eyes, rolled over onto my stomach and pulled my legs up underneath me. I couldn't handle this, not today. The tighter my eyes pressed together, the clearer my vision of Alejandro became. *He wasn't supposed to be in D.C.* He wasn't coming anytime soon. Why? Why did he lie to me? He started to say something, but my voice in my head was louder. He cleared his throat and his voice rose.

"Did you honestly think I was going to be okay with you hurting Sam? Threatening Lauren? Sam is my employee." His words hung strong in his tone. I felt Marshall's voice come from the pit of my gut. My tongue parted my mouth and I felt my lips become moist before he spoke.

*"Not okay, but figured you would understand the attempt I made, at the very least, keeping her alive."* His smug attitude wrapped around my body as his hand rested heavy on his gun.

"I'm not too understanding when it comes to people I value. Don't push me Marshall, you will lose. Where is she?"

Alejandro was standing square in front of me. I wanted to grab him, I wanted to push him, punch him, make him plea for his heart back. I want to watch him fall back alone and feel the same pain I had on the plane. I wanted Alejandro to ache like I had; I wanted his heart to burn to nothing more than ashes, like mine has. I hated him because he made me love him more than I've ever thought I could love again. I couldn't do any of that; Marshall had a gun in his waistband and there was nothing I could do about it. I was balancing between the intolerable confusion of fear and frustration. I was a visitor in Marshall's head with no ability to stop or change the outcome of what would happen.

*"I don't know where she is. Even if I did, I wouldn't tell you. Besides, it isn't Sam you should worry about. If I*

*were you ... I'd be more concerned with the woman you decided to fuck,"* Marshall sneered, taunting him for a reaction.

Alejandro flung himself toward Marshall; toward me. His shirt pulled tight against his body as his eyes fill with revulsion. I braced for the pain to explode in my chest when his hands found me. Instead I felt my body timber to the books behind me. My head hit the edge of the shelf. Marshall slid down heavy. We were on the floor, Alejandro's hands around my neck. The same hands that brought pleasure to my world, ignited a flame I hadn't had in a years, were now choking me. Marshall couldn't breathe and I felt his body begin to react and panic. I was scared to see Alejandro capable of doing this. Marshall reached up, grabbing at Alejandro's grip trying to break it from around his neck. Marshall thrust his hand around Alejandro's head. Everything Marshall did, I felt. I felt his fingers press into Alejandro's eyes and I couldn't do anything to stop it. Marshall increased the pressure in his thumbs and all I could feel was my thumbs start to blind the man I had given my heart to. Alejandro let go of Marshall's throat and I was able to breathe. Gasping, I welcomed the burning air that scraped down my throat. Alejandro stumbled back and brought his hands to his eyes. Scared by his aggression, I wished Marshall would have run, instead, he fumbled for his balance as he grabbed the bookshelves and pulled himself up. Marshall was trying to yell but only was able to breathlessly whisper to Alejandro.

*"You made a big mistake. One call and Lauren is dead. I'm the only one that can keep her alive and you just crossed the line."*

"If you so much as harm one hair on her head, I will not stop until I hunt you down and kill you," Alejandro snarled as he tried to rub the tears from his red swollen eyes. The anguish poured from his mouth.

"Going into business with me was the best thing you could've ever done. Look what you got out of the deal. Five years of technology that you could've never done yourself. If anything, you owe me." Marshall's voice cracked and I could finally breathe. My throat hurt like shards of glass poked unrelentingly at my trachea. Marshall pulled his head to either side to get the muscles to relax and stretch.

"Five years and now you're trying to back out of the contract with one week left. I gave you millions and for what? Nothing. Where's Sam?" Alejandro asked, demanding an answer. His eyes were still swollen and red but I could feel he was surging with anger.

"Maybe you should worry about Lauren and give up on Sam—just like you gave up on your brother," Marshall spat, deliberately prodding Alejandro. I could feel the bile creep up my throat. In my head, I was in love with Alejandro, but the body I was held prisoner in hated him.

"What did you say to me?" Alejandro turned toward Marshall. Slow motion clicked in my head and suddenly I saw Alejandro come at me in one sweeping motion. His expression hardened and his fists clutched tight.

Marshall back pedaled and spoke freely as my world crumbled into the unexplainable.

"You heard me. You gave up on your brother and now you'll give up on Sam and eventually Laur—"

Marshall's head bent back and slid down the bookcase as Alejandro clocked him upside the head. I felt the side of Marshall's face swell instantly and tears began to roll down from my eyes. The same hand that gently pushed my hair back from my face and tenderly touched my wounds a couple of days ago now inflicted disastrous pain; even if it was intended for someone else.

I knew what Marshall was doing. I could put two and two together. He wanted Alejandro to beat him, hit him so hard that I would feel the pain Alejandro could inflict. Do it while I was in his head, hearing every word, feeling every blow. Experience the awful side of him. Cause so much wreckage so Alejandro would have to live with the consequences. I was desolate. I was terrified I was going to watch the man I love get killed by the man whose body I was possessing, unwilling.

Marshall's body rose up off the floor as Alejandro pulled him up from the collar of his shirt. His face close to Marshall's I could smell his aroma fill me as I gasped for a breath.

"You're pathetic and not worth my time," Alejandro said as he let Marshall fall to the floor. I fell with a thud, hitting my head on the base of the floor lamp. I could feel blood mix with Marshall's hair as it poured from the gash in the back of his head. He started to walk away when Marshall said the words that would kill any hope. My relief turned to terror as I felt Marshall's fingertips press hard on his chest as he spoke. I expected his hand to move down to the waistband of his pants.

"And right there is your problem, you don't know any better. Spain. 1988? I was there." Marshall watched Alejandro freeze in his tracks. I felt everything I was freeze in Marshall's body. I looked into Alejandro's eyes, knowing what Marshall just said were words that were going to draw him in.

"I don't know any better?" Alejandro roared. His eyes filled with rage. Marshall struggled to stand up and I felt every part of his body that hurt. Neck, chest, arms and legs all throbbed with the pain Alejandro had unleashed on him just minutes ago. I felt everything Alejandro did to him, and all along he had no idea I was in Marshall's head.

"I had to make it look like a domestic dispute. I had to make it seem like I was her husband. She was working for our government and was about to report back to them my connection with Iraq. Desert Storm was over, my business was drying up and I needed to find a new client. I had to keep Grayson Industries viable. That meant I had to eliminate all obstacles in my way, including, Sarah Copland. I went to Spain where she was working a recon job. It was supposed to be easy. I would catch her in the room she rented, end it and leave before anyone knew any different. Instead, she ran down the street and I chased after her. We ended up in front of an apartment complex." Marshall took a breath, his demeanor changed as he shifted his stance.

"*Stop, just stop, Marshall ... you win, I give up ... please stop.*" I tried to communicate to him.

"Your brother, he should've stayed out of it. Instead, he had to be the hero. If he had just walked away, but he didn't. To be sixteen and have the ability to be so selfless." Marshall shook his head as he stared at Alejandro.

"*No! You selfish son of a bitch. Don't do this, Marshall. Don't!*" I screamed at Marshall. I watched as Alejandro's expression drained of all color. Suddenly, what I saw was a broken man, the same man that told me the story of his brother's death. His eyes raked with misery. His whole body looked dejected and misplaced. I saw the arrested space in his soul fill with hatred. The space created by the monster I happen to be occupying. I wanted to escape Marshall's prison, I wanted to grab Alejandro in my arms, hold him, heal him, kiss him so every painful feeling he was experiencing would vanish in my touch. I just wanted to take him home safe with me.

I hated Marshall, I despised everything he represented. He was the devil himself ascending from the pits of hell. "*I hate you ... do you hear me? I'd live a thousand lives wrapped in the confines of a five-by-five prison cell if it meant you would take your last breath at my hands."*

I felt Marshall's body as it became content with the pain he inflicted on Alejandro. Confidence swirled from his abdomen, uncontainable energy radiated through him entirely, but it wasn't enough. I felt the vile words exit out of his mouth; I wanted to stop him but I couldn't. He spewed venom from his forked tongue.

"No witnesses. I felt the blade push into his chest, cracking his ribs. It was suppose to be her ... but he stepped in front. I will never forget the strength I had to use to pull my knife from his body." Marshall's eyes wicked as he looked at Alejandro. His hand rested full on the gun at his waistband. I tasted every vulgar word as it poured from Marshall's mouth. My body felt every moment of his disgusting satisfaction as he broke the spirit of the man I love.

*"Please, stop, just stop, stop, it's killing him. Why can't you stop?"* I cried to Marshall, knowing full well he wouldn't listen.

No words came from Alejandro's mouth as he lunged forward and swung frantically at Marshall. I felt Marshall pull back his head, making Alejandro swing at the empty space. I didn't recognize Alejandro's eyes as he swung and thrust his way toward Marshall. Marshall laughed and I felt the horrid satisfaction rise from his belly when he realized he was torturing Alejandro with his words.

Unraveling Alejandro's pain one vicious word at a time. I saw death in Alejandro's eyes; I saw that he was going to kill Marshall.

Alejandro's fist connected with Marshall and I felt his body fall back. Marshall's hand off the gun as he landed hard, I could feel the vibration radiate from my insides out and across the hardwood floor. Alejandro's knees pinned Marshall's arms down at his sides and I watched as he pulled his rock hard fists back and slammed them down onto Marshall's face; my face. Before the first one left, the next one came crashing down. Pain radiated through my bones, causing ripples of devastation across my heart. Blood filled my mouth, draining into the back of my throat from my nose. My eyes puffed up and filled with tears, to the point where I couldn't see anything but an outline of a dark figure that stopped moving. I was scared of Alejandro, scare that he was going to kill Marshall and in turn kill me. My lips stung and burned as they swelled with blood. His weight shifted off my chest as he pulled his face close to Marshall's ear and spoke to him.

"Por último la muerte de mi hermano será reivindicado, ir al infierno hijo de puta."

*Finally my brother's death will be vindicated, go to hell you son of a bitch.*

The words flowed through my mind, and for the first time I translated all the words Alejandro said; only too late to make a difference. I shattered under his words. Nothing would vindicate his brother's death; nothing was going to bring Vincente back. His hands clutched at Marshall's throat; my mouth went dry and the familiar pain of being strangled rose in my body. I could feel Marshall trying to say something as Alejandro increased the pressure around his neck, squeezing the life out of both of us. I wish I prayed, wish that God would listen to my words, answer my requests, but he won't, not this time ... I relinquished to the idea that God's going to let me die at the hands of Alejandro and just like the pinprick said, except instead of dying tomorrow ... I will die today by asphyxiation, December fifth, two thousand thirteen.

"Lauren, do you see what he's capable of? Do you feel the pain? I hope so—" Marshall whispered out loud. The pressure across my neck lightened, but wasn't gone. He continued whispering loud enough for Alejandro to hear. "This pain, Lauren, this pain is the pain you'll know forever, just like the prototype in your head. Forever."

*"I hate you! I fucking hate you!"* I scream at Marshall until my lungs begged for a breath. Muted in his head, I knew my voice wasted on him, but I didn't care, I needed to release. I needed to get out the anger.

My mind hurt, my body was battered, and the man I loved was the one unknowingly hurting me. I wanted Marshall to die with so much pain he'd go to hell for relief. I wanted him to pay for everything he's done to Samantha, Roger, Doctor Finway and me.

I tried to make sense of what he was saying. I couldn't breathe and my eyes were swollen shut. I felt Marshall's hand reach to the front of his waistband and pull the gun free. It was cold and heavy causing my arm to ache. I felt the gun thrust hard against the side of Alejandro's head. Marshall's finger pulled back on the trigger; the pressure increased as I heard the hammer of the gun engage and felt Marshall's hand twist. The kick back as the bullet left the barrel was sickening.

"*Noooo!*" I screamed in Marshall's head. I couldn't lose Alejandro. *No, you're not supposed to die … it was me … I was the one that was supposed to die … not him!*

The room went dark and my body pulled away from Marshall.

I was still screaming as I felt my consciousness return to my room. My heart pillaged by my darkest fears. I can't lose Alejandro; I couldn't lose another man I loved. My skin burned, as if acid was slowly eating away at me.

"God, if you are mercy, if you are anything … please, please tell me Alejandro is alive, that Marshall didn't take the only reason I want to breathe," I slurred, determined to talk out loud. Determined to make my words more powerful than the reality that Marshall just pulled the trigger and there was nothing I could do to stop him. Tears flooded my swollen eyes, pouring down my cheeks and across my damaged lips.

My eyes were heavy; too heavy to open. Now, disconnected from Marshall my mind reeled in torment with the visions of Alejandro lying somewhere, bleeding to death ... I tried to get up, but felt different this time. I felt a wetness flow from my nose and a pain in my head pounding strong across my jaw and down the back of my neck. What happened? Why am I feeling this pain outside of Marshall's head? I reached my hands to my eyes; they were hot and swollen shut. I tried to open them but couldn't. My neck muscles started to spasm as I lift my head from my bed. My arms and legs weak under my movements I struggled into my bathroom. Impossible to see where I was going, I relied upon the familiarity of my house.

I pushed the door open and stumbled to the vanity. I had to see what Alejandro had done to Marshall, *to me* ... I was unrecognizable, even to myself. My lips huge with blood pockets, my nose twisted and flattened on the bridge, my vision blurred by my swollen eyelids. I couldn't tell if there were bruises across my arms and shoulders, but it felt like it. My body became too much for my legs to hold, I stumbled back against the wall. The last thing I remembered, my legs folding under me and sliding down to my feet, my face cold against the white tiled floor screaming for the man that damaged me, terrorized by the unknown fate of the man who had captured my mind, body and soul.

# twenty-three

I knew he was coming for me. Not because he told me, I could feel his presence draw near me. I never sensed someone's arrival before. It was like we were connected by intuition. I heard the smelly letters spread flat across the hardwood floor as he pushed my front door open. His rubber-soled shoes weighing light as he walked. He never called my name, but I could hear him stop at each room. My eyes still shut not wanting to face what I knew was bad. I had spent the last couple of hours on my bathroom floor and my body paid heavily for it.

The door swung open, my eyes still closed, I heard him gasp and the bones in his legs drop against the tile floor. His hands rubbed at my shoulder and pulled back the hair from my face. I could hear him push his face toward mine. Suddenly hope was thrust through my veins … carrying away my hardened fear. There was a chance I was going to live, and maybe even function as a normal human being some day if Roger could fix me. But I didn't want it if Alejandro was dead. I didn't want to breathe if he wasn't with me.

"Lauren, can you hear me? Lauren, who did this to you?"

A sense of relief rushed my skin as his voice filled my ears. I couldn't open my eyes or talk to him, but I knew Roger wouldn't stop asking until I answered. My throat sore and my body unforgiving, I tried to speak. He bent closer.

"Alejandro," I slurred without moving my blood swollen lips or my dislocated jaw. It hurt so bad to pluck those words from my throat.

"Lauren, who did this to you?" He still had his face pushed forward. His hand moved in a circle on my back. "Did Marshall?"

"No, Alejan—" My voice broke and I couldn't talk. Memories of what I last remembered flooded my mind. The feeling of Marshall's gun pressed firm against Alejandro's head, my finger pulling back on the trigger until it hurt, the sound of the hammer engaging and then nothing. Tears pushed past my beaten eyes, collecting in the crevices of swollen skin and broken cartilage as I lay on the cold tile floor.

My life was done. Over. Gone.

"Alejandro did this to you? I'll kill that son of a bitch." His body vibrated and I could feel his anger consume every part of who he was. Sometimes, one protests too much, could it be that he had some guilt? Guilt that he nurtured by inventing the precise technology that facilitated these exact results. I reached for him with my free hand. His anger wasn't going to help me stand up. I needed his help to stand up. I wanted to get off my bathroom floor.

Roger helped me to my feet, pain exploded, through every part of my body. My hand pressed hard to stop the sharp debilitating pain in my neck, my other captured my jaw to stop the throbbing. I knew I was in bad shape, and I had come to terms on the bathroom floor that if I was going to be disfigured forever, at least I would be reminded every day of what I lost. I was alive, and it was going to be for nothing without Alejandro. A spastic energy swirled in my gut and torn up through my heart, taking out my lungs and the cries burst from my mouth.

"Shhh, Lauren, it's okay, I'm going to take you to the doctor. We'll get you all fixed up, better than new."

Better than new ... words you say for used up and worn out appliances. I pulled myself together enough to shuffle down the hall with Roger.

"Let's go. Take me to Marshall's house. I need to find Alejandro." I push up from the wall, my heart beat at a panic pace.

"I think you should see a doctor," Roger piped up.

"It will be too late; he might be dead by then." I stumbled toward my front door. I was determined to get to Marshall's house. All the seconds counted, the hours I was on the floor didn't make the possibility that I will save Alejandro. *What if he bled out? What if he is close to death and I just get to him a little quicker I can save him? Have him in my arms again.*

I looked over at Roger as he studied my face. Confusion mixed with concern blanketed his expression.

"This isn't Alejandro's fault. I was in Marshall's head when they got into a fight." I sounded a little clearer as the swelling in my lips diminished.

"This happened while you were in Marshall's head? Using Marshall's recorder? Alejandro did this to Marshall—to you?" skepticism weaved through his voice.

"Marshall contacted me. He was in his library with Alejandro. They fought, Marshall held a gun to Alejandro then I blacked out. That's why I need to get to Marshall's house, now! Please ... will you please take me? I just need you to drive me there."

I tried to make eye contact with him. My neck rippled spasms as I clung to his arm. His eyes became constrained, the corners of his mouth wilted toward the horizon of the room.

Tears welled in my eyes, the immense pain and fear of Alejandro being dead owned my whole body and mind.

"Please Roger, I can't lose him ... I can't breathe without him. I have to do this."

Roger's focus became fixed as he whispered, "Marshall Grayson." He was still for a moment. Then spoke out loud, "Connect with Marshall Grayson." His eyes, preoccupied and filled with doubt, shifted around the room. What was he seeing? His eyes grew big as he mentally came back to the room. He grabbed my arm and helped me out my front door.

My eyes stung at the morning sun, the needle piercing pain was unbearable. I pulled my head to his shoulder trying to hide from the poison that easily found my weakness. He held me motionless, his body stiffened and I heard him mumble angry words under his breath. I was sorry I became such a burden to him, but I needed to get to Marshall's and I wasn't in any state to drive.

I felt his arms cradle me, protectively, possessively. I tried to look up but couldn't, the sun was bright. Roger shuffled me over to my wooden porch swing. He lowered me to sit, my hands sprung up to my eyes, trying to create barriers from the sun. I could hear Roger breathe heavy. I felt his lips press on my hair by my ear and tell me to stay. I tried several times to pull my hands away from my eyes with little progress.

"Roger, you need to take me." I pushed my face to the sky as I spoke up to him. He ignored me and spoke to someone else.

"You — I'm going to kill you, you piece of shit. You killed Marshall and now what? You come here to finish the job?" Roger's voice became frantic. I heard his feet shuffle across the porch away from me.

"Roger, what's going on? I can't see. Who are you talking to?" I forced my eyes to slightly open, just enough to make out a dark outline of a person standing at the bottom of the stairs. I blinked, trying to clear enough of the stinging pain away to find out who he was going to kill.

"*Lauren*! Oh, *mi dama*! Let me by." Alejandro bellowed as I heard his feet shuffle and mix with Roger's.

My mind flushed with confusion. Visions of his face as he hit me flashed in front of my eyes. The rage and complete hatred that radiated from his body when he was hitting Marshall was chilling. *Was he here to kill me? Did he kill Marshall? Was he coming back for me?* Questions pressed my mind at the same time flashes of our time together crushed against my heart. I wanted to touch him. Feel him. Was he real? He was keeping his promise.

"Like fucking hell if I'm going to let you by. I trusted you with her ... and look at what you did." Roger was blocking the stairs and not allowing Alejandro up on the porch. I felt my voice rumble from deep inside my throat.

"Roger, let him up. He isn't going to hurt me."

"How do you know, Lauren?" I could hear him turn to me.

"She knows me," Alejandro said.

"Please, Roger, trust me." I changed my tone to soothing. I heard Alejandro push through Roger.

"I'll be right here, watching," Roger called.

I felt the wood boards on the porch vibrate as Alejandro hurried his way to me. My eyes slightly open, I could see it was him. It was my Alejandro in the flesh. I felt the heat from his body reach me as he kneeled in front of me. He pushed my hair back from my face; fear climbed into my chest and pulled the strings of my pain.

"Lauren, sweetheart." He took his other hand and parted my knees pulling his body close to me, careful not to touch me. I flinched, at his touch.

"Alejandro." I felt tears pour down my cheeks and drop onto my hands as I reached up to wipe them free.

"Lauren, *mi dama*, shhh. I am so sorry!" He brought his hand to my temple. His cool hand soothed the fire that roared in my head. I couldn't say anything; my body trembled uncontrollably. He ripped off his coat and quickly wrapped it around me.

"It's okay, I'm here now and he will never hurt you again." I felt him kiss my forehead.

I wanted to talk, tell him how I felt, but I couldn't. It was as if my mouth was wired shut and sealed with cement.

I felt the rush of air as he stood up in front of me. I heard him walk over to the front of my porch and land heavy on each step as he left me alone on the swing. I was twelve all over again, watching my father as he left me sitting on the steps, abandoned. I pulled my arms tight around my waist, trying to comfort the chills that my body memorized that day. A private moment I forgot I owned.

I heard a low timbre conversation that became heated and lasted for several lengthy minutes. My vision cleared enough to make out the shapes of Roger and Alejandro. I saw Alejandro force his hands to his head and drop to his knees forcing his head down to the ground. I could hear him bellow in agony. I closed my eyes trying to build enough strength to go to him. I ached fiercely for him. I pushed my hands against the swing when footsteps clomped on the stairs and I felt the porch tremble as he hurried back to me. He lowered himself once again in front of me. Hands on his knees, he stared down at my feet. Ashamed at what he learned he did, he couldn't look me in the eyes. We sat there a moment, not touching, just feeling each other's presence. I saw tears drop and break against the porch he spoke soft delicate words to me in Spanish as his voice broke.

"What have I done? What have I done? Lauren, *mi dama*, can you ever forgive me? Please, please, forgive me, my despicable act. I would never hurt you. I adore you. I would rather die over and over again than hurt you. I love you with everything I am."

I put my hand on his head ran it down the side of his face and pulled up on his chin before I answered him in Spanish.

"Sé que no significa que me hizo daño. Te perdono."

He pushed up to me; unable to kiss my battered lips, he laid the side of his face against my chest. His arms locked around my waist and I felt him breathe me in. I knotted my hands into his tousled hair and wept. I was frightened by what I saw he could become.

Interrupted by a car door slamming shut, Roger drove away. My heart dropped into my stomach, this wasn't the way I wanted him to find out about Alejandro. I twisted myself to a standing position and I stared out in the direction of Roger's escape. The guilt raged and crept up through my body. Alejandro attentively held me steady for that regrettable moment before we went back into the house.

"You need to go to the hospital," Alejandro spoke quietly.

"I want to lie in my bed right now," I told him.

"I think you'd feel better if you went."

"I'm not going to the hospital." My face winced and my body tightened. He strengthened his hold on me.

"Okay. I'm here to take care of you now." He helped me to my bed, wrapped me in my down comforter and delicately climbed next to me. He grabbed my hand and held it to his face. It was exactly where I wanted him, next to me ... forever.

twenty-four

I was forced awake by a ringing in my ear ... it was Samantha Wilkins, someone that laid heavy on my mind, but I was unable to help. I wanted to talk to her, wanted to find out if she was okay and now was my opportunity. My eyes met Alejandro's as I told him what I saw.

"Sam is contacting me," I whispered to him. He sat up and became attentive.

"Talk to her, find out where she is." His voice mounted strong.

I focused on her name and connected with her.

*Sam, are you okay? Where are you?* I felt the words slip from my mind into hers. I waited forever for her to respond. I asked again, nothing. *What was going on?*

"She's not responding," I slurred to Alejandro.

"Not saying anything?" he asked desperate.

"Nothing, just blank space," I answered him. I didn't know what to do. "She's there, unable to speak to me; like something is blocking her from talking or even thinking out loud." Alejandro helped me sit up.

My head was heavy. I knew she was there. If I could just find out where she was, Alejandro could get to her. I minimized her communication file and pulled up my GPS. It opened like before, showing the world each continent a different color. The United States lit with a yellow aura. I focused on the east coast and there it was. Two bubbles lit bright red and the third was a faint pink. Only three this time, not four like before. I focused on the red bubble moving slowly across Virginia toward D.C. The text box popped opened.

Roger Clarke
Arlington, Virginia
Coordinates:38.53N,7.07W

Then the text box blanked to a spinning timer, it was recalibrating his coordinates for his location. I knew the other bubble was me, because it was blinking steady as it sat in McLean, Virginia. The third bubble, faint pink, was north. I focused on it and a textbox opened revealing who it represented.

Samantha Wilkins
Baltimore, Maryland
Coordinates:39.17N,76.37W

The textbox began to flicker and before I could register what was happening, it faded to an outlined shadow.

I was back at the map of the D.C area with two bright blinking red bubbles and one fading pink that decided to sputter to a tired stop and disappear. At least I remembered seeing Baltimore, Maryland.

I felt Alejandro's temperate hand press at my back, gently reminding me he was still there. I closed the GPS in my head and saw I was still connected to Sam through the prototype, but our connection had timed out. I was grateful the disturbing words that flashed diagonal across Doctor Finway's information the day he died, didn't find their way to her file.

"Sam's in Baltimore, Maryland," I said. Before he could ask a question, I continued, "That's all I know—Sorry." I dropped my chin to my chest and broke eye contact with him. I didn't see the point in explaining. Besides, I still had a hard time talking through my swollen lips. I pulled the comforter from my legs, the muscles across my shoulders and down the front of my chest reacted to the sharp ripping pain that followed. Alejandro saw my face writhe with despair and reached over to grab my hand.

"Wait, let me help you. Please." He held out his hands and slid them around me, strong, secure and warm. I quivered as they found the sore parts of my body. I watched him crumble from guilt as he looked at me.

"I feel a lot better now." I lied, looking into his worn eyes. I felt his muscles tighten as he started to lift me from the bed. My body rejected his attempt and began to shake.

"Are you cold? Let me get you something to warm you." My weight pressed back onto the bed, he was letting me go. I interrupted his motion, grabbing him tighter.

"No, don't go. I'm okay." I was desperate to stop my body from betraying me. He pulled close anchoring my chest against his, lifting me from the bed. My fingers drained white from clinging to him. His sweet smell captivated me as it filled my lungs. His moist lament eyes stared unblinking into mine.

"I'm sorry I hurt you. Sorry you had to experience that," he whispered. His eyes closed heavy trying not to get lost in a complicated despair. I pushed my hand to his face, he turned pressing his mouth to my palm. I desperately wished he could kiss me, rush the sparks he produced that ebbed deep in the locked away corner of my soul. Allow his lips to penetrate the shadows of dark demons craving to be tamed to slight imps. That's where we should've been. Instead, he pushed his lips to my forehead and softly warmed the deep worry lines that began to have a permanent place on my face. My body was broken, trying to heal from the damage Alejandro unwillingly caused me. I ached to be with him like we were before. I needed him to want me, to love me. But the way I was now, I was afraid my body wasn't going to trust him ever again. I got him back, God answered the one prayer I needed him too and now how can I ask for something else? A trust, an unabashed love we had before Marshall got a hold of me.

"Where am I taking you?" His lips brushed my eyebrows, his words quietly tangled in my hair as they found my ear.

"Bathroom." I pointed my silken pale red hand down the hall. I needed to get to the best place to contact Roger. He had to know something about Samantha; maybe he was able to see where she was using his prototype. Still he left, hurried along by his vision of Alejandro falling to his knees. Roger witnessed the passion between Alejandro and me and it must have devastated him. I couldn't do that to him again. The bathroom seemed to be the best choice to keep it private and between just Roger and I.

Alejandro supported me to the bathroom, his expression riddle with guilt as I shut the door behind me. I wish I could take it away, bury it in the past so we could regain our future. I pushed on the faucet and let the cold water run strong while I contacted Roger with my prototype. The sound of the water running in the sink felt normal. I thought my way to connecting with Roger. I was getting pretty good at proto-telepathy. We connected, however; he waited to say anything.

"Roger? I need to talk to you. Roger?" I felt like I was talking to an answer machine. The EQ bounced with every word I said and every breath he took as he punished me with silence.

"Please, Rog, answer me, I found out about Sam and where she is." Nothing still; only his breath caused the EQ to dance. I knew what he wanted me to do.

"Wish we wouldn't waste any more time, Sam is in trouble—she really needs you." I felt my heart wallop with anger as he still refrained from speaking. Something snapped inside of me. I knew I shouldn't have conceded to his silent treatment, but I had run out of ideas to get him to talk.

"You know, Roger, I am not going to apologize for meeting someone and falling in love with him. If you want to be a part of my life ... you're just going to have to deal with it. Don't make me choose ... I don't think you'll like the outcome." I had every intention to disconnect, when I heard him clear his throat.

*"Where is she?"* Dry words, belonging in a desert, climbed out uncomfortable from inside his head, blasting away the mirage he worked hard to create. I understood, focus on Sam and forget the rest. I can do that. I'm a pro at redirecting. I've done it for so long that it was second nature to me.

"She's in Baltimore, Maryland. That's all I got before her GPS bubble disappeared." I made my voice uneventful.

*"Bubble disappeared? How many were on the grid?"*

"Three—Sam, you, me. There was something strange before her GPS bubble was gone. It went from red to pink."

*"Was she able to talk?"*

"No, she couldn't communicate in anyway; mentally or physically. Like something was blocking her."

He took a group of long methodical breaths. I visualized questions swirling around his head, waiting to be answered as he exhaled.

*"Sounds like Marshall's disabled her prototype. We need to get to her. We don't have much time. The prototype evolves with the body, any long periods of disengagement, could cause irreversible damage."*

I tried to grasp what he was telling me. *Prototype evolves with the body – disengagement – irreversible damage.* Everything around me started to spin; my mind was searching for the definitions that usually came so easy to me. I knew in my mind what he said, but I just didn't really hear it. They skate around the truth until they'd get you to admit what you are willing to do for them.

Marshall's words set cruel in my gut. *Pain you'll know forever – the prototype in your head. Pain – forever – in your head.* I began to understand his and Marshall's encrypted words, almost like an out of body experience. This can't be true ... this can't be my fate. Bile began to swell in the back of my throat.

"I want to meet you. Take this prototype out of my head now!" I demanded. I needed him to answer my demands now. I wanted to hear him tell me. Tell what he did to me.

*"I can't, Lauren,"* he mumbled. I could tell he was holding something back.

"Sure you can, just come back here." I pushed my hands into the running water; the cool bubbles clung to my skin trying to clear away the insecurities of the day.

"*You don't understand, Lauren, I can't!*" he exclaimed. His words triggered my heart to hammer beats of despondency rough against my chest.

"I know it hasn't been two weeks, but—"

"*It's not about the two weeks — Don't you hear me? — Listen to what I'm saying — I can't take it out.*" He paused, I was silent and processing what he was saying when he finished his sentence. "*Ever — I will never be able to remove the prototype from your head — Never!*" He sounded pained, almost cruel, pushing his results of a test run I never asked for.

I felt my eyes roll up into darkness; the bathroom began to spin in my realization as my body fell to the floor. I must have hit it hard enough for Alejandro to hear.

**twenty-five**

I felt the something thrust across my back. Alejandro was pushing the door open. The skin on my arms stuck to the tile squeaking, as my body slid toward the tub. The urgency of his Latin dialect was provocative. Shivers didn't come close to describe how my body reacted when he said my name. He reached his hand down to my exposed side, balancing his fervent hand weightless in the curve of my waist. His long warm fingers pressed into my skin, his opposite hand cleared the metallic wet strands of hair from in front of my eyes.

"Lauren — what happened — can you hear me?"

I could hear him, but couldn't answer; I wished my throat was ripped from my body, I willed every organ in my body to malfunction. I rolled to my back, his hand slid to my stomach. I opened my eyes and watched his shoulder bounce up and back, not recognizing the motion until I became aware I was sobbing and his hand was moving with the muscles of my torment.

"Breathe, please just breathe. I'm here to help you. I need to hear your words. What happened?"

"Forever. *For fucking ever!*" I hollered.

"What? What are you saying?" Both of his hands cradled the contours of my cheeks. "Lauren, please baby, what's forever?"

"They knew it was permanent." Tears invaded my eyes as his thumbs wiped my cheeks dry. I saw in his face he started to connect the words and understand what I was saying.

"Who knew? Roger? Marshall?" His eyes narrowed, his jaw line pronounced while his lips pulled tight across his clenched teeth. I couldn't stop the automatic gasps for air that were inconvenient and rhythmic as they took over my body every time I tried to answer him.

"Y—s, they didididdd. This thi—g in my head is foreevvver." My body quaked, I was sobbing again. I was served a death sentence because there is no way in hell I am living like this … never.

He pulled me to his chest my face snug in his collarbone, I could taste his scent. His hands tightened around my back and in one motion, I was on my feet, embracing him.

"You're with me now, *mi dama*, I'll keep you safe." His hands pressed into my back making wide circles trying to soothe the awful untamed raw emotion that relapsed over and over in my body.

"Am I?" My eyelashes clung, melting with tears while I asked my question.

Two small words that I was supposed to identify with now, I am, even if I didn't know what *I* was.

"How am I safe? How can you save me Alejandro … you have no idea what this is this constant disease eating away at your humanity everyday … every fucking day, another piece of my soul, my humanity traded for what? *For what?*" I was uncontrollably shaking, falling deeper into the darkness that I have spent days trying to climb out of.

"Lauren, I will do whatever it takes to keep you safe. I won't let anything happen to you." His body surrounded me tight in a protective cocoon.

"It's too late, there's nothing you can do now." My body fell limp in his embrace. My eyes closed, my face replanted into his collarbone and I bawled uncontrollably against him as this huge bulge of regret kept tangling itself around what little humanity I had left in my heart. I wish Alejandro would have killed me when he pushed the gun toward Marshall … I shouldn't be here … I don't want to belong here anymore … not like this, it wasn't fair to Alejandro. My front door swung open and his body stiffened, pulling me tighter as I heard a growl pool in his chest. Immediately I recognized the voice that shouted my name, it was Roger. My head still buried in Alejandro's chest, I felt Alejandro take a deep breath.

"You — what did you do to her?" Still holding me tight, I felt my body raise and lower with his words.

"Listen, I need to speak to Lauren, alone." I visualized his hands out palms facing us, as if to say he won't hurt me. Too late; Alejandro held me even tighter, if at all possible.

"No, you won't. You have something to say to her, you have to get through me first." Alejandro readjusted his arms around me, tightening even more.

"This is between Lauren and me. You have nothing to do with this." I heard him take a breath and continue, "Lauren, you and I have a lot to talk about." His words twisted their way to my head.

"I don't think you understand me. She isn't going to be alone with you—ever again." My head still buried deep in his certitude. "So if you need to speak to her, you will do it through me." I felt Alejandro's hand slide up and off my back.

"Don't do this, I'm sorry. I didn't think about the repercussions of the prototype—with you. I didn't want to lose you. I should've thought about your feelings and I'm sorry. Lauren, look at me!" Desperation saturated his voice.

I didn't like what he was saying. I pushed my face deeper into Alejandro's chest and refreshed my grip around his waist. I wasn't ready to see him, to face the person who has altered my life forever.

"You need to leave. Get out of here." Alejandro sensed my body's rejection of Roger's words.

I felt him loosen his grip and lean me back from his solace. My arms still trying to pull him close, cold air filled the gapping space between us. His warm fingers caught my chin pulling my head to look at him as he whispered to me.

"I want you to go to your room. I will be there shortly." His eyes radiated deep green with flecks of brown. I tried to say something; he closed his eyes, dropped his head down and nudged my body to move away toward my bedroom. His stance was protective and demanding. I started to limp my way to my room, not making eye contact with Roger, when he spat desperate words toward me.

"Please look at me. I need you to listen to me. Lauren, please stop. You have to understand, you're the only one that can help me save Sam."

I stopped walking. Alejandro turned to me, motioning me to continue on.

"You understand—Sam needs us."

"Don't play her or me. If you know where Sam is, tell us now," Alejandro seethed.

"So you can swoop in and save her? Be the hero? Hurt her like you hurt, Lauren—no."

Alejandro straightened and began to approach Roger.

"Stop!" Pain shot across my swollen mouth and up through my nose. I slowly made eye contact with Roger. His eyes sunk, checks gaunt, and hair completely disarrayed, he looked awful. I wasn't willing to sacrifice anymore of myself or Sam. I am done being Roger's experiment.

"Alejandro, stop. Roger, you have done nothing for me or Sam. I trusted you. I loved you like a brother. You used me, and for what?" I felt the anguish well in my chest and catapult up my throat. I tried to hold back the tears and anger; stand strong as my body reacted to it. I couldn't, my eyes lost the fight with my feelings and I broke down in tears. Roger reacted and pushed his hands out to me.

I forced a word through my breakdown, hardly audible as I moved my body back from his advances. My hand pushed out to stop him. I didn't what him touching me, telling me thickened lies with false information. To me, he wasn't with me anymore, which made him nothing more than someone to be leery of.

"No."

Alejandro grabbed me and reached out, signaling him to stop.

"I didn't use you, Lauren. I didn't think I was. I wanted to keep you close to me. I love you—I've always loved you." Roger's words pierced my eardrums.

"Stop! I can't hear this. It's all bullshit, Roger! If you loved me, you wouldn't have done it. Nobody in their right mind would have done what you did. You wanted to control me. This isn't about love … what you did wasn't about love. Well, you lose—you lose." I looked him in the eyes, made sure he could see the abhorrence he created in my soul for him.

All at once it became too much. Something I couldn't squelch in my body rose up, some animalistic tendency took over and I leapt at him with all my strength. My arm broke free from Alejandro's grip and I swung making contact with the side of Roger's face. His glasses flew across the room and his head pitched low from the force. I pulled, trying to get free from Alejandro knowing if I wasn't hurt I would've been able to. I wouldn't have stopped hitting Roger until he hurt as bad as I did, but I didn't. I stood breathing heavy waiting for him to respond. Seething as the devastation pours into my thoughts, into my life, into every cell of my body. I was nothing more than a fucking experiment to Roger.

"Someday you will see that my intentions were honorable. Someday you will see it as a gift," Roger murmured.

"A gift? This isn't a gift! It's the worst kind of curse next to hell! You tell me the gift in me knowing I'm going to die tomorrow? What about that fact Roger? Picked to die by asphyxiation December sixth, two thousand thirteen! That's right I accessed the Langley file."

He looked at me like he had seen the devil himself.

"Yeah, I saw it all … I saw the file in that program you created with your prototype, the same file that said Doctor Finway committed suicide, and popped up with locks on yours and Marshalls information. The same file that recorded people's death years in advance. Was it you who marked me to die? Tell me you at least honored our friendship that much, because to think that some random fuck decided my fate would really piss me off."

He was frozen. Unable to answer my rant, he never knew I could access that file. *Don't trust anyone.*

The words of Doctor Finway flashed through my head.

"Lauren, that is a data-driven software. It's nothing more than a cross reference for the government. You plug in the information and it searches death certificates and replaces information. You didn't think the prototype was going to kill you?"

"Get out! Get the fuck out! I don't believe you—Get the hell out of my house!" I pulled Alejandro with me as he tried to hold me back.

"You heard her—leave now." Alejandro's voice rang over me.

Roger reached down picked up his glasses looked back at me and grudgingly walked out the front door.

I swung around and grabbed Alejandro around the neck. He pulled me again into his chest his arms wrapped tight around my back. For now I just wanted to be okay, normal, live my life like any other average person; even if it was only for one more day.

Roger didn't wait; he immediately tried to contact me. His name appeared in my right eye as Alejandro held me tight against his chest. Last thing I wanted to do was to talk to Roger. I hated him. Hated everything he stood for. He betrayed me, fed me to the wolves and had no intention to save me when they devoured me inch by inch. He was worse than Marshall. At least I knew Marshall was using me ... but, Roger, he sneaked into my heart ... plotted for our lives to use me ... Maybe our whole friendship was a lie, faked so he could have a guinea pig to test his shit out on. The devastation he caused me and Samantha, and even cost Doctor Finway his life! What excuse could he possibly come up with that would justify what he has done to all of us? The pit of my stomach churned as I reluctantly, accepted his connection and waited to hear what lies he was going to plant in my head.

*"Lauren, look I didn't want to have to talk to you this way, but you left me no choice. I have to tell you what is going on with the prototype, Marshall, Sam and the CIA."* Alejandro felt my back straighten in his arms.

"Are you okay?" Alejandro pulled me back from his body.

"Yeah, I think I should sit down."

"Let me help you." He grabbed my arm and helped me sit down.

"Do you think you could get me a glass of water from the kitchen?" I asked as I mentally prepared to engage in proto-telepathy with Roger. I watched as Alejandro left the living room.

"Okay, you got my attention; start talking," I stated out loud.

I heard Alejandro ask something from the kitchen.

"No, just talking to myself. Glasses are in the cabinet above the sink." I hated doing this, but it was the only way I would find out what string Roger had tied between Samantha and my freedom.

*"The prototype may seem like a curse right now, burdened with abilities that are life changing, I won't*

*argue that, but I want you to understand what I gave you."* Roger sounded proud.

My skin began to crawl; I couldn't believe what I was hearing.

*"What did you give me? I want to hear how much this is going to make my life better. Please, I'm waiting."*

*"Lauren, I gave you the newest prototype. You can control your body, your senses, desires, wants and even needs. You have the ability to learn and retain anything you read, see and study. Your prototype has a downloadable upgrade. As it keeps evolving I can upgrade it half the time. You'll be free from viruses, computer or organic. It is self healing and has programmable resistance to foreign germ warfare. You already know you have the ability to communicate to other prototypes, you can connect with other computers, hardwired or wireless-undetected,"* he spoke quickly.

Alejandro brought back my glass of water. Ice cubes floated, I was grateful, it was starting to get real warm in my family room. I thanked him and drank it down quickly. His eyes widened and I handed the glass back to him.

"Could you please get me another glass of water? I'm so thirsty." He bent down cupped his hand around the back of my head and kissed me on the top of my forehead.

I froze, his lips on my skin was so refreshing.

*Why was I giving Roger the time of day to fill my head, when I had Alejandro with me?*

Questions swirled ruthless in my head but one kept fighting to the surface. I collected my thoughts and asked him.

*"Why did I get hurt when I was in Marshall's head?"*

It was painful to get the words to transfer to Roger's prototype. I didn't want to go back there. Didn't want to remember what that felt like. I waited—no answer.

Alejandro returned with my glass filled to the top. New ice cubes floating pushing to the top one against the other. I knew what that felt like, to be on the bottom trying to push through to the top to see, breath, keep from melting down. I met Alejandro's eyes and told him thank you as I pushed my finger into the water trying to let the lower cubes experience the top.

Roger began to answer my thought I sent to him. At the same time Alejandro sat next to me putting his arm across my lap to rest his hand on my knee I saw the cuts and abrasions from the vicious experience I had with him this morning.

*The only thing that makes sense is all the other times when you were in Marshall's and my head you were watching recordings not live events taking place. This time with Marshall, you were in his head as the fight was taking place. You got hurt because you chose the wrong person at the wrong time.*

*I didn't choose him, he contacted me.*

I sent him my last comment. He didn't even wait for me to finish and he was talking again.

*He used a glitch in the prototype I discovered months earlier. I found that experiences can be shared between two prototyped subjects as they are happening. I thought it was just recordings — I was wrong. You've heard about twins — one twin gets hit across the face; the other twin gets the bruise. It's the same premise. Marshall called Alejandro to come over early today, knowing that he would be able to lock you in his head — knowing that you would feel everything Alejandro did to him. It all started when Marshall decided to cut Alejandro out of the prototype contract. Then he blackmailed me into installing the newest prototype in your head — he threatened me if I didn't do it — he'd expose me to the CIA. Tell them about all the work I had done with Grayson Industries. It was like he lost his mind. He tried to remove the prototype from Doctor Finway's head and killed him. Then he tried to disable it in Sam's head and well, you see how that went, but when he threatened to kill you, that was the last straw.*

I felt my body tighten and I just couldn't hear anymore. I felt like I was going to throw up. I needed to process what information he gave me. I disconnected with Roger. I didn't say goodbye; didn't acknowledge him; I was done and needed to give my focus to the man sitting next to me. I've wasted enough time and we still needed to find Sam.

Alejandro pulled his hand off my knee took my water and set it down on the table before he pulled me close to talk.

"I need to tell you something." His eyes started to glisten with grief.

I didn't know if I could handle anything else today. My skin twitched with urgent messages to my brain.

*"Don't let him go home tonight. Whatever he needs to tell you, don't let him out of your sight."*

"What is it?" I asked pushing my hand to his chest his heart beating fast through his silk button up shirt. With every beat my hand read his fear of my reaction. I put my hand to the side of his face, he tensed with my touch. I knew he needed to talk about what happened this morning.

"I want to be honest with you. That is important to me." Alejandro grabbed my hand in his huge strong grip, brought it to his lips and pressed firm to his heart as he continued to talk. "I need you to know that you're important to me." I watched him as he struggled to get the right words out. It was heartbreaking. I couldn't take it. My body was aching to get through this. I took a deep breath and told him what I thought he wanted me to know.

"Is this about Marshall? I understand why you did it. I was there, I heard what he said and I felt the words come from his mouth. I wish there was some way I could've stopped him from hurting you. I'm sorry," I whispered before I pushed into his chest, pushing so hard he stumbled back. I looked up into his face and saw the same teenage boy in the picture in front of the movie theater and the broken man standing in front of Marshall as he taunted him. I knew the look already. It was the same one he gave me when he left me in California.

"I killed Marshall. Soon the authorities are going to come looking for me. We don't have much time, maybe a day. It might just be enough time to find Sam."

I wanted to grab him, not let him out of my sight, but I couldn't do that, so I did the next best thing, I offered to go with him to Maryland.

# twenty-six

It was four in the afternoon and I was exhausted. I wished I had more time. I wanted to rest, my body ached, my mind was fuzzy and I was going to have to go back to the CIA in a couple of days. Some vacation this week turned out to be. I've lived more lifetimes in the last six days than I ever did in my entire life. I sauntered my way through the kitchen pulled open the garage door and reached for the keys on the hook I installed years ago to keep from misplacing them. I expected the door to drop against my back instead I felt Alejandro run his hand up and over my shoulder battling to grab the keys from me. It was strange to misplace the habit of the door hitting me in the back.

"I'll drive, you point." He passed me, rushed to the passenger's door, and held it open. His hand guided me to sit as he waited for me to buckle my seat belt. Once he saw I was compliant, he shut my door and entered the driver's side of the car.

"Baltimore, Maryland?" he asked.

"Yeah, that's where my GPS indicated she was before it malfunctioned and her location basically disappeared."

"You don't know where she is exactly?" He unbuttoned the top couple of buttons on his silk shirt.

"Not exactly — but I did see her coordinates and I should be able to plug in those numbers to the comput — prototype. We are a little over an hour away. Head west, you'll want to get on the four ninety five north." My voice broke off. I tried to keep from yawning, but my body wouldn't listen.

"Close your eyes. Once I get closer I'll need your help." He patted my knee softly reassuring me of his competence in driving this area. I forgot he used to live on the east coast.

"Thanks, but I want to stay up with you. Talk to me, keep me awake." My eyes hung at half mass, I could hardly make out his features, but I was determined to stay awake for him, for me. I wanted to live in that place where I could feel normal again.

"Tell me something about yourself," I rambled as he drove.

"What do you want to know?" He pulled his hand off the wheel and ran it through his jet black hair. Something I noticed he did when he was apprehensive.

"Favorite color?"

"Blue. You?"

"Green. Favorite time of day?"

"Early morning. Yours?"

"Same. What did you dream about being when you were a little boy?"

"A policeman. What about you?"

"President." I felt my eyes stare at the clock on the dash long enough to become blurry, looking straight through it, not blinking. My mind tilted becoming lost in the memory of my childhood dreams.

"I was ambitious enough to change the world. Or so I thought."

Silence filled the gap of time it took me to swallow and blink my stare loose from the flash memory of my silly childhood dreams. I had to know everything about him. Even things I didn't want to.

"Did you know that Marshall threatened Roger into installing the prototype into my head?" His slight Adam's apple bounced hard as he swallowed.

"No, I didn't know Marshall threatened him." His lips hardly moved as he spoke. I could tell he wasn't telling me everything. He was very careful with his answer.

"How long have you known about the prototype?" I stared at him, watching for his expressions to change. Praying with every cell in my body he would give me the answers I wanted to hear. He turned to look at me. I watched as his eyes began to answer my question.

"A while." He looked away refocusing on driving. Silence between us became thick before he continued, "Marshall, told me about it four months ago. I was looking to deal with another company from Japan. They had a similar technology but were still six months off from having a working prototype. About a week and a half ago Marshall contacted me, told me he had a prototype installed and ready for me to see." His head lowered and I watched his eyes fix to the speedometer waiting for my reaction.

"That's when Marshall called me. I fell for it, what an idiot!" I slammed my hand down on the dash pain shot up my wrist to my elbow. Alejandro's head bounced back looking to see if I was hurt. His body language indicated he had more that he wasn't telling me.

"The day he called me I flew out here. He and Roger met with me. I was impressed by the prototype. It did things that I never thought existed. Abilities way beyond I'd expected. We spent the day going over the formalities of the contract.

By the time we were done it was pretty late so Roger and I went out for drinks—a kind of celebration, for our deal. Roger drank way too much, I knew I shouldn't have let him ramble, but he wouldn't stop going on about this woman he worked with. How beautiful and brilliant she was. So naturally the more he said about her, the more I wanted to know. He must've sensed my interest because he wouldn't tell me her name. I needed to know who he was talking about, still he wouldn't budge. I left D.C the next morning." Alejandro shifted his eyes back and forth from driving to me and back. "She kept circling in my thoughts and I just couldn't shake her. Even when I knew I should be focusing on my business, she'd just keep coming back into my mind.

When Marshall told me he was coming to California, I couldn't help myself; I asked him to bring the woman." He pulled the car over as he finished his confession. I wanted to believe it was honorable, but frankly, I was scared.

"With every ounce of my honor, I didn't know the prototype was permanent. It was, in my mind, just the perfect excuse to finally meet you."

I didn't want to believe what he was saying.

"You told Marshall to install it in my head? What the hell is wrong with you guys? Do you honestly think I was going to be happy?"

"No, it wasn't like that. I told him to bring you to California. I didn't tell him to install that thing in your head. I just needed to see you." He looked at me with those familiar broken eyes. I couldn't fix it this time. He was the catalyst that brought me to where I was now. Forever altered, not natural, and never the same.

"I didn't ask for any of this. I didn't need this. All I wanted was to be a good CIA agent and do some insignificant side jobs for Marshall. Now I am broken and changed into something I don't understand. Something foreign, computer generated — something unnatural." My eyes blurred I didn't want to see anything anymore; I didn't want to live in the shadows of what I was supposed to be. I ached all over and it had nothing to do with the technology Roger put in my head ... I have be betrayed by everyone I've ever loved or trusted.

"Please Lauren. Don't say that—you gotta believe me—I'm telling you the truth—I don't want to lose you over this. I will fight for you. Please believe me." He tried to reach over and touch me. I jerked back. I didn't want him to touch me. I didn't want to own this hell anymore. I wanted to go back to my old life, my life before Marshall, before Roger, before Alejandro. I was done being stifled by their deviance; done with people damaging me by their own narcissistic desires.

My mind burnt with memories of shadows and shades of what I thought were real emotions. I was an empty shell waiting to be collected by my own visions of a superhero that didn't exist.

We both sat there for a soundless moment. Unable to repair the damage inflicted by words and events we never had any control over.

"Alejandro? Why me? You're a successful, smart, gorgeous man who could have anyone you want. Why are you willing to fight so hard for me? With this *thing* in my head?" My voice cracked, interrupted by my surging grief.

"I was intrigued the moment Roger talked about you. You don't see it? When I met you, felt your energy, our chemistry. You're amazingly beautiful, incredibly smart, and uncompromisingly vigilant. I've never met someone that was so protective and loyal. I want to be a part of that. No matter how small—give me that chance." I watched his eyes shrink to small specks of hope. His slight smile covering his teeth. I wanted to be that to him ... I wanted to make him my life ... but how can I? How can I trust?

"I want to believe you. In my heart I ache to be with you, my mind crusades for you, but the space that balances in between keeps telling me to run. I don't know if I can let that go." I didn't look at him when I answered.

I heard the car door close and when I looked up he was gone. I didn't know where he went until I saw him on standing outside my side of the car. Startled, I tried to push the lock down but missed. The door swung open and he was next to me. I wanted so badly to hate him, but I couldn't. I felt his hand quickly move to my seatbelt and force it to release. Fear mounted heavy in my chest. He pushed his body into the car, pinning me down in the seat. His upper body was pressing so strong against me. He lifted my legs out and pulled me outside the car. I didn't want to stop him ... deep down I wanted this. I wanted him to fight hard for me. I wanted to see if he was as honorable as he claimed to be. His hands cupped my jaw, holding my head still, making sure I was looking him in the eyes as he spoke.

"Listen to your heart and your mind. Let me work on the space in between. I will do whatever it takes. Tell me, will you let me in again?" He kissed me, pain churned across my mouth, but I didn't care, he tasted better than ever before. Pulling me into his body softer than he had ever before, his hands traced delicately across my back. The heat of his hands seared him into my skin.

"I'm so twisted up by you that I can't even find a way to breathe when you aren't with me. I love you, mi dama." His breath rolled across my flesh, before he kissed the sacred space behind my ear, drowning me in his scent. My most intimate spaces ached for him.

"I'll be your air ... I love you, Alejandro," I breathed as I felt his kiss leave a new ending to our story while creating a new page I'm willing to turn.

I felt the influence of my desires percolate in my head soaking my whole body with the rich taste of his vulnerability. I didn't care how dangerous he could be or how much he knew about the prototype. I wanted him entirely, every single part of him, his pain, his love, his fear, and his passion. I pushed my arms around him, nudged my forehead against his chin as I lifted to my toes to taste his lips sweetly against mine again. Our tongues skated the edges and danced together with the silent promises we were making. I pressed hard into him, hoping I'd melt into his chest and we'd be able to get back to that place where we were supposed to be one. He pushed me up against the car, desire swelled between us and my body spoke volumes ... he knew my answer.

twenty-seven

We were almost to Baltimore. Including our unscheduled stop on the side of the road, we were going to be in the city before six. All things considered, Alejandro was making excellent time.

I didn't ask questions to pass the awkward silence that filled the space between us. I decided it was better spent trying to find Samantha and where she was being held captive. I focused on the blinking cursor in the lower part of my right eye and spoke her name out loud. I hated this thing in my head. The prototype and everything about it signified betrayal, deceit and pure evil. Unfortunately, I was reliant upon it to help me find her. I watched as Sam's information appeared before my eyes and focused on the GPS icon causing it to glow bright. I navigated through the countries and came to our locations. I saw two bright red blinking bubbles. I assumed the one just entering Baltimore was me because it was pinpoint accurate on my location. The other one was north of us closer to the outskirts of Baltimore. I focused on the bubble and the textbox exploded open with all the information for Roger Clarke.

"Roger's location is the same as Sam's. The coordinates are exactly the same. I can't believe this, he must be with her," I shrieked.

"Well, that is a good thing right?" I could hear Alejandro's voice, but I still was looking at the GPS screen filling both of my eyes.

"I don't know." Before I finished answering him I minimized the GPS program and opened Roger's file in my eyes. I spoke his name out loud, attempting to contact him. I could feel Alejandro's glare burn through the side of my face. He never said a word.

Mumbled words pushed their way from my mouth, updating Alejandro to what only I could see.

"He isn't accepting my request. Come on, Roger. Answer me—please." I toggled between Roger's file and the GPS. I took the coordinates that filled the textbox, found the icon to connect to the internet and decided to take matters into my own hands. I did a search of his coordinates. I was numb as a harsh tingling reverberated and poured over the back of my head through my neck and down my spine.

"What is it? What do you see?" Alejandro asked.

"He's at a mental health hospital." Deflated but determined I searched encrypted files from the hospital. I might as well use this devilish thing in my head to find out what was going on.

"Okay, Sam, let's see if you are there," I said under my breath. "Are you a patient or is Roger?" I moved my eyes back and forth over the files, checking every access point that might lack the security software required to keep me out. "Bingo, there you are. Samantha Wilkins, brought in two days ago. Diagnosed with catatonic schizophrenia. Oh, no way. Symptoms observed, catatonic stupor, incoherent babbling, emotionally vacant. That can't be! Marshall institutionalized her? States here she's his wife. Claims no other relatives." My eyes were stinging; the desire to blink was hampered by the need for information. Without thinking, I pushed my index fingers into my tired eye sockets. Trying to use my lids as a barrier to rub in some relief, her information disappeared. I was looking out the window. I felt the car accelerate we were just minutes from the hospital.

*"Stop. Stay there!"* Roger's voice echoed in my head. My hands cupped my ears trying to stop the deafening words from inciting havoc in my head.

"Stop the car!" My lungs emptied and my throat burned as I screamed.

I was startled by Roger yelling at me in my head. *How did he do that? We weren't connected. I don't remember accepting his call.* I felt the car roll to a stop as I lowered my head to my lap. I couldn't imagine how I looked to Alejandro with my hands on my ears and screaming at the top of my lungs. "What's wrong?"

"Roger sees me; told me to stop."

"That's good, he can help us."

"No — not good. I wasn't connected to him."

"What?"

"I wasn't connected to him. He was able to get into my head without my permission, again!" The hate I felt earlier resurfaced instantly. As sure as I breathe or my heart beats, the hate I had for the prototype would never diminish.

*"Lauren, there's a coffee shop; it will be on your right side, a small shopping center. Meet me there. Don't go to the hospital,"* Roger barked loudly, unaware that I was seething at every word that came out of his mouth.

I didn't respond. I didn't want to go there with him. I just wanted to get Sam out of that hospital and Roger out of my head.

Alejandro spotted a Starbucks about three quarters of a mile from the hospital and pulled in. Roger's black Porsche Boxster was parked in front. My body teetered on the edge between hatred and hurt. I was ready to face Roger. I made the decision to cut him loose. I was done with his antics, done with his excuses. There was one last thing I had to do to be free of Grayson Industries, free of Roger. I was ready to continue my life with the man I loved. Alejandro pulled open my door and comfortably wrapped his arm around my waist. He paused, seeing waves of stress trounce the side of my face, he pulled me close and gave me a delicate kiss on my temple. The borough below my stomach purred, I was ready to be with him.

Roger was sitting in a secluded corner. His eyes wide, bouncing from one place to another like he was watching out for someone unexpected. His eyes froze on Alejandro. Roger's face checkered pale like he had seen a ghost. He adjusted his black-rimmed glasses across the bridge of his nose, something he'd do when he was irritated. I grabbed Alejandro's hand and pulled it to rest comfortably back around me. I wanted Roger to know I was with Alejandro. He stood as we approached, careful to make eye contact with us. I could tell he was preoccupied with something more than our relationship.

"Sit, we don't have any time." He pushed toward the middle of the table and spoke in a guarded whisper. I watched his head and followed his eyes as they darted around the room. "The CIA was at my house. They know about the prototype, know about Marshall's contracts with us. Lauren, they know about everything." His voice rose to an elevated low rumble. I watched as beads of sweat formed pathways to mingle with his dark brown eyebrows. His hand wiped at his brow as he continued. My mind clicked, every move, every word, every reaction played back to me in slow motion. I felt my eyes blink and I watched his lips move as his words came bursting from him slowly.

"Lauren, they want you — they know you have the prototype installed in your head. We can't let them get to you."

His words swam around my head as I realized he was talking about the CIA; I knew it would just be a matter of time before they were going to find out. I should have expected he was going to throw me to the sharks ... the feeding frenzy was going to begin to find me.

"*We*—what in the hell do you mean we? There is no *we*. Not only did you install this thing in my head forever, now you're telling me that I've lost my job with the CIA? How much more can you fuck up my life, Roger? Answer me that? How much more?" My blood boiled through my veins as I thought about how much Roger has used me, disposed of me taken everything I once was and striped me to nothing more than a weapon. I was seething when I stood up to leave. Alejandro pulled me to his chest and whispered for me to sit. I felt his body tense, using all his might to hold me still. I didn't move for several long seconds. I lowered myself into the hard plastic chair, facing the devil himself.

"I know there is nothing I could say to make this okay. I know that. I'm sorry; didn't know you would be the subject of a CIA manhunt." Roger's lame attempt to apologize. "But there's more you need to know." His hands damp and magnified from the sweat he kept wiping off his brow. I prayed he wasn't going to reach out to me.

I felt my body rock back and forth in rhythm with the words that poured from my mouth. "You're right, there is nothing you can say. Nothing you can do to change what you took from me. My freedom—my rights—my choice—*all gone*! So don't sit in front of me and tell me you are sorry—I don't accept." I shot up; my body held the full intention of escaping to the bathroom, but Alejandro grabbed me and

315

wrapped his arms around me again. I wasn't going anywhere.

"I won't let anything happen to you. Trust me." His voice pressed into my ear. Goosebumps shot across my skin as he moved the hair from my face and pressed his lips to my cheek. For that brief moment I knew I was going to be okay.

We held each other. I longed for him to take me away. Put me on the same plane that housed all of the pain I so desperately wanted to abandon days earlier. I was tired of being used.

"Hear him out. I'll be right here next to you." His words comforted me. I loved the way his lips brushed my cold, wet cheek, warming it just enough.

"What else can you tell me that would justify any more time wasted with you?" I asked Roger.

His silence was profound. Nothing between us, not a whisper, he didn't even clear his throat.

"Just as I thought—you son of a bitch. Nothing you tell me will change what you took from me. The day you installed this thing in my head, you sealed my fate—you took my life." The corners of my mouth chapped with cracks of constant worry ached to be left alone. Roger earned a one-way ticket to hell and I was all too ready to cash it in. I pulled out of Alejandro's embrace ready to leave this whole story behind.

"They found Marshall, dead. Homicide, but we knew that." Roger frowned as he stared down Alejandro. Playing with words to control me again, I didn't bite. Alejandro shrugged his shoulders as he continued to keep me from leaving.

"The butler found his body. They have a positive identification on you." Roger pointed his bony finger at Alejandro. "The gardener saw you stumble from Marshall's house to your car. They know it was you," Roger said. A look of complete satisfaction covered his face.

"Well, then it will be the gardener's word against mine." Alejandro pulled me closer. I could feel his heart thrust the doubt away with every beat in his chest.

"They have you on the surveillance cameras coming and leaving his house." I thought I saw a slight smile of pleasure amass Roger's face. "Now it's just a matter of time."

Alejandro lifted his arm from around me and pushed himself close and his lips brushed my ear.

"I need to talk to Roger—alone. Please trust me." His words unraveled the tether of my heart. My breath lost its way to my lungs as I began to drown in the same isolated fear I knew so well. "Please, give me a moment alone with him."

Alejandro's eyes closed and his brows furrowed heavy and for that small space of time, I understood his need. I kissed him, tasted his worried lips quivering for the desire to turn back time. My glacial hands forced their way to the back of his head, tangling into his sharp black hair. His hands pressed secure against the sides of my face, I didn't want our kiss to end as he pulled his mouth from mine. We held to the tight space between us before he followed my silhouette, first kissing my forehead, then my nose and finishing at the space between my lower lip and the bend of my chin. I knew he was memorizing me; saying goodbye. I tossed a glare at Roger, before I walked out and I didn't look back. I had a plan, and it was going to give me exactly what I wanted.

I pushed the button on my keychain and unlocked the doors to my 2004 Volvo. I didn't have much time to waste so I got into the passenger's side and immediately pulled up Roger's file. I had reservations about what might happen, being in his head, but the benefits out-weighed the costs at this point. I needed to see what Alejandro was going to say so I entered into Roger's head. For the first time, I finally felt like I had some control of this fucking thing in my head.

Alejandro was sitting in front of me. The flavor of warm French Roast rolled down my throat as I felt the cup pull from my lips. I hated my coffee black, and now I remembered why. Engine oil would have been easier to swallow. Yuck!

My eyes, Roger's eyes, watched Alejandro take a pack of sugar and manipulate it to fold in half without breaking it open. I watched him as he worked out in his mind what he was going to say. His lips pursed as he scraped his hand across the table, pushing the loose specks of sugar onto the floor. Brushing his hands together, he shook his head trying to move his hair away from his eyes. He looked desperate, agitated ... but determined.

I wanted to feel my heart drop into the special place I created deep in my body, just for him. However, I wasn't seeing him with my own eyes; I was in a Roger's head. I felt Roger's jealously, anger and frustration and how his heart pounded hard in his chest. I felt his anticipation as he waited to hear what Alejandro had to say. I felt him wish Alejandro would just disappear. Go back to California ... leave me so Roger could have me back in his life.

"Roger, I know you really like Lauren — you love her. I can respect that. I see your commitment and understand why you crave what she's not willing to give you."

"You really don't know anything about me," Roger quipped.

Alejandro took a deep breath as he cracked his neck. He was being patient with Roger ... it made me wonder what he had up his sleeve.

"I know enough about you, Roger ... I want you to know this about me ... I will fight for her. I will do everything in my power to protect her. No matter who gets in my way." Alejandro narrowed his eyes to Roger, both of them staring down one another.

"Don't you think she'll need someone who can help her understand what she is becoming?" Roger cocked his head to one side; I felt his glasses shift on his face.

"If I didn't care deeply for Lauren and what she desires, I would have taken care of this situation a while ago. I can see even through her anger — she still cares for you." I watched his hands communicate his desires as they pushed and pointed to Roger.

I soaked in the words he spoke so honestly.

Roger sat silent, brooding in his anger for a moment before he responded.

"What about when the prototype changes her, makes her stronger, smarter, more evolved than you? How will you protect her then?" Roger asked, his confidence radiating across the table.

Alejandro shifted in his chair. I could tell the look in his eyes had nothing to do with being intimidated and everything to do with control.

"That's why I'm here. That's why I'm choosing to sit across from you and leave my ego checked at the door. I need you to install the prototype in my head." I watched Roger's eyes meet Alejandro's. Stunned by his words, Roger was speechless. Instantly, I screamed in Roger's head.

*Nooooooo, God no please no ... Roger ... please say no!*

Alejandro's request devastated me. I can't let him do this. I have to stop him! He doesn't get what it is about. Every waking hour is altered and changed forever. I love him too much to let him do this. I love him the way he is; I love him unadulterated by this damn prototype in my head.

"I don't—" Roger was saying as I backed out of his head. I was in my car again, and needed to get to Alejandro before Roger agreed to do it. I'll do everything possible to keep it out of anymore people's bodies. It's dangerous and unpredictable.

Thoughts spun in huge circles around in my head. I didn't want to imagine Alejandro with this evil in his body.

I pushed the car door open and sprinted to the front of the coffee shop. I threw open the glass door so hard that the edge crashed into a display of Christmas gifts. Everyone's head turned, but I didn't care. I needed to keep Alejandro from making one of the biggest mistakes of his life, as honorable as it may have seemed to him. He was the only normal in my life ... I couldn't lose that now.

## twenty-eight

My eyes darted to the hidden corner. Alejandro was standing looking at me. My feet struck determinedly against the brown speckled floor. I didn't care that people saw the unrefined emotion that flooded my body. Tears fell from my face, leaving traces across my red cheeks as they dropped and landed on my shirt. My arms swung forceful, my strides were twice as big as my normal walk, almost as though I wasn't touching the floor.

Our bodies collided, like two trains coming at full throttle, and he stumbled back. My eyes locked on his, confusion snatched his expression, trailed by concern. His eyes rapidly searching for what was wrong. He grabbed, pulled me in and held me tight, unaware of what I had seen. I was consumed by the worry in his body.

I pushed him away; a torrent of panic took hold of me as I hammered my fists across his chest. Hollow thuds echoed, filling the coffee shop. Nothing but tears and howls of regret escaped my shattered spirit.

"What is it? Lauren, what's wrong?" He wheezed as he held me against his chest.

"Don't do it, Alejandro — don't," I begged.

"Do what?" he asked.

I looked at him through my tear-soaked eyes. He struggled to see what I knew. His eyes grew wide and his face glowed white when he realized what I had done. What I saw when I entered Roger's head.

"Why did you do that? Lauren, that was my conversation with Roger, you had no right to enter his mind." Anger flitted in the back of his eyes. He stepped back leaving me standing alone. "You had no business in his head."

"Yes I did. Alejandro, you can't — you don't know what it does; the pain, the isolation, the loss of control. You really don't understand," I groused. I needed to stop him, control him, and make him see that I was right this time. We stood facing each other in the crowded Starbucks.

He looked around, moved closer to me and spoke through clenched teeth to make our conversation as private as possible. My eyes focused on his mouth.

"I understand a lot more than you think. I'm sorry you had no choice, but this is different. I am choosing to do this. I want this." His face pulled back and I saw how much determination raged in his eyes. I had to stop him and if I failed then at least I told him what life was like with it in my head.

"Alejandro, you won't have any thoughts that are your own. Controlled by a machine in your head is not a way to live your life. Roger will be able to access your most private thoughts. You gotta believe me. You will always be changing—always wondering what's next. Waiting for the other shoe to drop, always questioning what, in your body, will change this day or the next." I pulled at his hands, twisting them to hold my face. I hoped he felt the heat saturate my skin, the truth I secreted from every pore of my body. I needed him to feel how badly I wanted him to forget the idea of having the prototype installed in his head. He pressed his lips to my forehead and answered my rant.

"Look at me. No, stop and really look at me." He brought his hands to my chin, holding my face as he spoke. I watched his eyes glisten with anguish and desperation. I recognized an ache that I created by being something he wasn't. Something he was willing to sacrifice himself for so he wouldn't lose me. "I am a grown man capable of making my own decisions. I know the risks, I know the benefits." I adjusted my face to break the hold he had on me.

"Why is this so important to you? Why are you so insistent? If you felt anything for me you wouldn't—"

"I wish you could see how incredible you really are. How can I make you see? What is going to happen when you evolve to a point where I'm obsolete in your world? I have a selfish side, too. If it means putting the prototype in my head to keep up—then I'm all in." I couldn't breathe after he spoke. To imagine him obsolete in my world didn't exist. It wasn't an option; however, having the prototype installed in his head, wasn't an alternative either. He wasn't going to budge on his ideas and I wasn't going to give in anytime soon. We were at a stale mate, a crossroads that if either of us decided to turn someone would get hurt. So we barreled on, going forward because right now Samantha needed us.

I looked past Alejandro to Roger. He was rubbing his palms against the table, the cuffs of his dark yellow shirt folded off his wrists, quaked as they tangled with the edge. He was shuffling information around, using the prototype, his eyes bouncing from left to right and top to bottom in circles. Whose file was he rummaging through? I walked toward Roger without acknowledging Alejandro. I wanted to confront him. I knew he couldn't see me with the files open in his eyes. I could sit next to him and he still wouldn't know I was there. That's how deep the files absorbed your senses. It's a strange feeling when open files surrounded you, sound disappeared and all you could see, feel or hear was the files in your eyes.

I took advantage of his vulnerability and entered his head. I wanted to know what he was looking at. I wish I hadn't. I thought he would have been looking at Sam's files, trying to find where she was or what we were going to do to save her. No, instead he was in classified files from the CIA, files overflowing with information about me, my career, my education, and my associations. Lines of poignant dates in bold, scattered throughout the entire document. Photos I had never seen and no idea were taken popped open, cascading one on top of the other.

My head spun thick with every moment he was plotting to use me. The agreement to work for Marshall, the small jobs we did together, and the words he saved for me as his friend. All were lies, planted to use me. I swallowed trying to wet the back of my throat that went painfully dry. Uncontrolled questions wrapped in betrayal popped into my head, not expecting an answer. *Why was he doing this? Why my file not Sam's?*

*"I knew you would enter my head – just now and earlier today – I know when you're in here. Come on, Lauren, I've had this in my head for months, did you honestly think you would enter unnoticed?"* I took a deep consuming breath as he continued. *"I can detect any breech, any access. Unlike you, I have evolved for a longer period of time."*

Chills jerked my body and the palms of my hands became drenched. I was scared. A fear that was unexplainable. Not like the fear of the boogie man under my bed as a child, or the fear of bodily harm or even losing my life. It was a fear of no control. No way to stop this thing installed in my head. The unchallenged and unregulated power of the prototype had become incalculable.

My mind spun as he kept talking. *"There are applications I have installed in my prototype that have become independent self updaters, the same one's I will need to install in your head soon. It's the best intrusion detection system available. It recognizes security breaches and alerts you immediately. I made sure I have the best cryptographic and firewall software available. So, the next time you want to enter my head, knock first."*

My eyes cleared and suddenly I was staring across the room at a young girl with shoulder length brown curly hair that bounced as she reached across the counter. Her smile unable to hide even her lower teeth as she took drink orders from the line of people waiting for their daily caffeine infusion. Part of me envied her simple existence, whether it was true or not.

Without any warning, the muscles throughout my entire body burned with pain. Like poison saturated every fiber of my soft tissue starting at my neck and working its way down through my torso, arms and eventually my legs. Even as I stretched to release the ominous toxic energy, I felt my body giving in to a fever. I was a prisoner again, but this time possessed by something taking over my prototype and my body.

I remembered Roger telling me that with the prototype in my head I wouldn't get sick. My body was immune to organic or computer viruses. So why was this happening? I looked at Roger for an explanation. I must've looked healthy, no sweat dripping from my forehead or pale skin with sunken eyes. No evidence of the affliction on my outward appearance. I looked normal, while in my mind I was becoming sicker by the second. What was going on in my molecular structure? Why was I feeling this way and yet nobody could see it? I looked at Alejandro. He flashed a crooked smile as a reminder of our earlier conversation.

"Roger, something's wrong with me. I feel like I'm coming down with the flu." I felt my face flush and a sharp shooting pain behind my eyes. I don't remember the flu feeling like this, not so intense. I just wanted it to stop. My body gave up and I began to convulse as the chills worked from my core out. I watched the room enter a vacuum being sucked and twisted into my eyes. Instantly, my eyes rolled up into the back of my head and my body fell hard to the cold tile floor.

I woke up in the secluded corner of the coffee shop. Roger was typing on his laptop and Alejandro was holding me, my head resting on his lap. He pressed wet brown paper napkins to my forehead. He was saying something under his breath as my eyes started to focus.

"She's awake. Are you okay, Lauren? Do you know where you are?" Alejandro's hands cradled my head and rubbed the space between my ear and chin. I loved him touching me ... His hands so warm, his touch so delicate, I wish I could tell him how much I loved him.

"Alejandro, you must look into her eyes. Are there any red spots in her irises?" Roger was stressed and hurried. "I'm almost done configuring the upgrade that will stop the virus."

I looked at Alejandro, opened my eyes as wide as I could, I didn't speak, I couldn't. I tried to move my hands to touch his warm skin, I couldn't. My legs, the same, I was paralyzed. Visions of my life flashed so real in my head. I was in a wheelchair with a breathing tube attached to my throat. I closed my eyes, trying to blink away the image only to have it change to my body in a pine box coffin, alive but unable to tell anyone that I was. This had to stop. Tears crashed over my eyelids and tickled as they ran down the sides of my face into my ears. I couldn't reach up and wipe them away. Alejandro took his fingers and pushed the tears dry.

"No red spots in her irises. What does that mean?" Alejandro reported, his eyes glued to mine, ready to announce any change. "Good — the red spots means the virus corrupted her prototype. I needed to download the patch to the IDS she has and I never got a chance to. We still have time." I could hear the keys on his laptop click and bounce quickly as he worked to save my life.

"Sweetheart, don't cry — stay with me. Keep looking into my eyes." Alejandro' voice was filled with trepidation. "I'm right here."

I tried to speak. I wanted him to know that I loved him and didn't want this to be the end of us; whatever *this* was. I wasn't able to make a sound all I could do was blink as I watched his eyes fill with worry.

"Got it—here it is. Lauren, you have to access the file in the prototype that says updates. Once that's done, we can remotely download the patch." He turned toward me, staring into my eyes, making sure I understood.

I maneuvered my way to the file and had it open waiting for Roger to initiate the download. How was I going to tell them I was ready? I doubt Roger was going to enter my head to see, especially if I was truly infected with a virus that was attacking the operating system of my prototype. I frantically blinked my eyes to tell him I was ready. Hoping he understood my visual communication.

"You're ready?" he asked.

I closed my eyes tight and opened them several times, hoping he was able to make me okay again. My head trembled while Alejandro kept me secure on his lap. The smell of wet cement on a scorching hot summer day burnt deep in the back of my throat. Side effect of the virus, I had no idea, I wouldn't know until Roger downloaded the patch to fix it.

A dialogue box opened and all the anxiety was carried away by a huge wave of relief that crashed down hard on my soul. I clicked the last button to start the download and I watched the timeline fill to a green color. The names of the files flashed quickly in my eyes causing nausea with each change. I minimized the file in my vision and gazed up at Alejandro's worried expression. Wishing I could tell him that no matter what happens, I loved him. He rubbed my cheek and mouthed the same words back.

The patch finished downloading and a prompt popped up in my eyes asking me if I would like to restart the prototype. I didn't want to but knew I had to in order for my body to function again. I chose yes and prayed that it was going to work. I watched as Alejandro's face was swallowed by a black fog. He disappeared to nothing; a thick black nothing that made no sound, no smell of hot wet cement, nothing. Even the warm touch of my lover was gone. I was completely alone in the dark, unable to hear, see, smell and completely paralyzed.

# twenty-nine

My eyes felt like they were glued shut with rubber cement. I tried to open them only to feel the crust on my eyelashes fighting to keep them together. I pressed my fingertips at the base of my eyelids trying to scrape the gunk that held firm to my short thin lashes. It took several lengthy seconds to realize my arms moved, my hands clutched and released. I could feel the refreshing softness of sheets rub against my naked legs as I raked and bicycled to get the covers off. I wasn't paralyzed! My eyes were still stuck shut; it was strange when all I could visualize was the back corner of the coffee shop and Alejandro holding my head. I couldn't possibly be there anymore because I smelled sautéed garlic and onions. My fingers pried my eyes opened and finally I could see where I was.

The room was unfamiliar but incredible. Cream-colored walls wrapped with substantial elegant dark brown crown molding, and between the solid walnut head board were two oil paintings of the Baltimore harbor at sunset. Covering the sliding glass door were hammered satin and suede curtains that

332

alternated stripes in shades of dark brown to velvety tan. The room was breathtaking.

Roger stood over me. His tired eyes behind his glasses filled with satisfaction as he smiled and looked at me.

"Hi, welcome back," he said.

My eyes darted around the room, suspended confusion filled my mind.

"Where am I?" My throat, painfully dry, stung when I asked him.

"Baltimore Inn," he answered, pushing his glasses back up from the bridge of his nose.

"Why?"

"Your place isn't safe. I didn't want to take the chance of getting caught."

"Not safe? Caught?" My lungs burned as I brutally gulped a breath of air.

"Lauren, you've been passed out. We had to get you somewhere safe. Somewhere the CIA wouldn't find you." His eyes shift back and forth behind his black-rimmed glasses.

I could see he wasn't comfortable. He paced the room, the light brown carpet changed to dark under his feet. He crossed the room and sat in an elegant wingback chair. He bounced his legs nervously as he ran his hands up and down his black corduroy pants. I watched, mesmerized by the way his pants seemed to crease and fade with every stroke.

"Where's Alejandro? Sam?" I asked.

Roger stood up and crossed to the other side room, his way of avoiding a stressful topic. I asked again, "Where's Alejandro; were you able to get Sam?"

When he turned and faced me I knew he didn't get her and for that scratch of time, I was afraid he was going to tell me Alejandro left, again. Anxiety pulled the air from my lungs ... I couldn't breathe. Fear flicked its wicked tongue across my skin, inviting the lonely girl back.

"She— well, I couldn't—" He stumbled over his words. He was conveniently interrupted by someone coming into the hotel room.

Alejandro walked into the room; my train of thought broke free from Roger, from where I was and what I was asking. My body surged with that spine-tingling retreat that possessed me when he was in the room.

"You're awake—how do you feel, *mi dama*— okay?" Alejandro asked as he made his way to me, putting his treasures on the small table. His shirt was wrinkled and pulled loose out of his Levi's. His hair was unkempt and dark circles cradled his eyes. He looked like he hadn't slept in days. He bent down kissed my forehead then my cheek and last my lips. I liked it; a lot. He was warm, soft and delicious against my mouth.

"Yeah, I'm okay," I answered against his lips as I took a bottomless breath, tasting deep in the back of my throat his essence.

"Where's Sam? Did you get her?" As twisted I was up about liking her and hating her; there was a part of me that was very protective of her. She and I possessed something life-altering that no other women on the face of the Earth shared.

"Roger should tell you, he's the one that went there; I stayed here with you." His eyes broke from mine.

"I don't care who tells me. I just need to know." My breath escaped me, pressure rose into my chest and across my face. Roger cleared his throat and began to tell me in limited details what happened.

"You were out. I planned on your help to get Sam, but the virus was a little stronger than I had anticipated. So on Friday when Alejandro was here with you, I went to see how I could get Sam out of the mental hospital." He pushed his fingers behind his glasses rubbing his eyes before sliding his palms down across his cheeks. The stress permeated his body.

"How long was I out?" A twist of angst coiled into a knot low in my belly.

"Thirty-six hours—a day and a half." Roger was matter of fact with his answer. I assumed he thought about the mathematical probability of my surviving the virus.

"Lauren, you weren't alone—ever." Alejandro piped up.

"Sam?" I asked. My eyes locked on Roger, waiting for the rest of his story.

"I went to the hospital, told them I was her brother. I wanted to see her. Find out if she was okay." He paused, his eyes lowered to the floor. "She wasn't there."

"What do you mean, wasn't there?"

"Terence took her from the hospital. No sign of them anywhere, gone. The only thing we have is his signature and one eyewitness that can identify him."

"This is your fault, Roger! If you never stuck that thing in her head, she wouldn't—" I stopped from saying anymore.

"She wouldn't what?" he asked.

"She wouldn't be missing," I told him.

"Stop. This won't help her now." Alejandro broke the tension between us. "I know Terence, he's my employee. If he has her, I have to believe she's okay."

Roger walked to the other side of the room, mumbling under his breath.

"How do you know? What if Marshall told him to finish her off? One last thing before he died. Let me see into your memories, Roger." My eyes followed him.

"No," he and Alejandro answered in unison.

"Why? Are you afraid of what I might see?" I asked.

"You've been unconscious; I don't want to take any chances," Roger scolded.

"But you can take a chance on Sam? Leave her out to die? How can you stand there and not let me in ... Let me see the file, Roger!"

"Lauren! Sam didn't have a virus that nearly killed her," Alejandro replied. "Besides, I will not risk your health right now." His face stern, his words colored the room as he spoke with a commanding voice.

"I agree with Alejandro, you're just too weak right now," Roger answered as he walked around to the other side of the bed.

"Might as well wish she had the virus, anything would be better than what she is now. Why did I get a virus? You told me I was immune. Did you lie to me?" I pushed him to answer me. Roger stared at the floor. His face flushed to a luminous red. He was working out how he was going to tell me that he let me down. How his fucked up technology wasn't as good as he claimed it to be. Maybe he'll admit he shouldn't have installed this thing in my head until he had it completely updated. Maybe he'll be man enough to tell me that he should have thought about my safety first. His head raised steadily, making eye contact with me.

The pit of my stomach tightened. My jaw hurt from the anger settling in my muscles. Everything I was today was because of his selfishness. Because he was more concerned with a machine than humans. The cool air of regret brushed along the entry of my nose as it burnt down the back of my throat. I knew when he looked at me he wasn't about to apologize or tell me something that I wanted to hear.

"I didn't lie to you. You had some virus protection, just not the one to stop that virus." He continued to look me dead straight in the eyes. I felt strange; I knew he was trying to tell me something.

I looked over to Alejandro. His expression was frozen in shock. He pulled one of the pillows across his chest. The muscles in his arms flexed. His hands clutched at the pillow and I could hear the feathers break under his grasp. *Did he know what had happened? What was I missing?* I glanced back at Roger as he spoke in coded words and confusing confessions.

"The virus was strong ... and hidden deep in the operating system. I didn't think — think you'd be so affected by it. Lauren ... I didn't think — I didn't think ... I didn't expect that it would penetrate and become so entrenched and twisted into it. Didn't think it would wreak so much havoc in the body." His physical stance became protective. His eyes darted between Alejandro and me.

I struggled to understand what he was trying to say. His words snarled my thoughts. I should've known it was something he did to me. A familiar wave of betrayal swelled in my soul. I knew it so well now.

"You gave me the virus? Why?" I wanted to get out of the bed. I struggled to push up on my knees but a massive conveyer belt pulled me back to the mattress; it was Alejandro using all of his strength to stop me.

"Don't do it. You need him still," Alejandro whispered into my ear, his arms wrapped around my chest and my skin surged with his touch, I ached to hurt Roger. I hated what he stood for; I hated that he kept pushing me, testing me in the sickest ways.

Alejandro adjusted his arms across me and my body rested heavy against him.

"It wasn't something I planned. It happened when you entered my mind this last time. I set a booby trap of sorts, to keep people from accessing my prototype. *You shouldn't have entered my mind.* I didn't think it would affect you like it did."

"More excuses? It doesn't matter that you didn't plan it. It still happened. You're so hungry for this prototype to be successful, you're willing to kill and maim people to do it? *Who are you?* You're not the person I loved and respected." I wanted Roger to hurt ... God, I wanted him to feel my pain. I got up from the bed quickly, making sure Alejandro couldn't catch me. My eyes spun in my head and the room joined in the spin ... I lost my balance and fell back into Alejandro. I wasn't able to leave.

"Lauren, stop." Roger lunged for me.

"Don't touch me — ever again." I pushed my hands out to stop him. The prototype had been in his head for six months and it released a beast in him that made him unbelievably strong, so much stronger than me.

I was spent, done with people who didn't work in my life anymore. Roger broke me, took my life from me and plunged me into the darkest corners of my humanity. I only had words that could hurt him deep enough to make a difference.

"I hate you. You are dead to me. More than dead, you are nothing to me. Get out!" I stared him down to look away.

"Tell her what I did for you." He looked past me to Alejandro, his eyes narrowed, like he had something he had to tell me.

"She told you to leave," Alejandro said as he pulled his arms tighter around me. I was completely content in the choice of words I spat at him and the answer Alejandro gave.

"Someday you will thank me for this, you'll see," Roger whispered.

"I will never thank you for ruining my life, ever!"

Roger looked up at me one last time before he grabbed his wallet and keys off the small table and walked out the door.

I turned to Alejandro and rested my head against his chest. His heart beat settled me and mellowed the seditious questions that ravaged my mind.

*What did I just do? Did I think this through? Handle the prototype without Roger? What about the CIA?*

Alejandro pressed his temperate hand to the side of my head and pushed against my ear. His soothing lips warmed the middle of my forehead as he answered my thoughts. Pressure trapped my breath and for a threadlike moment, I was twisted into believing nothing was what I expected.

**hindsight**

I never fully understood the meaning behind the saying, *hindsight is twenty-twenty*. I guess because it was never really relevant in my life — until now. If all I had to do was turn back to change my future, I never would have let my emotions hold my rational thoughts captive. I would have fought against every moment that led me to where I am...

Now I'm shackled to a technology I barely understand and in love with the man who knowingly funded it. Do I find a way to put to rest the burden I have become, or am I resolved to exist with the prototype for the rest of my life?

Eternity is such a long time.

**Book Two**
**The Possession Series**
**~Coming 2015~**

# about the author

By day she teaches computers at an elementary school; by night she dawns the cloak of motherhood, wifehood, and authorship. Worried that she's irritating her husband as she clicks away at her laptop until three in the morning, she's penned a New Adult trilogy titled The Wilson Mooney Series.

She is finding her way through self-publishing and is truly learning to let go with every curve and bump in the creative process. Gretchen de la O is a mother of three boys, a believer that anything is possible, and a lover of life.

Her newest work, Prototype, is the first book in an Adult Romantic Suspense titled, The Possession Series.

### Where to find Gretchen de la O:
www.gretchendelao.com
**Also on:**
Facebook, Twitter, Pinterest, Instagram and Google Plus.

### Find other titles by Gretchen de la O
**Amazon.com**
**BarnesandNoble.com**
**Smashwords.com**

Have Questions?
**Email them to:**
gretchen@gretchendelao.com

**Please send all correspondence to:**
Gretchen de la O
P.O. Box 416
Canyon, CA. 94516